END OF REASON

Dana Steele

*To Tresa —
Who lets me talk ad nauseum.
Always brings a smile to my face.
I adore our time together!
Dana Steele*

Copyright © 2020 Dana Steele

All rights reserved

The characters and events portrayed in this book are fictitious. Any similarity to real persons, living or dead, is coincidental and not intended by the author.

No part of this book may be reproduced, or stored in a retrieval system, or transmitted in any form or by any means, electronic, mechanical, photocopying, recording, or otherwise, without express written permission of the publisher.

ISBN-13: 9798642093498
ISBN-10: 1477123456

Cover design by: Trisha Waddell
Library of Congress Control Number: 2018675309
Printed in the United States of America

*To those who believed in me, and also to those who did not.
Adversity and support are both fantastic fuel for motivation.*

CHAPTER 1 — DURBIN

The journey on foot to the Black Swamp was a long one, but the rumors told of fresh, sustainable water that still lay unclaimed beyond it. Abundant and clean water had become quite the commodity since the catastrophic societal downfall referred to as the Collapse; the majority of settlement disputes revolved around the control and distribution of water and other resources. Everyone's survival was heavily dependent on access to water. In the flatlands, most of the area's water had become stagnant, making settlers ill, if hydrated, and the risks of drinking dirty water outweighed the benefits. Attempting to gather water from one of the few flowing rivers usually found a person dead; as territorial settlers guarded their supply fiercely. Patrols of settlers would cruise the riverbanks and lakeshores of the countryside armed with rifles that announced a settlement's claim to water before questions could be asked. And so, rumors of a vast freshwater source — stretching as far as the eye could see — were tempting to follow.

But this old man, weathered from years on the road and traversing the once-plentiful farmland, knew quite well of the water source. Its old name was Lake Erie —he'd grown up there in the Black Swamp. In the days of youth, the region was a cultivated land of plenty —well irrigated— overflowing with harvest, feeding masses of people every season. Mighty rivers flowed through the farmland to the lake, delivering yearly spawns of walleye, bass, and carp. Rolling hills surrounding the red, green, yellow, and brown patchwork fields several kilometers to the north and south, providing bounty after bounty of corn, soybeans, wheat, barley, lettuce, apples, and pears. Between the rocky beaches of the shores of Lake Erie and the cultivated farmlands stood the sentinel named the Glass City, a mix of concrete of mirrors. The city thrived on the lake's freshwater, and copious industry: fishing, chemical production, medicine, petroleum processing, and automobile assembly, it boasted a bustling seaport of mammoth tankers, railyards with shipping containers, electricity production facilities, and numerous machines were produced there...

That was before the Collapse.

Now, every crumbling road, rail, and waterway leading into and out of the Glass City was littered with metal carcasses —old-world vehicles stripped of all their valuable fabrics, wheels, fasteners, and glass. The machines lay brittle from rust, with trees growing through their flaking red-brown frames. The superhighways that climbed into the sky and wound through the sweeping farmlands decayed with each passing year, the concrete turning to rubble, the asphalt windswept and rain-washed to black dust. Roads were merely a subtle guide to nomads and travelers now; teasing, overgrown paths in the wilderness suggesting the potential presence of a wayward village, or struggling settlement that lay just off of traveled routes known mostly to merchants and traders. The roads could take a traveler through the burned down suburbs, past vacant warehouses and schools and shopping centers, derelict pastures and ranches and dairy farms. The threadbare highways could lead a modern-day adventurer to any of the previously flourishing cities if they were traversed long enough. This old man, Michael Durbin was aware that cities were a deathtrap after the Collapse, and assumed that the Glass City was no different —ravaged by the power grab and resettlement, the constant battles for safety, supremacy, territory, resources, and survival. He remembered clearly the days of the Collapse, the revolution, the downfall of society, the mass egress to less populated areas to escape the unending peril of murder and violence that erupted... the days when titles such as 'family' or 'friend' suddenly meant nothing —when everything abruptly ceased to make sense—

—*Click*

He instinctively dove to the cracked roadway he, simultaneously unsheathing a long bowie knife from his boot, tucking it blade side to his wrist under his sleeve, the dark walnut hilt grasped firmly in his hand. He rolled to face the sound of the hammer of a gun cocking into position.

Not today, Durbin thought, *I am not in the mood for guests today*. He waited for any other sound.

Slowly from the small thicket of gnarly, shadow-casting trees appeared a dirty, skinny young man. Black mud thoroughly covered his dull brown clothes, some caked into his short blond beard and matted into his long stringy blond hair. He held a matte grey-black pistol out in front of him, pointing it at the old man.

"You can get up now, old man," Commanded the muddy youth, pointing the business end of the pistol at his knees then twitching it upward. "Nice an' easy like."

The old man feigned feebleness and took his time getting up, groaning as he brought his knees under him, grunting painfully as he fully stood, the asphalt gravel grinding under his tattered combat boots. He distractingly brushed the dust from his heavily pocketed drab-green pants.

"You hidin' anything good in them pockets there?" asked the muddy youth, pointing his pistol at several pockets on the old man's vest and jacket. "We always lookin' for bullets and blades, food, too. Actually, that vest is purty nice, oh, and that hat? Maybe we take that, too."

*We...*thought Durbin, as his eyes darted left to tall rustling grass across the road where two more men arose. One donned a torn and puffy green coat, the other tried to wrap his long grey trench coat around him, weighed down by sloppy mud. These men were soaking wet in appearance, black liquid dripping from their pants. *Probably went under the road in a storm drain* he thought, observing the gentle concave incline of the roadway.

All three scavengers slowly came closer to the old man, deliberately threatening him with their posture and movements, elevating their shoulders and clenching their fists. Their wet boots made slurping and slopping sounds with each step. "I'll ask nicely once more," said the muddy youth with the pistol, his finger on the trigger, "what are we takin' from you today?"

"You don't want to do this," said Durbin, keeping his

stature as meek and vulnerable as possible. He shrunk his posture slightly, slouching almost to a bow, while he adjusted his grip on the hilt of the bowie knife in his hand, allowing the long sleeves of his red shirt to conceal the blade. He held up his empty hand timidly. He took care not to stand to full height.

"Oh, but we do, old man, we do." snarked the muddy youth, darting his eyes at each of the wet men to the left and right. "See, we low on supplies, and we hungry… and camp's gettin' way too big as it is."

Maybe because your resourcefulness is terrible? Durbin thought. These guys acted more like simple Loners than hardened scavengers.

Quietly, trench coat man and puffy green coat man stepped behind Durbin. He spied each of them in the edges of his peripheral vision over each shoulder. He again shifted the bowie blade in his hand under his left sleeve. "I have skills, perhaps I can help with your troubles?" pleaded Durbin, monitoring the movements of the wet trench coat man behind him to his left.

"We don't 'ave any need for an ol' sandbagger like you." said the muddy youth, nodding quickly to signal the approaching trench coat man.

And the man wearing the grey trench coat had come within arm's length to his left. The muddy youthful leader had severely underestimated Durbin. In a swift movement, Durbin turned to his left brandishing the bowie knife as he swiped it at trench coat man's throat, releasing a cascade of hot red blood.

Durbin simultaneously kicked backward at the muddy youth's left knee, breaking it and sending him falling backward bow-legged and screaming as a deafening pistol shot rang out. After the old man's dagger slashed through the tender throat of trench coat man it was heading toward the throat of the puffy green coat man when Durbin realized he wasn't there. The puffy coat man lay on the ground, quivering, eyes wide open, with a raw open gash in his forehead where the muddy youth's accidental pistol shot landed. He gave a dismissive shrug as he continued his spin on his heel to face the muddy youth who had fallen and slid down on the slope towards a storm drain under the road. His pistol had dropped out his hand as his broken leg failed to keep him standing. He was gasping for breath, the intense pain gripping him as his jagged yellow-white bones escaped his flesh.

"Well now your camp is three men smaller," Said the old man, standing over the suffering muddy youth, with mud caked in his stringy hair, a single wet black leaf clinging to his bottom lip, the faint smell of urine and coppery scent of blood on his pants. The old man observed the youth's heaving chest and bulging blood vessels straining in his elongated neck as he struggled for breath through shock and panic. Air flowed through his clenched teeth with a wet whistling breath.

Then Michael Durbin raised his leg and stomped his boot down forcefully on the muddy youth's neck, crushing his airway.

CHAPTER 2 – CALEB

The scrawny fifteen-year-old could not believe what he'd witnessed. From the seclusion of the tree covering a short distance from the roadway, Caleb Hurst watched in disbelief as the grey-bearded man he had tracked for days dispatched the bullying scavengers with ease. The man appeared fragile in front of them before seeming to slash throats with bare hands, fire guns without touching a trigger, and knock over men with barely a glancing kick. He hadn't seen much of what happened after the skinny man was kicked and fell backward beyond the side of the road, but Caleb was suddenly questioning his plan to seek this man's assistance.

But, on the other hand, he knew that should he fail to get help, or if this man were a cold-blooded murderer, the fate of his home would change little. He rummaged his thoughts for some time, watching the bearded man loot his felled attackers before continuing on down the road in his intended direction. Caleb stuck to the cover of trees lining the roadway, hoping that the bearded man would make camp soon with the sun setting. Caleb wanted no business with vile scavengers after dark —or anytime, rather— and felt his opportunity to approach the bearded man would be tonight at camp.

Caleb tucked the end of his wooden recurve bow under his elbow to keep the string in place as he rose from a crouched position and trekked after the bearded man. He kept his path just inside the first row of trees to avoid detection while, but still keeping sight of the bearded man. The setting sun cast the land in orange and golden light, white rays piercing the clouds and sliding in between tree branches that had not yet yielded fresh leaves. The dull remains of the cobbled pavement somehow managed a glisten or two in the setting sunlight, and Caleb took that glimmer as a sign of hope.

As the golden radiance of sunset began to fade, Caleb quietly grabbed a few handfuls of dandelion leaves and was fortunate to have pulled some with roots while moving swiftly down the path. Blindly he slapped the plants against his thigh, knocking loose mud and dirt before rubbing away the rest. Then, he tucked some of the leaves and roots into the pockets of his worn denim pants and pocketed jacket and softly nibbled on the rest. In his mind, it was no substitute for rabbit or goose but he'd decided he wasn't making a fire again tonight. He intended to share the bearded man's fire this evening while asking for his help.

After nightfall, the bearded man had lit a modest fire under the covering of trees several dozen meters away from the road. The ground sloped below the edge of the road but remained dry enough for comfortable sleeping. The bearded man sat on a rotting log, using a red scrap of cloth to clean up the pistol he had retrieved from a dead scavenger. He inspected the barrel and removed the magazine, gently flipping it over in his hand a few times before snapping it back into the grip of the gun. Occasionally, he would glance around, peering into the darkness that stood silently outside of the reach of the yellow flicker from the campfire.

Caleb cautiously approached the makeshift camp, careful not to make much noise and draw ire from the bearded man. He stepped as silently as he could, thinking back on the last few days of tracking this man. Setting camp several hundred meters away, waking at daybreak, to be led down the solitary road that the bearded man continued to follow. Strangely, the bearded man kept to the old partially paved roadway, straying only temporarily to hunt or relieve himself and then to make camp. A few times a day he would harvest plants from the brush and overgrowth on the side of the road. He effortlessly grabbed berries, dandelion leaves, and roots for consumption and nourishment. While observing this resoluteness in foraging, Caleb felt confident in his decision to seek this particular man's assistance in saving his village.

But it was not all confidence as, this morning morning, Caleb awoke and found the bearded man's camp cold and deserted. Panic rose in his chest as he began to think that his past few days of tracking were now wasted. He hoped beyond hope that the bearded man had stayed true to his pattern of keeping to the paved road as Caleb slung his bow across his back and took off in the direction they'd been walking the night before. He ran on the side of the roadway, the dormant tufts of grass silencing his footfalls, continuing to keep to the tree line to stay hidden when he could. After running several kilometers, Caleb finally caught a glimpse of the bearded man standing on an elevated portion of the roadway, being approached by a thin, muddy man holding what looked like a gun. That was when Caleb dashed farther into the tree line and watched in disbelief as the violence ensued. It terrified him.

And now, Caleb stood just a few feet outside of the glow of the campfire, able to see the gentle breath escape in a fog from the mouth of the man who had so brutally defended himself that morning. He was trembling slightly, scared to approach the bearded man in a way that would find Caleb joining the scavengers dead on the side of the road. Fear and relief fought within him making movement difficult. He quietly took a deep breath, relaxed his nervously clenched fist, raised his open hands in front of him in a sign of peace, and softly walked closer to the edge of the campfire glow.

Before the light illuminated Caleb, the bearded man spoke without raising his eyes.

"I was wondering when you would approach me face to face." He spoke clearly to Caleb. He didn't sound old, his voice had no waver nor gravel. His voice was deep, full, but also reserved.

Caleb stopped just shy of the tiny clearing, the flames throwing orange figures on Caleb's denim pants, and muck-brown jacket. The top buttons were missing, but the flaps were held down by the bowstring slung across his chest. He was shocked that this man knew he was there.

"H—How did you know..."

"I have traveled around long enough to know when I am being tracked." said the bearded man. He looked up at Caleb, squinting slightly in the campfire light. "Two days from my count. Why have you been following me?"

"I, uh, am seeking help for my village," Caleb said, his voice cracking slightly. It was the first time he had spoken aloud in days. He stepped more clearly into the light of the fire, his hands still open in front of him raised up in surrender.

"Huh," the bearded man grunted, shaking his head slightly as he slid the pistol into one of the many pockets of his brown vest. He wiped his hands with the scrap cloth he'd used to clean the gun. "I would have been less surprised had you began with 'I come in peace.'" The bearded man stood from the sitting log and adjusted his clothes. Caleb looked at him puzzled by his comment.

"Well, I do, I guess," replied Caleb, sensing a decreased tension between the two of them after what he could only assume was an attempt at a joke by the bearded man.

"My village is sick. People are falling ill from the water. People are dying. I was looking for more water sources, then I found and followed you, then I saw how you navigate the environment, and your knowledge of plants and—"

His words came out in a deluge of desperation and anxiety as the stress of the last two days came cascading from him.

"Slow down, kid," commanded the bearded man, softly gesturing to reassure Caleb. "Have a seat." He motioned to the duffle bag-sized log lying on the ground, close to the fire. After Caleb sat on the log, the bearded man continued.

"You have some skill at tracking," said the bearded man. He looked to be studying Caleb's face while awaiting an answer.

Caleb stayed assertive, studying the bearded man's face in turn. He didn't look that old at all, maybe later forties if Caleb were to guess. *No older than Dad, probably.* Up close he didn't look grey. He had some silver in his amber-colored beard, and he appeared bald under the wide brim of his brown hat. His face was slightly weathered from many years in the wilderness, but he appeared much younger than he feigned when the scavengers attacked. His green eyes had a concerned look to them. And the way the bearded man moved appeared efficient to Caleb. He thought back to tracking and how everything this man did seemed to be as conservative as possible. He spoke directly and pointedly, driving to whatever information was relevant at the moment. He wasted no energy. In contrast, Caleb bobbled his words and fidgeted with his hands, repeatedly coiling and uncoiling his fingers in his lap, bustling with nervous energy.

"What is your name, son?" he asked, tipping his chin upward. "And where is this village of yours?"

Caleb was eager to offer his hand. "Caleb Hurst, sir. And the village is Bridgetown. It is several kilometers that way." He pointed away from the traveled road with his other hand. Then the two of them shared a firm warm handshake.

"I know where it is, Caleb. My name is Michael Durbin. Friends call me Michael. Most people call me Durbin." He released Caleb's hand.

Caleb breathed a sigh of relief to have a name to match the man. He felt his whole body relax and suddenly realized just how chilly the night air had become. The smell of the dying winter was fading, an icy dirty smell of melting snow and thawing mud. He was grateful to be near a fire tonight.

"What troubles this village of yours again, Caleb?" inquired Durbin, though his facial expressions gave away that he already had an answer.

Caleb stumbled over his own tongue, "It's my sister — well, not just my sister. You see, Trina has been caring for everybody; Mom, Dad, nearly everyone else. They're sick. Swollen faces, so weak they can't move. They have a hard time breathing. Some have even died. It is affecting most of the people of Bridgetown."

Durbin stroked his auburn silver beard gently. He nodded his head in thought, as Caleb longed to know what he was thinking. "And what were you planning to do if you found freshwater?"

"Well," Caleb started, twisting his face in confusion, "I figured I would just take everyone to the new location."

Continuing to nod slowly Durbin replied, "These people are ill, yes? Can hardly move? Can hardly breathe? How do you suppose these people will travel? And if they get there —"

"I don't know!" burst Caleb, twisting his face further from confusion to frustration. Durbin's questioning of Caleb's judgment and planning caused him to lash out unwittingly. He felt insulted, though Durbin had said nothing of offense. "All I know is that my people are sick and I am searching for ways to help them!" The sensation of the night's chill had left him now, replaced with the burning of self-doubt and shame of not knowing how to care for his parents and village.

"Alright," Durbin said in a comforting tone, motioning again for Caleb to calm down as he discreetly surveyed the edges of the small clearing, straining his ears for sounds of unwanted visitors. "You made quite the effort in tracking me, and have shown much courage in approaching me here in camp tonight. The least I could do is see you back to your settlement. Let us get some rest, and at daybreak, we will make for Bridgetown. But I caution you, son, I am no medicine man."

CHAPTER 3 — DURBIN

At daybreak, Durbin rose from the makeshift bed next to the smoldering remains of the campfire. He placed his hat upon his bald head and looked down on the young man — *he is a child* — sleeping on the opposite side of the fire. Caleb was long and thin, his head a wavy mess of mousy brown hair that reached his chin. Caleb's face looked soft, unmarred by the rigors of nomadism. His brown jacket wasn't very tattered, suggesting he had enjoyed the security and confines of Bridgetown without much incident. The good condition of the jacket and denim pants indicated that he was not left wanting for supplies, or that Bridgetown has had at least some sort of trade or access to fresh materials. His boots were also brown, well-worn leather with thick soles that held dried mud. Beside him lay a recurve bow, tan in color, with a dull finish from years of use. It was strung taut and laying over a matching tan leather belt quiver stocked with about a dozen arrows adorned with blue and green fletching. There were tiny splatters of dried blood on the quiver.

Durbin shook his head with a shiver. Something about looking at this sleeping lad brought on memories of his own son —now gone ten winters. He drifted into a thought of whether his son would have wielded a bow at this age, or would he have preferred other methods for hunting game? His son was always building things, helping out the village with organization or construction. His son had a great talent for those sorts of things.

Caleb stirred with a slight twitch next to white smoke

rising from the fire pit and his hands went straight for his bow. His tense brown eyes focused on Durbin's face and then relaxed. Standing up from his dirt mattress, he collected himself and his bow, blew into his closed hands and rubbed them vigorously.

"You ready?" asked Durbin as he patted his numerous pockets, ensuring that all his personal supplies — knives, pistols, ammunition, rags, striking flint, and food — were in place.

"Yeah, I'm good to go," Caleb replied. Then he added, "It feels better to not have to track you down this morning."

"Lucky for you I have been sticking to these old roads," chided Durbin, as he kicked dirt and mud to snuff out the fire. "But that changes now that we are heading to Bridgetown."

Together, they walked out of the thicket of trees that bade them camp and protection and began their trek through the yellow brush of wild wheat, untended for years. They marched through rigid leafless shrubbery, some beginning to bud with increasing temps and sunlight. The occasional mulberry tree offered bitter berries for light breakfast and energy to continue. The vegetation was revealing sparse greenery as nature finally whispered itself back to life from its overdrawn winter slumber. Geese would honk in offbeat melody as they flew overhead. Robins would greet the men by perching on tall stiff stalks of foliage before jumping away to retrieve straw or animal fur for their spring homes.

By the end of daylight, they were halfway to Bridgetown. The swollen springtime river ran just outside of sight to the right. They could hear its washing rumble, hissing, and gurgling, but a wall of trees and various changes in elevation kept it out of sight. They planned to follow the river as closely as possible as Bridgetown sat on a series of bluffs along this river. Durbin instructed Caleb that they would be keeping to the high ground as much as possible while tracing their path along the river. Since the Collapse, rivers had a tendency to fill the floodplains frequently, unexpectedly, and drain slowly. All floodplains and riverbeds were dangerous to travelers on foot. Particularly in spring, the floodwaters of snowmelt could rush from upstream, filling the floodplain and washing away anyone ill-prepared. The receding waters could leave mud and sediment so deep and viscous that a grown man could be sunken to his waist with no means of pulling himself free becoming a meal for badgers and crows. *Yes, the high ground keeps us visible, but it is still safer.*

After hiking up and down the gentle slopes of the river valley for the duration of the sunrise, Durbin and Caleb made camp in another thicket of trees, far from the more traveled roads. Caleb readied his bow and crept upon a gaggle of geese to hunt for dinner. Durbin showed a rare burst of emotion as Caleb returned with his bow on his back and the black neck of a goose in his hand. Plunging his knife into the breast of the goose to carefully remove the succulent meat, Durbin smiled greatly, excited to be eating meat.

It's been too many days of berries and leaves and roots, he thought as he slid a stick through each portion of fresh meat. He held the goose breast into the fire and patiently waited as the fat sizzled and popped in the searing flames.

During their evening meal, Durbin listened to Caleb as he shared stories of growing up in Bridgetown. He relayed memories of the small community that banded together on the riverbanks. The old sawmill over the river that had still been running until just a few months ago fascinated Durbin. The fact that the community thrived in an abandoned small town was just as interesting. Everyone up and left the original Bridgetown after the Collapse. No one remembered its original name. Caleb's family and other settlers had stumbled upon houses full of supplies, clothes, building materials, even fuel. However, like most of the survivors at the time, none really had the foresight to realize that their resources would eventually run low. And without solid leadership, any community would likely dwindle away their resources without means of restoring them.

Durbin listened intently as Caleb told of his parents, who welcomed him into the world in Bridgetown during the first year after the Collapse. They were businesspeople. Number crunchers. Pencil pushers. It was clear by Caleb's words they had no survival skills. It was indeed a miracle that they and Caleb survived. To further the miracle, Caleb's older sister, Trina, was only 4 years old at the time of the Collapse. And by Caleb's word, she is strong, resourceful, smart, and means the world to him.

Durbin wasn't convinced that the only reason Caleb tracked him was Trina. *Surely, he knows those people are sick beyond healing. Surely he knows that any healthy people need to leave that place.* But Durbin kept his thoughts close to himself as he had grown accustomed to doing. There was no sense in causing the boy any more worry. They had only a few more hours of hiking until arrival at Bridgetown, and Durbin decided to reserve judgment until he saw the situation of the inhabitants for himself. In fact, Durbin reserved most his words for the evening and allowed Caleb to carry the conversation before turning in for sleep.

The morning brought a surprise of fog clinging to the trees and rolling slopes of the riverbank. Along with the unexpected fog was a welcome rise in temperature, and the stillness of the cloaked morning was occasionally pierced by chirping birds or a rustle of wings.

Durbin and Caleb continued on their path loosely following the meandering river valley with the intention of arriving at Bridgetown by midday. Durbin made the effort to reciprocate last night's conversation by selectively sharing some of his own background with Caleb to pass the time. He informed Caleb that he had traveled south from the lakes and hills up north. He sadly told of how many of their lakes had either dried up, had gone stagnant, or were fiercely protected by madmen with more rage than sense —and more ammunition than patience. As such, Durbin had been on the road over a fortnight, leaving when the last heavy snow began to melt, though his travel was inhibited by recent light snow falls. He hesitantly revealed that he was heading towards the Erie Lake in search of some shoreline along that great body of water that was salvageable for a settlement.

The fog slowed them down, made them more vigilant regarding their surroundings, but still, they kept hiking the river valley. Durbin found himself relaxing slightly, letting down his constantly rigid guard in the presence of this boy. Meeting friendly people in today's environment was not common. One would just as soon shank a person and steal their belongings as realize that there can be strength in numbers, or try to understand another's skills for the sake of survival, or just let bygones be bygones…

Durbin shook his head as he realized he wasn't entirely innocent in this world. How many times had he taken a life? How many strangers had he passed without so much as a greeting? How many suffering stranded travelers had he ignored as he pressed on about his selfish goals? How many settlements had he left in the dead of night because of his mistrust of its leadership? Or worse, how many times had he snuck into a settlement and stolen ammunition, striking flints, coats or boots while its inhabitants slept? Or what about those inhabitants he'd befriended merely to steal from? *I have been no better than those scavengers from the other day. This world has brought out the worst of us all...*

But as he looked over at Caleb, he caught himself wondering if this world really did bring out the worst in everyone. Caleb tramped through the brush, wheat, mud, and fog with an innocent determination. He had tracked Durbin in passionate earnest, desperately seeking support for his home. His voice carried no malice. His eyes revealed no hunger other than that of hope for the salvation of Bridgetown. He carried his quarry with a pride of provision as he returned to camp last night with their meal. *Not everyone in this world is selfish, Michael.* He could hear his wife's words in his head from years ago at Camp Moon —just as clear now as then. *She was wrong then*, he thought. *But maybe she isn't wrong now.*

Durbin cursed himself for entertaining the thought that Caleb is disingenuous. He tried to understand that Caleb's experience in the world was one of community and survival of "the whole". He had no reason —and no teaching— on how to be selfish. He had no reason to be dishonest. The world miraculously had not shown him that side of its fallen nature. Durbin tried to remind himself that the biggest challenges the world has thrown at Caleb have been food, heat, and water.

And the sound of the water nearby was indeed becoming louder. The rushing sounds of grand rapids between the rocks under the surface of the swollen spring river were beginning their shouted whisper, washing away the last vestiges of winter and its snowfalls. They were closing in on Bridgetown now, but the fog had failed to release its grip on the river valley. Durbin felt the ground beneath his boots become firmer as he realized they had reached the point where the remnant highway met with the bluff over the river. To his left, he saw several burned-out or dilapidated remains of homes long abandoned. Bridgetown was just over the next hill.

The fog shielded the town from the river. Much of the fog was so thick that one house could not be seen from another. As Durbin and Caleb reached the top of the hill, it was difficult for them to make out the concrete bridge that crossed the river. Young trees had made roots in the cracks of the concrete, their scant foliage shadowed in fog. The bridge itself seemed to melt into white mists. But above the fog, one could see the sharply pitched black roof of the sawmill at the end of that bridge. Also leading towards the sawmill, was the crisscrossed steel of an old railroad bridge. Below the bridges lay concrete canals and locks streaked green and black with mold, moss, and slime deposited by the water. On the other side of the canals, the water could be heard rushing under the bridges, but it stayed out of sight. Other than the sound of the flowing river, Bridgetown was eerily quiet.

Caleb picked up the pace, making way towards a structure that was nearly invisible in the mist. As Durbin inspected the building through the grey covering, he spied the rare sight of electric light emanating from a variety of square and rectangle windows. Some were still intact; others he could make out the sharp edges of broken glass creating jagged lines within the panes. More of the building became visible as Durbin came ever closer. It was in decent repair, with white metal siding stained with mildew, a dark grey roof that appeared full of grittily textured shingles; it became obvious that this was a house. A small, rusted silver pipe stuck out of the side of the wall and bent upward to the trees compromising the canopy that seemed to trap the fog inside Bridgetown. On the next wall that stood adjacent to a canal, Durbin could make out the slow steady spin of a waterwheel.

He followed Caleb to the far side of the house, where he was opening a solid brown windowless door. Durbin slowly spun around as he observed that the house they were entering was the only one equipped with electricity. There were several houses around, some with holes in their dark-colored roofs, some with walls missing completely, some charred black from fire, and one half of a house, its splintered wood revealing that the other half had slid into the river below. He stepped into the house and gently closed the door behind him.

Inside the house was surprisingly warm. The soft yellow-white glow emanating from the ceiling gave light to a coppery red wooden floor, randomly covered in crushed and torn patches of dirty greyish-green carpet. The walls were a collage of crumbling drywall and peeling paper. An empty table sat in the middle of the room surrounded by three chairs, with one of them missing a wooden backrest. Beyond the table and chairs was an open threshold to a kitchen area where a faint buzzing sound could be heard. Caleb weaved around the table, into the kitchen, and turned left.

    Durbin followed; the worn carpet and wood transitioning to a chipped, cracked, moldy, sticky linoleum floor that once boasted a black and white marbled pattern. Blocking a window was a large metal and plastic box swathed by various colored wires and black and grey tubes that were inserted into rectangular receptacles in the walls. The buzzing sound was coming from inside the box as it rattled the rusted silver pipe that rose out of the top, turned toward the wall, and led outside. Durbin continued left, through two more rooms similar to the entrance room. One featured a drab green couch that was missing a cushion, resting beside an end table with a variety of cups, a teapot, twine-tied bundles of dried herbs, and a book titled "Home Remedies"; the waxy cardboard cover yellowed with age. The next room offered a path to a wooden staircase leading up.

    While ascending the stairs, Durbin twisted his nose as the air became less musty, but took on a tinge of death. A sickly-sweet scent hung in his nostrils; it stunk not of decay, but of sickness. His footsteps plodded heavily on the staircase. As he approached the step, he could hear faint sobbing, accompanied by raspy, labored slow breathing. He could finally see into the top-most rooms of the house. The partition wall stood with a large hole in the plaster, revealing the room beyond, the wooden studs and laths somehwat intact with others splintered and frayed. Between the broken laths, Durbin spied Caleb with a raven-haired female of the same height in a tight embrace, Caleb's shoulders shuddering. Durbin's boots quieted as he stepped onto the level floor with greyish carpet. Two small beds lay to the right filled with many frumpy blankets. One of the frumpy masses would rise and fall with intermittent raspy breathing sounds. The other lay inanimately still. Stepping closer to the moving blankets Durbin saw the round swollen face of a woman struggling for breath. Red and blue blotches littered her gaunt complexion. Her sunken eyes stared without seeing at the cracked ceiling above, her lungs making a sucking sound as they clung to life.

Durbin could hear Caleb and the female break their embrace and begin walking towards him. He turned away from the dying woman and prepared to meet the raven-haired female with Caleb.

"Michael," Caleb paused as he turned to reveal the young woman, his face streaked red with tears he had just wiped away, "this is my sister, Trina."

Durbin compared the features of the siblings. They were nearly the same height and shared the same brown eyes and small pointed nose. Trina's hair was black as night, and extremely long, as locks fell over her left shoulder past mid-length of her white, red, and blue flannel shirt. Although the oversized shirt hid her frame, she looked no bigger than her brother. She stood stone-faced in front of him, and he could not discern if she was untrusting or disinterested.

"Michael Durbin." he said plainly to her, declining to offer a handshake.

"So, you are here to save us, Michael?" Trina sniffed, starring through her new acquaintance.

CHAPTER 4 — TRINA

The hardest thing in the world had to be sharing bad news. But bad news was the only news ever shared in Bridgetown. And bad news seemed to come constantly in droves. Then, since last autumn, it seemed to have gotten worse.

Ed Maxwell died.

The Big Bridge has a new hole.

The waters aren't receding.

The Saw Mill is out of commission until a new swingarm can be fabricated. But Ed Maxwell is dead, so no one knows how to do it.

Samantha Gaylord fell sick.

We lost two makeshift bridges in the last flood.

Jungen's house fell down. Then his boat was found capsized in the river.

The potato crop was rotten.

Bernie's canoe got a hole in it, and now it is harder for him to gather fish.

Samantha Gaylord died.

The waterwheel used for grain somehow became split down the middle and is only half as effective as before.

Three houses burned down in the past year.

Robert Aaron fell sick.

Scavengers took our cattle from outside of town.

Half of the Gaylord house fell into the river.

Robert Aaron died.

Bernie's dog went mad and attacked one of the Price children before being shot.

Mom fell sick…

And then the first thing I have to say to Caleb upon his return is that both Mom and Dad have died.

She hugged him tightly as he wept. She stroked his curly mousy brown hair gently as his tears soaked her shoulder. She whispered words of comfort softly, knowing all too well that comfort will not come for days. She rubbed his back lovingly, vaguely aware of the footsteps coming up the stairs. Those footsteps belonged to the gruff-looking man standing before her now. This man with a pocketed fishing vest who just sauntered upstairs of her house while she consoled her baby brother now orphaned…

Trina stood as a statue as the words, "Michael Durbin" echoed in her skull. She felt her soul rise up from the depths. It soared past fields of blue and green, over bright red brick buildings with flags waving in the wind, over crowds of children playing on the playground in the sunshine, through seas of people dressed as monsters and animals who suddenly exploded one at a time in splashes of dark red. Her soul quickly changed directions and flew into a forest of black gnarly trees with sharp branches cloaked in the rainy darkness. She saw her mother's face, bright and young, smiling down at her before picking her up and spinning her around. Then the youthful face grew white and round and sickly looking, coughing and coughing and coughing before wheezing in a body consuming heave—

SNAP!

Trina's soul crashed back into her consciousness, more aware of this Michael Durbin than before. She fixed her eyes from the cracked drywall to his auburn silver beard after asking, "So, you are here to save us, Michael?" She sniffed and shook off her tension.

"You haven't been here long enough, so I will save you the trouble. There is no one here left to save."

Out of the corner of her eye, she watched Caleb rub his tear-streaked face, and sniff in a childlike fashion. Her heart sank. *No one but the two of us.*

Michael Durbin, however, did not move. He just stood there, calm and collected and stone-faced as if the death of every inhabitant of Bridgetown meant nothing to him. As Trina's mind began to settle from the mile a minute racing speed it had grown accustomed to in recent weeks; she was more able to focus and decided to attack his silence with more questions.

"Why are you here, Michael Durbin?" she asked pointedly.

Durbin shifted his weight and sighed deeply. "Your brother sought my help with your village. Instead of turning him away —or worse— I placed my own journey on hold. I came here at his request." He held out his hands and gestured broadly, "Either we are too late, or there was never much hope."

To Trina, the words were cold, but not rude. He was not wrong. Once half the population of Bridgetown fell ill, the younger inhabitants fled. All except Trina. Only she remained to tend to those who fought for breath, who wheezed into death, whose lungs filled with fluid, suffocating them, whose bowels loosed uncontrollably, sapping them of whatever rare nutrients she could get into their failing bodies. Since last autumn, all who fell ill had died. At first, it seemed a coincidence, then the wheezing, and swelling and diarrhea quickly turned into a death sentence. Trina had held each of her parents till their last breath, silently praying for someone, anyone, anything to be able to save them. But even the thawing winter brought nothing —nothing but the death of her parents. That, and this road-weary, bearded man with serious green eyes who stood before her and her brother and offered nothing but snide words.

"I'm sorry, Trina. Caleb," Durbin said softly, trying to offer solace. He turned to address Caleb. "On the way here, I told you there may be nothing we can do. These people contracted a waterborne illness; a bad one. The medicine to heal them doesn't exist anymore."

"Then maybe we should leave before we get sick, too, Caleb," Trina interrupted.

Durbin looked at her with his head tilted at an angle that indicated surprise, with one raised eyebrow, his mouth slightly turned at the corner. Trina shook her head dismissively, *I am not stupid, I understand when a situation is lost*, she thought before returning to the room revealed by a giant hole in the laths of the plaster wall.

"Caleb," she called back loudly to the other room, "head over to the Maxwell's house and grab some supplies. They had plenty of useful stuff left when they died."

He did as he was told. He bounded down the stairs quickly, his boot heels thundering lightly then disappearing

Trina then opened a wide but shallow drawer from a deep brown bureau with a warped top. From it, she pulled a hard, black case slightly bigger than her hands. She snapped open the fasteners and checked its contents: a knife, a striking flint with a handle, several meters of parachute cord, a compass, and two white tubes that looked like fat straws with hexagonal ends. She closed the case and set it on the warped shelf, then reached deeper into the drawer and retrieved a shiny silver and black revolver with a black grip. Beside it was a box of copper and silver rounds marked with .44. She took the black case and firearm and tucked them both into a black leather coat after wrapping it around her. She proceeded to the closet door beside the bureau and produced a black recurve bow with a brown stripe down the center. With it came a long black belt attached to a quiver filled with arrows adorned with blue and green fletching.

Trina felt the weight of the leather on her shoulders. She smelled the slight hint of spicy earth from the coat and felt something in her change. The weight of the gun in her pocket was comforting, the feel of the bow in her hand was empowering. She wrapped the belt and quiver onto her back and then slid the bow over it, the bowstring across her chest. She turned and poked her head into a hole in the wall like a rooster as she looked up at Durbin.

"What journey were you on, Michael Durbin?" she asked. She pulled her head back out of the hole and walked around the wall to face Durbin. "Caleb and I will help you accomplish it."

"You'll what?" he choked. His eyes opened wide, and brow raised in reluctance.

"We cannot stay here," Trina continued, "this place is dead. There is nothing left for us here. We will need a new home. We will help you with your journey the best we can, and when we find a suitable home, we will let you be." She pressed her words into him. She suddenly felt overcome with urgency.

"Trina, it is not safe to travel in large groups. It attracts attention. Scavengers, Loners…" He diverted his eyes from her and looked back towards the dying person swathed in blankets.

"Three is nothing of a large group. And you would leave Caleb and I to find a new home for ourselves? We have hardly left Bridgetown or the river valley in our lives. You could at least guide us to a new home. Surely you have seen plenty in your years." She had resolved not to take no for an answer. This man could still help them, though maybe not in the way Caleb had planned. She was surprised to see him turn and start down the stairs.

"Hey!" She chased after him, the stairway thundering again with footsteps from thick-soled boots—louder this time. They made their way out of the house, the big brown door slamming open against the side of the building, the thud deadened in the thickness of the fog. Durbin spun around on the cracked and overgrown concrete sidewalk to face her.

"Michael!" Trina called to him in a tone that she was trying to exude more command than desperation.

"Look," he said sternly, getting very close to her face. She could smell campfire in his beard and roasted meat on his breath. "I am sorry that I was unable to help your family or your village. But I cannot be responsible for the two of you. With little experience in travel…" Durbin trailed off.

Trina pressed her pointed nose up to Durbin's, "I am not asking you be responsible for us. I am not asking anything at all. I am telling you that we are abandoning this cemetery, and joining you until we find a suitable home."

Durbin pulled his face away from hers with a muffled growl as he looked up at the sky blocked by thick green trees. Caleb materialized from the fog with a large, tan satchel on his back. "What is this about finding a new home?" he asked.

"We are heading back on the road again to find you two a new home." Durbin surrendered.

Trina could feel her face warm up with the notion of victory. Finally, some good news.

CHAPTER 5 — DURBIN

Durbin wrestled antagonistically with himself in his mind. He had no business in this morgue. He had nothing to offer Bridgetown. He had little to offer these strong-willed children who reminded him so much of his own. This Trina, who was headstrong, and beautiful with her dark features, looked so much like his deceased daughter. She was so young when she was taken from him. His son was also so young. And Durbin found himself missing them terribly. The aching pity and sadness caught him by surprise as he remembered their last days and weeks at Camp Moon, in the early years after the Collapse.

His daughter, Celina, was an eager, energetic, and decisive twelve-year-old who knew exactly what she wanted. She could broker deals with anyone in camp with sweetness and persistence, though it was not for selfish gain, or to put others out. She was merely a determined individual, and if she wanted help carrying firewood to their cabin, she talked someone into doing it. If she wanted someone to take her fishing so she could catch dinner, she found a method to con them into it. And then she would present her catch of river trout to Erin, her mother, and offer a deal of, "Hey, I caught it, you cook it," as she flashed her toothy adolescent smile and turned away with a flip of her long dark hair.

Abbot, his son, was a mere ten years old, and his quiet personality was a faint candle to Celina's vibrant light. He was trusting, hardworking, and determined in his own right. He let his effort speak for him, as he was not a boy of many words. His command of language was good enough, but having Celina as a big sister meant taking some liberties when it came to being social. And so, Abbot expressed himself and his worth for Camp Moon through actions of construction, and harvesting, and organizing, and gardening, and cleaning.

They spent the first five years post-Collapse in the secluded safety of Camp Moon. It was nestled in deep woods rippled by ravines and high hills in the river valley. Being a former Boy Scout camp, it was equipped with several dozen cabins and a few lodges along with private access to clean water. Its 150-plus acres were well hidden and generally surrounded by a river and man-made lagoons. Anyone who wanted to come to Camp Moon had to be deliberate about their arrival. Celina and Abbot grew up in Camp Moon, in the first few years after the Collapse, knowing little else about the world prior. The children were not grieved by the lack of electricity or plumbing. Not having fuel for motor vehicles was not an inconvenience to them, for they knew nothing other than boating or walking to their destinations. They were so inherently innocent, having been reared in the quiet remoteness of the camp with a dozen other families struggling to survive. Durbin was foolish to think that society would build around them, and the world would regain its sense of reason.

After surviving at Camp Moon for five years, after ignoring the perils and plight of the world outside of the camp for five years, after being a devoted husband to Erin, and father to Celina and Abbot for five years, after being a friend and neighbor to other survivors for five years, tragedy struck.

Michael and another Camp Moon settler named Daniel had left camp for a few days to hunt deer in the woods to the north and east. After kissing their families goodbye, the pair ventured out into the wilderness with bow and rifle, backpacks full of camping gear, and a netted cot for dragging home their quarries. Their hunt was successful; they nabbed two fair-sized female deer and three plump geese. Four days later they were heading home.

Within a mile of Camp Moon, the smell of burning wood became overpowering. The canopy of the forest blocked any view of smoke, but the light wind blew the scent from the direction of Camp Moon. Daniel and Michael hastened their pace. As they came to a ravine close to the north side of camp they could hear the crackling of wood —too much to be a campfire. It was one of the cabins. No other sound could be heard save for the roaring of flames. No yells for help. No screams of fear. No one was shouting for the children to run elsewhere. Daniel and Michael dropped their wild prey and ran down the ravine, dove through the clear cool water, and ran back up the other side.

The camp itself was empty. Multiple cabins were burned nearly to the ground. A handful of bodies lay face down scattered about in the clearing. One of the burning cabins was Daniel's. Both men ran headlong toward their cabin's screaming for their children. Michael's cabin was on the other side of the camp and pressed on harder. The entry door with crescent moon shaped cut-out had been left open, and articles of his clothing were strewn about outside. Michael burst into a sprint shouting, "No, no, no!" slipping on blood as he dashed through the open door.

The dresser of clothes was knocked over. His silver 9mm with the word "EXODUS" engraved in the side and its ammunition were gone. His water purifying drinking straws were gone. All of his combat gear was gone. All of his waterproof boots were gone. The food pantry was raided. What few canned goods they had left were now gone. The letters R-E-D were painted on the wall in blood. Then against every fiber of his being, Michael walked into the bedroom of his cabin.

His heart was not prepared to see Erin, Abbot, and Celine lying in a corner, the children with their faces buried under Erin's arms, bullet wounds in their torsos. Erin had been stabbed dozens of times in the chest and stomach. Michael then fell on them. He wept bitterly, hopeless, helpless, shamefully punching the floor and cursing himself for not protecting his family. He lay there all night and for another day. At some point during his despair, he heard a single gunshot ring out across the camp.

He had no business in Camp Moon anymore.

He had no business in Bridgetown.

And now, he had no business caring for these orphaned teenagers who had no better chance of surviving in this vile world with him than his own children had of surviving without him. *This is a cruel place*, he thought as he kicked a rock away from him.

Bridgetown was now miles behind them. They had crossed the river via the concrete bridge that ran past the abandoned sawmill. They continued north for a short distance before turning toward the Glass City. They were a hapless trio of adventurers, moving quietly by foot during the day, setting up camp in any cover they could by night. Durbin had to laugh at their appearance. He recalled fantasy adventure books and games he would engage in as a youth. He always found it funny that the protagonists were a motley crew of individuals who seemingly had no qualms about traveling with strangers. They were so trusting of the accompanying muscle, or brain, or mage, that the heroes would never stop to question their motives or history. Their goal was the only true thing uniting those characters. Their goal, all too often, was to save the world from a cosmic terror, or a sociopath bent on enslaving all of humanity. And Durbin laughed to himself. Our 'lofty' goal is to find a home with water.

CHAPTER 6 — CALEB

Caleb's heart was twisted mass of conflicted emotions. Without time to fully process the circumstances; he learned his parents were dead, lost nearly every person from his village to illness, and uprooted himself and his sister from the only home they have truly known. He wasn't sure if he should be excited, or scared, or grateful for his newfound companionship with Durbin, or upset, or grieving the loss of his parents. Now, Durbin tells him they are on their way to the Glass City.

Caleb's father had told them that they fled the Glass City in the days of the Collapse. He said that when all the money disappeared, then people began to get desperate. Order began to slip away as consequences were no longer being upheld. When the government failed to implement measures to have the military paid, or allow police forces to resume compliant order, several groups of armed citizens began to assassinate government officials. With no accountability, smaller groups began to murder regular citizens without reason. Doctors were gunned down in the streets because of angry men who lost their wives to medical errors. Wealthy businessmen were ambushed and knifed by people who felt they lost their life savings by their swindling; left bleeding in their regal offices and marbled lobbies of towering merchant centers. Public spaces were randomly bombed by desperate individuals who had lost their grip on reality as society was crumbling around them. The President had a heart attack and died soon after, and due to the unchecked violence levied on municipal and federal leaders, no one filled the helm. Violence erupted further. Houses, neighborhoods, cities burned. He told Caleb the darkest reaches of humanity had been exposed and they escaped the city seeking safety and trust of outlying communities. Caleb's heart was scared.

It was the story of his family leaving the Glass City that found Caleb uncomfortable with the direction of their journey. His father's account of the Collapse always stuck with Caleb when he ventured out of Bridgetown. The attack of the scavengers on Durbin a few days past was all the proof that Caleb needed to be assured that there are humans who had not regained their decency or respect for life. And now they were well on their way into a lion's den of sorts. Caleb's heart grieved with the loss of humanity.

As they made their way across hills and floodplains, old dirt roads, over and under shambling bridges, through fields of grain that slowly were giving rise to fresh greenery, were obstacles that slowed their travel. They carefully plodded through the increasing amount of sloppy wetlands, and Durbin explained that they were making their way into the edge of Glass City. Their intention was to find high ground and survey what they could of the city ruins. There was noticeable caution in his voice as he said their best option was to find a way to a tall abandoned hospital building several kilometers outside of the Glass City proper. He said the height would give them a view of the area, perhaps even the Erie Lake, and they could better plot their path. The thought of rising above the Black Swamp had Caleb's heart curiously excited.

Trina stopped Durbin. "Would the hospital have supplies? We could find medicine there to help other settlements. We could prevent another Bridgetown."

"I am afraid not," said Durbin. "Any supplies would most likely have been scavenged or used years ago. Whatever meds and instruments that were not taken in the early days of the Collapse would have been picked over in the years following. Only after the brigands who killed off the doctors and nurses realized they would need someone with medical knowledge."

"I don't understand," Caleb spoke up. "Why were people so ugly to each other?"

Bushes on the sides of their path yielded small colorful ball of nourishment. He reached out for some red and pink berries and offered some to his sister. "For years, in Bridgetown, we worked hard to help each other. Keep houses standing. Fighting off bandits. Fishing. Rebuilding every spring. We were people. And we were in Bridgetown together."

"Desperate people lack reason," said Durbin dryly. Caleb had the feeling that Durbin didn't have a real answer other than that. He tried to understand, though the remark made little sense to him. In Bridgetown, desperation forced the village to work together more intently. These stories from his father and from Durbin made desperation sound like a poison that turned one's mind against their fellow person. It made Caleb feel grateful to have been raised in a community that banded together in the face of adversity.

"Our terrain should get interesting here in a few kilometers," Durbin warned. "Don't get excited about the multitude of houses and such you'll see. Most aren't safe. And if you see a body, let it be. We aren't making friends, and we aren't digging graves." Durbin went on to explain that Loners and scavengers were known to booby-trap homes after salvaging from and abandoning them. Sometimes they ripped the floorboards open just inside of doorways, sending unsuspecting entrants to fall into cavernous basements below. If the bandits were still nearby, they would often rob and kill the victim, or let them suffer from broken bones until starvation took them. In the early days, explosives were rigged to tripwires, but it had been so long that Durbin wasn't sure if the explosives would still work if triggered—and he expressed rather intently that he had no intention of finding out. Other, more heinous machinations were also devised, but Durbin stopped short of describing them.

The trio climbed up a steep embankment and stepped through a torn chain-link fence, peeled away and rolled back to reveal an opening, setting foot on a proper street, more intact than any surface they had walked in days. The pavement was cracked, but it was not overgrown with foliage like many of the previous routes. The dried vine-covered chain-link fences lead to squalid houses; and burned, partially standing structures as masses of bent and twisted sheet metal of abandoned warehouses. Between the street and the buildings stood scorched trees, some untouched beginning to bud new leaves, and many with broken limbs, weighed down by bulbous black cables and metal girders and rigging. The occasional car that was oddly parked or flipped over was encountered, the wheels, engines, and seats often removed and salvaged.

Caleb looked around at the destroyed and dilapidated landscape with a sense of awe. He had never been this close to the Glass City before. The amount of desuetude was a revelation to him. Trees were found erupting from the debris of broken structures, and in some cases, the trees appeared to knock over buildings, uplift smaller structures from their foundations, and others crushing the roofs with mighty limbs.

They cautiously avoided sinkholes, stepped over befallen street lamps and signs, mottled with oxidation and burn marks; and traversed tilted upheaved slabs of asphalt and concrete revealing earth and tree roots and ancient red brick falling from their underbelly. Some of the streets buckled and rose at steep angles, or fell sharply to muddy caverns made from eroding waters flowing through the unchecked sewer system. Crossing their paths were thick black rubber cables that hung from rusted steel poles that towered over their heads. Standing water could be seen in some of the sinkholes while brown flowing water could sometimes be seen and heard rushing under the buckled and beveled portions of the streets. They avoided places with rushing water, as Durbin cautioned them that the flowing water could erode the surface beneath them, and carry them off to wherever the water flowed.

Amazingly, they saw no other people.

Caleb didn't know if he should be relieved. He was, after all, searching for a new home. And despite all of Durbin's knowledge of the area, his erratic pathfinding instilled in Caleb a sense of uneasiness. They would turn down random streets, which all looked the same to Caleb with their wild disrepair.

The desolation and narrow paths continued until they came to an area where the majority of the houses were built of brick and stone. The bulk of the structures still stood, but their windows had been shattered, and several no longer had a roof in place.

"Almost there," Durbin said as the last house in the row gave sight to a large watershed area low lying and forested. Slick black and brown trees trunk stuck out of the surface of the water at various angles and some floated like boats in liquid currents that more swirled than flowed. Part of the street had eroded into the watershed lake, and the trio stepped away from the water to the left side of the street. And that was when he saw it.

Sharpening its top-most edges on the clouds above them was a monumental concrete and glass tower. The panels of glass that remained reflected the midday sunshine in an eye-burning glare. At the top level of the 'L' shaped towered hung an arrangement of letters that spelled "MEDIA HOSTAL" though the letters were spaced oddly, and it was apparent that some letters were missing. Multiple concrete and glass panels had fallen away to reveal large holes in the side of the hospital. The debris had fallen about 100 meters down to the ground crushing cars, and green entrance awnings. The hospital was the largest thing that Caleb had ever seen.

A tall circular marble fountain in front of the main entrance was tilted and half-submerged in a hole where its foundation had given away to flowing water. Barricades of scrap steel panels, rusted from the elements, stood in evenly spaced patterns with orange and white barrels. One single tree growing sideways outside the main door was covered in white blossoms, an unusually beautiful and timid sight compared to all that Caleb had seen the last few days.

"I am not sure what we will find inside," said Durbin, leading the way around the steel barricades. "We are heading up as high as safety will allow and get a lay of the land. With any luck, we will be able to see Erie Lake and survey the entire Black Swamp."

"It looks like twenty or thirty-something flights of stairs," Caleb said, shielding his eyes from the light as he looked at the top of the building.

"And those holes in the walls don't look promising," said Trina.

"No, they don't." Agreed Durbin. "So, we will tread slowly and safely."

CHAPTER 7 — TRINA

Trina Hurst was in awe of the size of Media Hospital. The glass walls climbed into the sky. As she stood near the entrance and looked up, the clouds raced past the top of the building giving the illusion of the walls swaying to and fro. It had a dizzying effect on her and she shook it off as she followed Durbin into the shattered glass entrance of the abandoned medical center.

Her eyes took longer to adjust to the darkness inside. As they did, she could make out the long curved reception desk, riddled with bullet holes. More holes, craters, and gouges were evident in the marble pillars that created a pathway to a series of elevators. Streaks of dirt lined the floors, and as the darkness melted away she could even make out faint footprints in the dirt. She touched her black bow, pulling the string more tightly to her chest which pressed against the revolver in her coat pocket. Durbin's words repeated in her mind — *I am not sure what we will find inside.*

Trina walked between the battle-worn marble pillars to the elevators. Some were closed, the dull grey doors not opened in years. One had no doors and the elevator car inside was lifted up several inches. And one had no door and no elevator car in sight. Trina stepped close to it and could hear the echo of dripping water down below. It was too dark for her to see anything in the shaft.

Durbin had walked off down the hallway, into bleaker

darkness, where the light from the shattered glass entrance had difficulty reaching. He motioned for them to follow him. Caleb spun as he walked, taking one more look at the sunlit lobby before venturing into the dark with his companions.

She stepped softly, but Trina's boots still echoed lightly on the marble floor. She followed Durbin to an irregularly shaped turn where he opened a heavy metal door. It squealed loudly in protest as the hinges groaned and creaked. They stepped inside to a concrete stairway with a rickety handrail. The metal door shut behind them with a resounding thud that rattled the pipe-shaped handrail up the concrete-lined staircase. Looking up, Trina observed the stairs winding the vertical corridor with sharp turns and corners. Sunlight was visible.

With heavy sighs of preparation, the trio started up the concrete stairs, the pipe handrail wiggling and vibrating frequently. The reverberations would wobble high up the staircase and disappear until one of them would bump the rail again sending more shockwaves up and down the cylindrical metal. Trina guessed they were on an outside corner of the hospital. Large cracks and even whole areas of displaced concrete allowed plenty of light to see and climb by. It cast hard angles of luminescence that created knife-edge shadows around the corners. Occasional gusts of wind would whistle down the stairway, whipping Trina's long black hair around her face. Her legs began to burn as they climbed ever higher. Every couple of turned corners they passed a metal door. Some of those doors bore a number indicating the floor they were on, some had worn off over time. More and more sunlight came through the increasing holes and cracks in the wall casting even more sharp-angled shadows on the stairs and doors and dust could be seen falling gently like snow through the rays of light.

Higher and higher Trina climbed, the cracks and holes in the concrete increasing in number and size, pebbles of debris falling from her boots. Ahead of her, several steps up, Durbin came to another heavy metal door. The number "45" was stenciled on it in green paint, faded over the years.

"Top of the line," he said as he pulled the door open, a brief metallic screech piercing the air as the door was pulled from its resting place.

The hallway beyond the door turned to the right and proceeded down a long corridor intermittently interrupted by tan painted doors and open doorways. A light wind hummed and buzzed throughout being fueled by broken window panes and funneled through random thresholds. Partway, Durbin made another right turn. As Trina went to follow him something at the far end of the hall caught her eye. The wall was missing completely, revealing the world outside. And just before the missing wall was a couple of wooden framed armchairs, and a barrel with the faint air of smoke rising from it. Someone has been here recently. She let Durbin go on along his hall as she went to investigate the other direction.

As she made her way to the end of the hall she saw that the multitude of doors led to patient rooms, some with bed frames holding flattened and torn mattresses, some with blinds ripped from the windows, some lacking windows at all. Vials and syringes and plastic fluid bags lay everywhere, accompanied by wires and hoses and dirt-covered or moth-eaten linens.

Cracked and shattered monitors hung loosely from the walls, some swaying in the wind that blew through the high rise.

Trina came to the wood-framed chairs at the end of the hallway, looking into a smoldering fire in the barrel. Next to the barrel was a small, circular table with two reddish-brown colored books on it. She stepped closer to the edge and looked out.

She now stood so high above the trees that she could see large swaths of the Black Swamp. Far off the distance, she spied giant white fan blades that rose above the tree line. There were countless deserted homes, offices, warehouses, and retail centers in various states of repair as far as she could see. The spindly sticks of trees recovering from the winter filled in the spaces between structures and roads. Trails of glistening water made their winding paths where the land sat lowest, looking like glassy fingers winding crooked the wilderness. Closer to the hospital, brown and green winter grasses and weeds forced their way up through broken concrete slabs and faded, debris filed parking lots creating a mock roadmap of green lines on a canvas of white and grey. The usual rubbish of flipped over rusted vehicles was also prominent —fallen warriors left where they lay. Trina peered straight down the sheer face of the hospital, a dizzying hundred meters down, and the wind picked up slightly as if to push her back away from the opening of the wall.

"Hello, young lady," came a soft man's voice from behind her.

Startled, she screamed as she spun around on the shards of glass on the floor, and for an instant, she felt like was falling backward off the ledge. She threw herself forward in desperation and landed on her knees next to a wooden framed armchair with faded green upholstery. She winced as chunks of glass pressed sharply into her knees and the palms of her hands. A short, boxy man with a long white goatee rushed over to her feet.

"I'm am sorry to have scared you, my dear." He said softly, placing his hands just below her shoulders and guiding her to her feet. "But tapping you on the back would have sent us both over the ledge." He smiled up at her, genial blue eyes sparkling behind his black square-framed glasses.

Caleb and Durbin appeared around the corner, running toward them when Durbin suddenly slowed. He continued walking toward her as the white-haired man patted her back with a mallet of a hand. "It will be okay, child." He reassured her.

Trina looked down at the white-haired man quizzically. She felt foolish for being frightened by him. He was a short, stocky man with very broad shoulders and thick hands. His long white hair was pulled back in a ponytail and his square black-framed glasses complimented his long white goatee. His cheeks were round and protruded above his genuine smile as he looked up at her.

"Paul?" inquired Durbin as he came closer to Trina, "How did we not see you as we came up?"

"Honestly Michael," Paul said, holding his arms wide to welcome Durbin in a friendly hug, "You were so loud coming up the stairs, I had plenty of time to hide. Scavengers haven't been up here in years, but I wasn't taking any chances."

"You live here?" asked Trina, trying to remember if she saw any signs of habitation throughout the floor.

"No, no," Paul denied, releasing Durbin from a back-patting hug. "whenever I am passing through, I make sure to spend a few days up here, looking at the city. Offering a prayer or three as necessary."

Trina realized she understood very little of what Paul was saying. *Was he a nomad? No real home? Offering prayers? Why would anyone not want to have the security of a home?*

"Still trying to save this fallen world, Paul?" Durbin asked jokingly. "We are surveying the land to chart a path to Erie Lake. These are my companions, Trina and Caleb." He gestured to each of them in turn.

Trina felt a warmth in her heart to be labeled as Durbin's companion. Perhaps it was the stark hesitation he held toward her joining him initially. Or perhaps it was the makeshift father figure she felt him becoming in the last few days since leaving Bridgetown. Or perhaps, despite the initial startle at his entrance, it was this Paul fellow who had the ability to calm her with just an amiable smile.

"Pleasure to meet you both," Paul said cordially, and he led Trina passed Durbin and Caleb and down the hallway that she had forgone upon arrival to the floor. "If you need knowledge about the surroundings, I would be your man. Though I will warn you, Micheal, the Glass City is much different than it was when you were younger."

They continued on down the hall toward another end that showcased another missing wall and treacherous ledge. Trina carefully avoided dried blood splattered on the tile floor, and the new ledge held a sight even better than the previous.

Where the previous ledge offered her a view of trees and residential ruins, this new direction allowed her to see the Glass City proper. Off in the distance was an army of tall buildings making up a battered and time-worn skyline. In the center, standing taller than all the rest was a skyscraper made of mirrored glass. Many of its glass panels intact it reflected the sun's late-day radiance in brilliant searing light, illuminating the smaller brick and limestone architecture that stood around to pay it homage. The Glass City itself still resided several kilometers away from Media Hospital. And the space between was filled with water flowing through low lying troughs and valleys, trees reclaiming their space, crumbling red and brown brick warehouses, grey limestone dwellings, and the occasional bell tower perched atop a church on a hill.

Paul raised his hand up and placed it on her shoulder. He pointed with the other hand.

"Despite all that has been thrown at us, this is still a beautiful sight." He said with that unending softness in his voice. "To the right of the city, all of that crisscrossing scaffolding and those thin smokestacks are the remnants of the Refinery. Don't let the beauty fool you. The Glass City is filled with all sorts of vile creatures that refuse to see the light of this world. Magnates of treachery and murder, fallen souls who seek their own purpose and slither like snakes in the swamp. You can't see it from here, but the streets are all waterlogged. One would need a canoe to effectively navigate the murky canals of downtown."

He moved his pointing hand slightly to the left pointing to a gleaming white triangle that had a large central pillar and appeared to have stripes that fell at angles similar to the triangle. The base of the triangle was barely visible above the trees, with small blue and red squares placed sporadically on the base. It occurred to Trina that it was a giant bridge.

"That suspension bridge off in the distance has been named the Spire." Paul continued. "The inhabitants there pretend to defend the Glass City —from what? I don't know —the Marauders already own what's left of the city. So in reality, they are merely isolationists with sniper rifles and tactical advantage over any who would claim the bridge as their own. And over there…"

His hand pointed even further to her left, and she followed his finger to the solitary massive hill which was near the Spire but appeared even further away. "That is probably your next destination, Michael. That is Trash Hill. It is nearly as tall as the point at which you stand now. And you will have a much better view of Erie lake from there. However, the best path takes you passed the Spire. If they can see you —and they will— they may just shoot you."

Trina felt her heart rise up in her throat. Why would this seemingly meek and softly spoken man send them on their way past a group of violent brigands?

"Do they not entertain travelers at all, Paul?" asked Durbin. Trina had not felt his presence behind her while she gazed out over the Black Swamp.

Paul shook his head and pulled at his long white ponytail. "I wouldn't count on it, Michael." He stepped away from Trina and the ledge that he seemed much too close to without worry. "They *cough* welcomed me into their camp once. But after the second person started to take a serious interest in my sermons, they took my Bibles and burned them before threatening to do the same to me."

Paul leaned against the wall some distance from the ledge and slowly slid to the debris-covered floor, pulling a strip of wallpaper down the wall with his back, revealing a grey powdery solid wall underneath.

"That book of yours will get you killed, Paul." Durbin chastised his friend coming to sit next to him on the floor.

"If only I could be so honored." Paul flitted back with a smile on his face, that Trina felt reflected his heart.

She stood there quietly taking in the friendship of these two men. They both carried with them age and experience, as well as a sense of fatigue. She could tell that there was more to their banter than the words that were spoken. There was an unsung camaraderie between them as if their paths had crossed several times before. But at the same time, it seemed to her something deeper. Something older. No, these men knew each other before the Collapse, she thought. And her mind began to wonder about how much these two men had seen. About how much the world had changed during their lives. About how much it must hurt to see the state of the world, and then together realize that they are relics from an age past. Trina recalled so little from her days before Bridgetown, that this world was all she had known. The stories about civilization prior to the Collapse were only stories to even her. She didn't anticipate the world ever returning to the stature once held in those stories. She wondered if deep down, these two men sitting on the floor wearing their tired faces felt the same.

In contrast, she looked to Caleb, who stood at the ledge, his elbow wrapped on an exposed steel girder, him leaning over the ledge with wanton abandonment. He kicked thick shards of glass the size of rock salt off the ledge and followed them with his eyes until they were lost in the distance. Caleb, on the other hand, was convinced he could make the world a better place. He just lacked the means and know-how to make it happen.

Paul cleared his throat and spoke out to her and Caleb.

"I recommend the two of you enjoy one of the quality beds up here. It is a rare commodity for travelers. I assure you that we are quite safe all the way up here. In the morning, I will be heading south, toward the windmills. I will be needed there soon."

The sun had begun to set, and the mirrored skyscraper in the center of the Glass City reflected a molten orange glow on the sycophant structures around it. The trees below cast long shadows and the tendrils of water filling the streets contrasted lightning white edges with orange gleams of twilight. She vaguely remembered Durbin telling her that he was going to visit with Paul a little longer before she walked sleepily to the first intact bed she could find. She gathered up dirty linens and did not care about the smell of moldy wetness as she gave herself over to sleep.

CHAPTER 8 — DURBIN

Michael Durbin sat with Paul near the ledge on the top floor of Media Hospital. Dusk had settled in and the orange and pink and purples of the sky reflected in the lenses of Paul's square spectacles. Paul quietly stood and had started a new fire in the barrel with a striking flint and wood he pulled from a nearby room. It occurred to Durbin that Paul sought refuge in this hospital often. He had stashes of materials everywhere, hidden in closets, tucked under unassuming shelves, books lined up or stacked on flat surfaces shrouded in shadows.

Paul placed a short, thick hand on Durbin's shoulder before sitting his short blocky frame on a chair across from him.

"You aren't one to take on traveling companions, Michael," Paul said softly. His tone was mildly pretentious, laced with a desire to know more. "Where are you off to?"

Durbin sighed deeply, his shoulders rising and falling as he looked up at the cracked and peeling ceiling above him. "The Irish Hills are not safe anymore. Marauders and Loners are getting more violent. The water quality is lower than it has ever been. The lakes up there are all growing sick. I started down here to make a path to the Erie Lake. Surely such a large body of water will have stayed clean. So I decided we should head to Trash Hill and survey the land closer to the lake. Coming here was a way to get our bearing on the landscape"

Paul shrugged casually. "And the youths? Your philanthropy is often wound around some self-benefit, yes?"

"That's not fair, Paul." Durbin protested.

"But it isn't untrue," Paul said to him, looking over his glasses, his elbows on his knees and hands clasped lightly as he leaned closer to Durbin.

Durbin shook his head. "The children have nothing to offer me, in fact, their companionship poses more risk than anything else. They can survive well enough in the sanctuary of a settlement, but the harshness of the wilderness and the savagery of scavengers or Marauders is too much for them."

"So why take them from their home?"

His voice was defensive when he spoke. "Trina demanded to join me, Paul — she would not take no for an answer. They hail from Bridgetown. Nearly everyone there fell ill and died, including Trina and Caleb's parents. Protection was there no longer. It was only a matter of time before they, too, fell ill or were taken by brigands." Durbin tried to mask the sadness in his voice, the growing pity he found himself feeling for Caleb and Trina.

"And this has nothing to do with your own children, Michael?"

"I don't know." Said Durbin, looking intently at Paul, searching his face for any trace of wisdom. Paul was one of the first people that Durbin encountered after his family was murdered at Camp Moon. Like nearly all post-collapse run-ins with

Paul, it was a chance meeting of sorts; Durbin running north toward the Irish Hills, Paul hiking south on the same nondescript trail. Their casual greeting along with Paul's inherent meekness and aura of kindness ignited Durbin's emotions and he fell on him, weeping bitterly. Paul sat in a makeshift camp with Durbin for two whole days, praying with him, reading to him from one of his many books, and listening to Michael's deepest cries for his family to be back in his arms. Paul stood quietly by as Durbin would randomly break into a cantankerous rage, unbridled fury, and desperate angst about hating the world until he would collapse from the eruption of emotion into a pile of human tears once more.

"This is different." Durbin continued. "These kids are older. For the current state of the world, they are thriving. They don't need me. They just want my help finding a home. People... would never really leave Bridgetown. They don't know the Black Swamp. Caleb was born after The Collapse —he knows nothing of how the world operates outside of Bridgetown. Trina is decisive enough, but still lacks knowledge of the ways of the wilderness. But, chances are, whatever home they choose will not be suitable for... someone like me. And wherever I settle this time will probably not be suitable for them"

Paul stared at him for a long minute. "Do you feel responsible for them?"

Durbin paused a long minute before answering. "I feel the need to right the wrongs I have done."

"You did not abandon your family, Michael. We have been through this." Paul chastised. His words were more fatherly than sharp, more pointed than rude.

"No, not that," Durbin replied, "I have made my peace with that. It is everything else. The thieving in the night. Making friends with settlements only to take advantage of their kindness by hoarding their resources. The scores of men I have had to kill in the name of defending myself..."

Durbin drummed on his knee rapidly with his fingers, a small amount of frustration building within him. He wasn't frustrated with Paul. *This is what Paul does. He forces you to look within yourself.* And it was the introspection that frustrated Durbin so. Bringing to the surface all the lack of innocence that plagued him, Durbin was forced to realize, yet again, that he was just as guilty as any scavenger or brigand that resorted to violence.

"Yes. I see." Said Paul. It was obvious that Paul had more to say. But Durbin was not prepared for it. "Have you made peace with the ones who killed your family?"

Durbin turned his head sideways, trying to process Paul's words. "Do you know who killed my family?" Beads of sweat formed on his brow as he felt his face redden with anger. Thoughts of torturous vengeance on the person who took his family from him flashed in his mind's eye. He wanted to jump out of his chair, but Paul raised a calming hand.

"I am afraid I do not," Paul stated leaning close to Durbin. "And I fear what you would do if you ever found out who did."

"I try not to think about it." Durbin agreed, his heartbeat settling slightly.

"Michael, I am not trying to upset you." Paul continued, "I have known you for years. I know that you are a drifter of sorts now. You chase whatever suits your fancy. I am just trying to lead you to think about what could happen to these children if something." Paul looked to the ceiling as if it were to offer him the right words, "pressing…were to arise. Abandoning these innocents if you were to get word of your family's killer would not right any wrongs. I understand that you are not seeking them out, that the killer may very well be dead. But these children are a long way from the only thing they have truly known as a home. And you are taking them even further. I don't think Trash Hill will have any better answers for you."

"I have to try. I have no home. They have no home."

"They also have no guidance. No parents. They will need that from you, Michael." Paul paused for a long moment with his mouth open before he resumed. "I will be making my way to the Windy Well to the south of here come sunrise. If Trash Hill yields disappointment, seek me out there."

"Windy Well?" Durbin raised an eyebrow inquisitively.

"It is a protected settlement at the far edge of the Windfields. Very noticeable from a distance by the massive white and silver windmills." Informed Paul.

"If things don't go as planned regarding the Erie Lake shoreline, we will seek you out there. You have always been a great friend, Paul. Far better than I deserve."

CHAPTER 9 — TRINA

Trina was awakened from her deep sleeping by what felt like violent shaking. The earthquake rocked her, teetering her body from left to right. Before her eyes opened she realized she was in the top of a forty five-story building, and threw her body off the bed only to realize that Durbin was only gently shaking her awake.

She squinted her eyes at him, shielding her eyes from the bright morning sun bursting through the floor to ceiling windows. Her heart and mind mellowed, and she grounded herself in reality once more. *I wish I could get my nerves under control.* She felt that since her parent's deaths, she jumped so easily, felt so on edge, and it drove her crazy. Her head was clearing from her sleepy haze as she followed Durbin out of the room. Caleb was sitting outside the room in a torn chair eating from a can of beans.

"The bed was nice, right?" he said with a smile, his teenage awkwardness showing as he scooped more beans into his mouth with a bent spoon. He held the can with a dirty linen to protect his hand from the heat as faint wisps of warmth could be seen rising from the open can.

"Do you want some warm food to follow it?" He asked, very eager to offer. "I will put a can on the fire for you."

Trina nodded. "I would love that Caleb."

His joy was comforting and encouraging. Trina then

found herself looking for Paul. She failed to wish him goodnight and wanted to at least greet him good morning. She watched Caleb pull a can opener from his canvas backpack and begin working on a can with a faded white and green label. He removed the paper label before placing it into the fire barrel.

"Paul left for the south windmills earlier this morning," Said Durbin, placing a few cans in his backpack. "He gave us access to his food stash hidden a few floors down. He and I grabbed some for us all. Feel free to take some from here," as Durbin gestured to the cans on a circular table with a chipped green covering.

The table showcased a large supply and variety canned goods. *Must have taken them a few trips to bring all of this*. She looked over the seemingly ancient cans of corn, carrots, beets, and beans, and ham and shredded chicken, trying to decide what would be worth the weight of carrying. She separated two cans each of beets, beans, and shredded chicken, lightly rubbing the rusted edges as if to try to remove the orange and brown spots of oxidation.

"Trash Hill is our destination?" she asked Durbin, sliding the cans into her backpack.

"Yes," affirmed Durbin, "with any luck, the height that close to the edge of the lake should give a good view of the shore, and any potential land for settling."

"What do we do about the Spire?" Trina asked, recalling Paul's warning about snipers and unwelcome visitors.

"We will stay as far from it as we can, but I would like to not take longer than necessary to get to Trash Hill," Durbin said as he grabbed unclaimed cans from the table and moved them into an adjacent room. Trina heard the cans being placed on a laminated countertop, then the sound of a light door slamming against hollow wood.

Caleb handed Trina her can of beans wrapped in a yellowed towel with a silver spoon poking out the top. Hot steam swirled around the handle as it escaped into the air as smell of molasses and barbecue entered her nose. She ate silently and hungrily, happy to have warm food. Still, the warmth of the beans in her mouth failed to quell her worries about traveling near the Spire. She was nervous about encroaching on territory owned by hostile individuals. Back in Bridgetown, traders would come to town, bartering clothing, furs, leathers, food, ammunition, firearms, but no one meant any harm. In addition, they were always welcoming newcomers to the settlement. Unfortunately, the sloppy eroding waterlogged riverbanks were not desirable to most travelers.

She took another look the the end of the hallway, and over the ledge to view beyond the Glass City. She focused her gaze on the single white pillar on the suspension bridge the made up the Spire. *I can't spend my time being afraid.*

Trina wondered what was waiting for them out there. Durbin maintained the notion of a vast, freshwater lake, but she was beginning to doubt it. Even from the top of Media Hospital, she couldn't see the great lake she heard so much about. From the highest point she has ever stood, she could see streams of water winding through the residential areas, carving their way through and swallowing the lower lands, with houses or vehicles riding over the surface like unpoppable bubbles, trees —

currently stripped of leaves— grew wherever they could find a way; through structures, out of cracks in the concrete, overtaking greenspaces. The Glass City was so far off. *Is the lake beyond there?* She didn't distrust Durbin, quite the opposite in fact. It just felt like they had traveled so far, and are no closer to finding a new safe home.

She looked around at the relative safety of the top floor of Media Hospital. *They were protected by height. The stairways were loud, offering protection from looters and scavengers. They had beds. They even had a place to store food. Where did Paul get all this food?* she thought, sliding another spoonful of warm beans into her mouth. *But getting potable water all the way up to the top floor would be a grueling chore, and that would be only viable if the water across the road was safe. Of course, it couldn't be any worse than our water in Bridgetown.* She shivered slightly at the depressing thoughts that seem to arise with even a mention of her abandoned home. Then she shivered more as a blast of cold wind howled through the hallways, blowing shut a distant door with a thunderous boom that resounded back down the hallway.

"Maybe staying here isn't a great idea." She said to herself.

Caleb looked at her quizzically as he finished packing his backpack and bow, strapping his belt quiver around his waist. He then turned and poked his head into a room. "You ready, Durbin?"

Durbin appeared behind Caleb and looked over at Trina as she finished her food, placing the can and towel on a table beside the fire barrel. "You ready to head out, Trina?"

She nodded, bringing her coat around her body, and

gathering her own backpack and bow. The relative comfort of Media Hospital had been enjoyable and quite welcome after several days on the road sleeping under the cold blue and black abyss. She was slightly sad to be leaving, and even more sad she didn't say goodbye to Paul. *There is just something about him.*

After securing their provisions, Trina, Caleb, and Durbin descended down the concrete stairway to the ground floor and weaved their way through the darkness to the front lobby they had encountered the day before. They traversed the debris of glass, concrete, and steel as they wound their path around the base of Media Hospital. Durbin directed them down a broken road pointed towards Trash Hill.

The journey through the suburban ruins of the Glass City was mostly uneventful, much to Trina's pleasure. She was startled once by a possum that clumsily fell out of a pile of twisted gutters and scurried across her path. A falcon screeched from overhead that broke their silence as they slowly walked through a narrow alley of bricks.

As they left the potential danger of the residential areas and moved into the more wooded wilderness, Trina felt it was safe to begin talking again.

"What is Trash Hill?" she asked Durbin.

He slowed his steps to walk beside her. "It is exactly as the name states." He said with a snicker.

"Before the Collapse, we were a mostly civilized society. We didn't throw our trash just anywhere or burn it. There were large trucks that collected our trash from our homes and stored it at a specific location. Over the years, they piled it higher and higher, added dirt, and piled more trash. The result was the largest mountain in the land."

Durbin's rare smile made Trina think that he rather enjoyed talking about the old world with them. She worried about bringing up history, unwilling to dredge up doleful memories. She wanted to ask him what he was like before the Collapse. Did he have a family? How did he learn his skills of survival? What was the Glass City really like before all the destruction and neglect and chaos? How did he and Paul meet? Instead, she went with a different topic.

"Michael, what happens if we don't find what you are looking for from Trash Hill?"

She half expected him to stop in his tracks and chastise her for her doubt and lack of faith, but he did no such thing. They continued in stride up and down small ridges, while weaving around thin tree trunks that directed them like guideposts up a slight incline and away from a growing ravine.

"If the viewpoint of the tallest hill in all the land won't show us something useful, then I fear we are no closer to either of our goals... And then we follow Paul to the Windfields and Windy Well"

Trina liked the idea of following Paul and meeting up with him in what sounded like an established settlement.

"How does Paul know of these places?" she asked.

"Paul travels the entire Black Swamp," Durbin answered. "He goes from settlement to settlement, sharing his message of salvation and peace in efforts to quell the violence that this world insists on embracing. Also...Paul just seems to *know* things..."

They climbed ever further up the ridge, on the left lay rubble and old foundations of broken and washed away buildings, while splintered and eroded walls piercing through the ground pointing to the skeletal branch canopy formed by flood traumatized trees. To their right swirls of brown water, looked deeper and more ominous with every step. Trina noticed that water expanded much further to the right now, and it appeared they stood above a riverbank. She would have guessed it was the same river that flowed past Bridgetown, though she could not be certain. This river was far wider, with tall buildings on the other side stacked with crumbling red or grey bricks, missing windows above bent and twisted metal fire escape ladders.

But, about a thousand meters downstream, in the middle of the swirling waters stood a giant squared column of white. Trina followed it up to a convex bridge hovering over the water supported by the single column. Scores of thick round white steel cables all anchored at the column and strung to the bridge platform. Much like Media Hospital, the column appeared to scrape the sky.

Caleb's voice broke Trina's fascination with the monumental bridge. "Hey, Durbin, what do you suppose this is?"

Caleb had stopped to view a wooden sign, deliberately placed, one meter wide, and nailed to a tree at about 2 meters height. Crudely painted on the wood was a large red circle and with a giant cross through it. Trina thought it looked much like the cross—hairs on the scope of Mr. Maxwell's favorite gun back home in Bridgetown. The red paint had dripped slightly before it dried, giving the appearance of running blood.

Trina briefly heard a faint whistling buzz sound before the tree beside her spat splinters in her face. She and Caleb both screamed as Durbin threw himself onto them, pushing them behind the sign and down the ridge towards ramshackle foundations and crags of concrete. She tumbled, head over feet, her shoulders plowing through the wet earth, her bow smacking the back of her head and springing her into another backward somersault till she came to a stop on her side in a soft mound of decaying leaves and rich black soil.

Durbin swore under his breath, rubbing his knee as he rolled off of his face, wet leaves in his mouth and beard. "Stay down." He commanded.

Trina looked back up at the ridge. It was just high enough that she could no longer see the bridge called the Spire. The trees and the sign were intact save for the splintered chunk where bullet had landed. She touched the cut where a chunk of the tree slashed the flesh of her cheek.

"Did they shoot at us?" she asked quietly. She wasn't sure why she was being quiet. The Spire was so far away that no one was going to hear them.

"They certainly did." Affirmed Durbin, sitting up and surveying the ridge and the city ruins around them. "Though I am not sure if they missed on purpose or accident."

"That was awfully close for a warning shot." Said Caleb, his hand over his heart, his chest rising and falling with rapid breathing.

Trina was shocked that one could shoot from so far away with accuracy. Miss or not, she found it amazing that a mark could be identified and targeted from such a distance. She adjusted her bow on her back and wondered if she could manage such a feat with it.

"Thank you, Michael." She said sincerely, standing to her feet and reaching out for Durbin to help him up. They grabbed each other's forearm, and Durbin grunted as he regained his balance. "You okay?" she asked looking down the knee he was rubbing.

"Yeah. I'll be fine. Just have to walk it off." He said, shifting his weight and walking in cautious circles. "Let's stay below this ridge until we are well past the Spire. Apparently, they want no visitors."

They continued walking in their intended direction. Aside from the crumbling foundations, Trina noticed the earth under them had an odd quality. It appeared swirled and whipped, almost fluffy. It looked as though the land had been swept away and redeposited many times over the years. Even the layout of fallen trees was in overlapping and ill—shaped circles, the debris from the many deteriorating structures also fell along the paths of churning circles frozen in their motion.

Flood season is even more destructive here than at Bridgetown, she thought.

Cautiously, they resumed their path under the cover of the ridge. A shadow was cast down upon them as they crossed under a portion of the bridge leading to the spire. The tight cluster of trees hid them from a clear view. Looking up, Trina could see the occasional hole in the bridge surface, steel girders bent downward as rusted rebar poked out of choppy concrete resembling twisted metal fingers. She could see wood planks and sheets of red, green, or blue steel covering some of the holes. She hoped no one was up there waiting for them to pass underneath.

Trina then realized that after they crossed under the bridge, their backs would be to the Spire. She grew worrisome about how close the Spire was, whether there was a lack of tree cover, and the ridge on their right appeared to become smaller further along the trail. *Would they shoot us in the back if we are heading away from their camp?* she wondered. She suddenly felt a distaste for snipers, for individuals who would dare shoot without knowing the objectives of their human target. A strong distrust began to rise up from inside her.

"Michael, I don't trust the people up there. If they would shoot at our faces without knowing our intentions, why wouldn't they shoot at our backs as we are leaving their territory?" She was unable to mask the fear in her voice.

Durbin looked up. Looked forward. He looked to the ridge and to the arranged lines and piles of ruined structures to the left. He then gazed down at the ground and shook his head.

"We should probably seek better shelter beyond the ruins over there," he said, pointing to the jagged walls of bricks and cinder blocks, the disheveled rooftops sunken, crumpled, collapsed, and strewn about, no longer home to any buildings. It was an old neighborhood ravaged by time and repeated floods. Splintered timber and wooden frames and scaffolding lay everywhere. And jutting out from a section of wall Trina could see the tangled figure of a man's leg adorned with a tan combat boot.

"Grab the thickest log or board you can carry, keep it muddy," Durbin ordered, picking up a splintered shaft of lumber from the mud, "if they start shooting, we split up and seek cover behind the thickest walls we can find. Stay low. Use the wood as a decoy from behind a wall or other cover before you move in a different direction to another wall."

"Where do we go?" asked Caleb, already making his way to cover.

"Just away from the Spire. But do not move alongside the bridge. Move away from that, too. And stay low!" Durbin's voice was sharp with controlled panic.

This must be what he was talking about when he said he didn't want us joining him, Trina thought. She felt foolish for leaving Bridgetown now, but it was too late. Her home was so far away. And out here in the wilderness of the Glass City she was so exposed, the full realization of danger abound. She was uncertain of what to do. She felt completely reliant on Durbin while the snipers potentially waited for them to cross under the bridge, as Durbin commanded them to split up. She began following Caleb, moving toward the broken walls and flood tasseled earth. She placed her hand on a red brick wall that came to her shoulders, it's sharp chipped top edge scoring her skin. She looked up to see that they were all clear of the cover of the bridge and she could see the white rails at the closer end of the Spire, still a fair distance off, but much closer than where the sign with the red paint stood. She continued to trace the brick wall with her hand, while she eyed the white railing of the Spire, following it to the giant white column in the middle when saw the bright glimmering flash of a lens flare.

She gasped and dropped to the ground where she stood as a sound of —*vvssshht thud*— collided with the wall protecting her, raining pebbles of red brick on her head. "RUUUUN!" she shouted over to Caleb who dove behind a grey wall of cinder blocks. She sat with her back against her shield wall realizing she forgot to pick up a decoy. She slapped the mud frantically, clawing at it looking for a log or board. *All this debris and no decoy for me?* She raked the ground until she found a wide flat board, wet and stained with deep brown streaks. She tugged at it and it wouldn't move. She brought her boots under her and squatted for leverage, digging further to feel for the angle the board sank into the mud. With a grunt, it pulled free, about one and a half meters long and tapered at the buried end. Trina frantically looked around at her surroundings looking for cover to move to that wouldn't expose her on her path. Her nearest cover was about 10 meters away. But the remnant walls began to cluster more beyond that point.

How fast can they shoot, she thought. *I have to find out.*

She planned to run to the right of her current cover, then make her way out of range from there. She held the tapered end of the board in her hand, feeling its weight strain her forearm as she revealed it from behind the wall. She heard the whispering buzz sound again as the board splintered in her hand and she immediately bolted to her right. Her heart raced as her boots slipped in the soft earth. She clawed the mud for traction as she dodged debris in the mud, her bow slapped her repeatedly on the back of her thighs. She neared the grey cinder block wall, much taller than her last wall of provided cover, and she dove for it.

She landed flat on her belly, sliding behind the protection of the wall as another bullet hit the wall with a —*crack* — raining down pebbles of grey brick where she had dived from. *That's too fast.* Her heart was pounding so hard she couldn't hear Caleb calling for her, waving at her from a few dozen meters ahead —where the partial walls were taller and more clustered together. She had a narrow path ahead, a corridor of sorts if the walls were only a few feet taller. But she wasn't certain if she could make the path and roll to cover in time. She had left her splintered board behind with the last distraction. She looked for anything to use as a decoy, needing it even more desperately now. Poking out of the ground, she found a rippled swath of muddy fabric. She crawled over to it, wrapping her soiled fingers around the lined and pulling. It gave away easily, with a light tearing sound, and she pulled free what looked like a wet brown, window curtain. She balled it up and focused down the alleyway ahead bordered by two brick and wood walls. It grew ever longer as she stared down the path, Caleb and his wildly waving arm grew more distant.

She prepared herself by digging her boots into the soft earth, ready to launch herself forward as she tossed the filthy ball of linen upward and outward, hoping the shooter would mistake it as her making another dive. Then she was off. Her boot slipped in the mud; she heard a bullet slice through the linen flying to her left. Then the ground became more solid under her feet and she propelled herself into the space between the freestanding walls. She tried to count out the seconds, desperately hoping the decoy linen bought her enough time, but she lost count as time seemed to nearly stop. She plodded clumsily, moving slower than she ever had in her life to the end of the wall. She planned to dive left behind an even taller section of the tan brick wall. She launched herself forward and left as the air was cut by yet another bullet shot from the Spire. Trina felt something pinch her calf hard.

She screamed in pain as she landed face first in the soft earth once again. She rolled over, looking up at her current cover, grateful that the shambling wall was long and tall despite missing bricks. She sat up and looked at her calf. She looked down expecting to see blood where the bullet had bitten her during mid-dive, but there was none. The was only a swath of mud, and as she rolled up her pants leg, there was only a red welt where the mud had ricocheted into her flesh. The last bullet had missed as well, hitting the ground and spraying mud with substantial force. She sighed heavily, thankful for the poor marksmanship, and surveyed the walls for her next action.

Ahead of her was another broken wall, mostly intact with a window frame opening beckoning her. The wall behind her, she saw, provided enough obstruction to allow her to climb through the window and change positions undetected. *It also puts more distance me and the shooters at the Spire.* Across the mud filled adjacent to her, she saw Durbin also crawling through a window. As his boots finally slipped through, she watched a brick above him explode into red shards. Durbin stayed low and wiped the mud out of his eyes. When he could see, he locked eyes with Trina and he waved her off in the direction of Caleb.

"We have to get out of range!" he called out to her. "You alright?"

"Yeah, only been hit with debris," she called back to him,

rubbing her leg.

"The walls here are taller. Stick to them as you can. We have to move that way." He pointed in the direction she last saw Caleb; a group intact houses and structures where the ground above the muddy alleyways.

She nodded in agreement and looked ahead to plan her new path. Her pulse slowed to normal; she felt more in control now that the walls were taller. She had time to breathe. She had time to think. She pressed onward, the frame of a door opened a path to the next set of walls that once belonged to a house in the shadow of a majestic bridge. She continued to squat walk, allowing the bricks and wood to conceal her movement as she made her escape. The sniper had focused their attention on Durbin. Intermittently, she would her bullets impact the bricks, or wood, sending a spray of fine debris impacting the earth around him. He seemed to stay one step ahead of the shooter, and she began to wonder how to thank him if they made it out of the situation alive. After navigating several more sets of walls and more intact structures, she realized she had moved beyond Durbin. She looked back to see him nestled in a corner, placing his brimmed hat onto a large stick he had pulled from the soil. He raised the hat to the wall line, just barely visible to an onlooker. He moved it toward a window opening in the wall. He held the hat so that only it was visible in the opening, but no shots rang out. He jammed the stick into the mud leaving the decoy as he walked to the edge of the wall opposite the window and waited.

After several minutes, Trina and Durbin continued crawling through windows, and over half-standing walls until they met up with Caleb. Together they scrambled over the terrain until Durbin looked back at the Spire, comfortable with the space and obstacles between them and its imposing white obelisk. He leaned against a wall of splintered wood, it's coarse siding frayed and worn, and sighed deeply. Caleb ran up to embraced him, catching Durbin by surprise. With a startled jerk, Durbin wrapped his arms around his shoulders, patting him softly. Then Trina followed, unable to control her overwhelming gratitude to be alive, she swung her arms around Durbin's neck, stifling back tears. Caleb sobbed on them both, and Trina could barely make out the words as he said, "Forgive me."

"We wouldn't have made it without you, Michael." She said with a vulnerability in her voice.

"No," said Durbin, "I wouldn't have made it without the two of you."

CHAPTER 10 — CALEB

On Durbin's command, Caleb went running. He darted in between walls, over knee—high ones, and through shoddy thresholds. He dove through broken window panes. He kicked up mud behind him and zigzagged through the labyrinth of bricks, mortar, and debris. When he finally spared a moment to look back to the Spire, after Trina had screamed 'run'; the rain of silent bullets against brick had showered the area with coarse pebbles of red, white, and brown. He saw Trina struggle for a decoy. He watched her frantically plan a course through the labyrinthian rubble. He watched her appear to get shot as she dove for cover. All the while, he was safely out of range. And he felt guilty for it.

Durbin and Trina dove over the last set of walls, finally far enough from the Spire that the shooter had given up. Caleb ran to him. He was overcome with grief from his cowardice. A hole formed in his chest as he thought about what he would be doing if they were killed in this ruined neighborhood, and he still alive merely because he ran. *I placed my own survival above everyone else's.* He jumped on Durbin and tried to crush him with a hug; sobbing and begging the man not to hate him.

"Forgive me..." he cried, "forgive me. I ran. Forgive me."

"I told you to run, Caleb," whispered Durbin. "There is nothing to forgive."

Durbin's hands felt strong yet soft on Caleb's shoulders.

And in the next moment, he felt Trina embrace them both as well. Durbin placed his hands on each of the children's' waists and the three of them kneeled down together in the soft earth. Then they rested their backs against the rippled green metal siding of a single, freestanding wall. And they wept. They held each other, taking in the moments of being alive. Grateful for their survival. Grateful for each other.

One by one, they each calmed down and collected themselves. Durbin stood first, grunting himself to his feet. He reached for Trina's wrist and helped to ease her out of the mud. They both grabbed a hold of Caleb and pulled him upright. He patted the dried mud off his drab-colored jacket and pulled his bow around him.

"I don't want to go through anything like that again," he said refusing to look in the direction of the Spire. "I felt like we were being hunted." Though the moment had long passed, he still shook from fear and adrenaline.

"No one can promise that, Caleb," said Durbin. He rubbed his bald head which appeared vulnerable without his round brimmed tan hat. He then stroked some flecks of mud out of his auburn and silver beard and continued. "People don't have a good reason for their actions anymore — if they have any reason at all."

"Then I will work on being more vigilant." Caleb said.

He meant it. His moments of helplessness —which felt more like hours— as he watched his sister and survival guide being fired upon by an enemy unseen rattled him deeply. He felt responsible for bringing the bulletstorm on them by stopping at the unusual marker on the trees. He felt that if he had just paid more attention to what Paul was telling them instead of hanging off the edge of the hospital tower, enamored with a view, then he would have noticed that they were approaching the Spire and that more caution was necessary. He was so caught up in the adventure that he'd forgotten its inherent dangers, and they all nearly paid the price for it.

"We all will," quipped Trina.

"Yes," said Durbin, "Let us compose ourselves for a moment. Then we continue on to Trash Hill."

The path to Trash Hill was more of the same. They blazed trails through the never-ending waterlogged, residential wasteland. The trees were packed together, but smaller, thinner, soft and rubbery. The earth below them was the softest yet. The concrete roads and sidewalks they were fortunate enough to happen upon were covered with thin films of silt. More streetlamps and utility poles lay scattered and tossed about the landscape. Small valleys were filled with water, with stopsigns breaking the surface, and partially submerged trucks with their cabs seemingly floating on the surface like glass and metal and plastic bubbles.

They continued walking for the majority of the afternoon. The overgrowth cleared slightly, and they happened upon a tall chainlink fence with a portion of it sitting on a series of rollers rolled to operate as a gate. It sat partially opened, with no one guarding, save for a blue sign with the only visible yellow letters spelling LASS ITY. Under that was crude, hand-painted in an off-color yellow the words TRASH HILL.

Durbin led them into the open portion of the gate where the ground began to swiftly slope upwards. Caleb looked up and saw that Trash Hill was a steep mess of yellow and red steel panels, all standing vertical, creating a mazelike corral towards the top of the hill. Dotting the path were porcelain sinks, and refrigerator missing doors, broken pieces of bookshelves and end tables, splintered laminate countertops and various scraps of steel, metal storage drums of rust, yellow, blue, and grey. Broken glass shards lay about like sand most looking dull in the cloudy skies. As they continued higher, the scenery became more macabre. Broomsticks and rippled rebar were thrust into the ground like pikes, featuring the skulls of deer, or the full skeletons of buzzards and squirrels. Some were topped with cadaverous fish, their hinged maws seemingly swallowing the pike.

Caleb pulled his bow from his back and revealed the quiver at his belt. He gripped the bow firmly. *Vigilant*, he thought, and he followed Durbin through the winding corridor of steel.

Soon they reached the peak of Trash Hill. The summit was surprisingly flat, with a variety of makeshift steel shacks making up a battlement of sorts around the perimeter. The shacks made a tall wall and they could see no sign of Erie Lake. But straight ahead, propped against a blue makeshift shed was a ladder that reached to the top level of the shed. And above that was a table and a small chair. It appeared to be a balcony of sorts.

Caleb was making his way to the ladder when he realized that he wasn't even sure what he would be looking for once he stood on top of the shed. Instead, he called for Durbin.

"There is a ladder over here, Durbin. You can see out from up there."

Durbin had begun making his way towards the ladder when they all heard a loud clanking of metal and a shattering of glass come from one of the red sheds. Suddenly from the doorway of the shed, burst a figure banging a wooden rod on a dented steel saucepan. He slammed it hard and rhythmically, varying from fast to slow, and then the figure began shouting.

"You'll not ravage my home, Marauders," he cackled maniacally. Caleb pulled an arrow from his quiver watching the man run erratically toward Durbin.

"Trash Hill belongs to Lassity! And Lassity will sooner see you dead than his home besmirched!" He bound awkwardly toward Durbin, who turned to look at his attacker banging together cookware. Lassity had plastic bags on his feet that rustled as he clumsily plodded the ground. On his knees were skating pads, one lime green, the other pink and missing plastic rivets, the protective shell flaying with each step. He wore no pants but was covered with a ripped chest protector worn by baseball players. His extremely long and wiry white beard and stringy hair were as untamed as the wild inflections in his voice, his eyes were yellow balls swallowing beady black pupils.

Durbin patiently waited for Lassity to come closer, and in a swift motion, Durbin caught up both his arms under Lassity's armpits and interlaced his own fingers behind Lassity's head. He spun the vagrant around hard enough that one of the plastic bags flew off his foot revealing long yellow talon-like nails on his toes. Durbin slammed him down on the ground firmly, still pinning his arms up in the air, the saucepan and wooden rod falling to the ground with a metallic ring.

Caleb nocked an arrow and pointed his bow at Lassity, slowly closing the distance between them, threatening him from further action. But Lassity struggled fruitlessly against Durbin's submissive hold, grunting and wiggling, his calloused feet gouging the glass speckled dirt. The feebled man turned his restrained wrists lacking the dexterity to claw at Durbin's face with yellow dagger-like fingernails. Durbin just casually dodged his flailings by tilting his head left and right.

"Inner. Rage BURNING!" Lassity fumed with desperation. "Unleashing dragon. Dragon! DRAGON!" he spat furiously at Caleb. Lassity continued to roar comically while Caleb and Trina looked on, uncertain of what to do. Then Trina approached him. Caleb kept his bow trained on Lassity's chest.

"Lassity, is it?" Trina asked, stepping closer to the withered delirious man as Durbin tightened his hold on him. Lassity's skin was darkened by years of grime and dirt, his bones pushing against his thin weathered skin, his joints enlarged and reddened with inflammation. Caleb noticed she softened her look to pity for the brainsick fool.

His exaggerated huffing and roaring ceased as his gaze settled on Trina. He twisted his head sideways against Durbin's arm and smiled a toothless smile.

"Ah, Lassity has caught the pretty lady's eye? And she has caught Lassity's, I am sure." He said, mimicking kissing motions and making sloppy wet sounds with his lips.

"You can let him go, Michael." She advocated for the pauper to Durbin, without removing her stare from Lassity. Caleb fixed his nocked arrow on Lassity with an even tighter draw string than before.

Durbin relaxed his grip and allowed Lassity the use of his arms once more. He scrambled to his feet, his motions bumbling and ungainly. He sucked the spittle through his lip as a shiny strand of drool clung to his thin unkempt beard. Caleb remained ready with his bow, but looked down the shaft of the arrow toward Lassity's head.

"Yes, the lady brings the pleasure to Lassity," he said, his maniacal yellow eyes looking her up and down, "The pleasure, indeed..." he hissed as he thrust his hips toward her, the leather protector over his torso popping off his body to reveal his sagging manhood flopping aimlessly.

His lewdness seemed to strip all the pity from Trina. Her soft look changed to one of disgust and revile. To Caleb's surprise, she balled up her fist and swung fiercely at Lassity's face, striking just below his left eye. He fell over onto his right hip and slumped into a heap of dirty skin and bones.

Durbin stifled a laugh and quickly turned to climb the ladder on the makeshift shed behind him. Caleb un-nocked his arrow from the bow and returned it to his quiver. *Vigilant.* He sprung over to the ladder to hold it in place as it screeched against the metal roof of the shed under Durbin's shifting weight.

Trina rubbed her fist as she approached Caleb to hold the ladder so he could join Durbin at the top. There was a loud crunch as Durbin could be heard jumping on the corrugated metal of the roof of the shed.

"It's safe for one of you to come up," Durbin called down to them.

Trina nodded to Caleb as she gripped the long cold rails of the silver ladder.

"But what about you?" Caleb asked looking back to Lassity lying as a mass of junk on the trash-filled earth.

"I will be fine, brother," she assured him with a wink and a faint smile.

With a nod, he turned and scaled the ladder, the mud on his boots causing him to slide lightly on the rounded rungs. Short screeches of metal on metal chirped again as he shimmied to the top. Durbin grabbed Caleb by the arm and helped him up over the top. The roof was difficult to walk on, with the metal shaped into tight sweeping arcs of rounded ridges and valleys. The metal bowed under the weight of the two men, with a slight springiness that coupled with the sheer elevation of Trash Hill caused Caleb some disorientation.

The communing clouds overhead rippled back towards the horizon where they met with the Erie Lake. At the line hard to distinguish, the clouds turned into white feathers that cut the surface of the water and returned back like waves. Far below, Caleb expected to see the waves crashing on a beach, but instead, the waves broke on random rocks or partially submerged vehicles, or ramshackle structures long brutalized by waves and wind and half-sunken into the lakebed below the stygian water. The water crept into any land it could, swallowing any beaches under its murky brown greyness and swirling currents. Caleb could not fully believe what he was seeing. There was no shoreline. The Erie Lake, massive and ominous, had no finite end where it met the Glass City and the Black Swamp. They were all intertwined as a melded mass, none of them distinguishable from the other. It stretched beyond imagination, and the waves lapped at the skyscrapers of the Glass City. It flowed toward the Spire and swallowed the land around the cooling tower of a long-abandoned nuclear power plant. The random white-crested waves showed no prejudice as they frothed through the grey water in the distance, and then through the brown water closer to the Black Swamp. Below them, at the base of Trash Hill, the water smacked mercilessly and repeatedly against the earth, eroding it away. Green and reddish-orange iridescent trails floated in and above the water with ominous intent, dissipating into the distance and through the finger-like rivers that bled into the city.

There is no usable land here. The water is not drinkable. What are we to do now? Caleb felt his spirits fall. A crushing chasm of emptiness opened in his chest. *Have we wasted all this time? Had we risked our lives passing the Spire for nothing?* Caleb stomped his foot into the metal underneath him. It rippled and bounced slowly, as if made of something other than metal. He grabbed the chair that began to topple over and placed it securely in the grooves from which it had been knocked loose. He sat down on the chair and rubbed his forehead vigorously, his brain switching rapidly from desperation to frustration and back again.

"Paul was right, wasn't he?" Caleb finally said after finding words. "We don't have the answers we seek up here, do we?"

"Not the ones we seek, no," Durbin said calmly. Caleb

sensed a tinge of discouragement in his voice. "But we have answers about Erie Lake."

Durbin placed his hand on Caleb's shoulder. "This thing doesn't end. The lake and the swamp are one. The Glass City is merely an obstacle in their way, overcome by them both. The ground is oversaturated with moisture. The trees soaked to their cores. The pollutants in the ground have bled into the water, poisoning it. There is no place to build here. And all that remains upon this hill will eventually wash into the sea. No, we cannot build a new settlement here or anywhere along this lake."

Then Durbin directed Caleb's vision past the Glass City skyline, past the Refinery's skeletal girding and structures, and farther inland away from Erie Lake, back in the direction of Bridgetown. Somewhere past the tall tower of Media Hospital, and beyond the Glass City skyline, Caleb could see the faint figure of giant windmill turbines, their image distorted and masked by the overcast sky.

Durbin pointed over Caleb's shoulder at the silvery-white windmills, so far away they looked like tiny toys resting amongst the trees. "Out there is the Windfields. Paul also said he was heading that direction, to Windy Well. I told him that if our plan fell through, we would follow him there."

"But that is far away from water. What about water? What about food? How will that help us?" Caleb was lost in frustration, and desperate for resolution.

"Windy Well is an established settlement, according to Paul. Maybe getting away from all this soggy land is what we really need to be doing. Maybe we have been going about finding a serviceable home the wrong way."

"We." said Caleb, looking up at Durbin, encouraged by his inclusion of them. "Okay, let's tell Trina."

Durbin helped Caleb position himself on the ladder safely, while Trina held the base. After both had stepped foot on dirt again, Caleb relayed the unsatisfying news about the Erie Lake's lack of habitable shoreline.

"So, we are now heading in the opposite direction. Toward the Windfields?" Trina asked as they turned away from the sheds and makeshift battlements that made up Trash Hill. Lassity had woken from his haymaker induced nap and sat in the shadows of an awning over a porch of one of the distant sheds. He rocked back and forth rambling incoherently as the trio began the descent from the summit settlement of Trash Hill.

"It is a fair distance away," Durbin informed them. "And the trip shall be made longer by us avoiding the Spire and the Glass City at all costs." He then looked up at the overcast sky. The clouds had gathered densely and grown dark in color. "And it looks like a storm may slow us down more."

Caleb was not fond of storms. The powerful wind gusts would blow down barns outside of Bridgetown. They would rend the roofs from some of the more compromised homes. Lightning strikes would start fires. Occasionally, tornados could develop, creating such powerful cones of swirling grey destruction that whole forests and communities would be eradicated completely. He hoped that they could find a suitable shelter if a thunderstorm blew in.

They continued down the steep, walled in slope leading down from the Trash Hill summit, Caleb recalling how ominous the piked skulls and skeletons had looked previously. At the base of the monstrous hill, Durbin lead them away in a direction different than whence they'd arrived, taking them north, farther from the Spire. This area was gouged with deep water-filled ravines and washed-out bridges. Intact shelters were non-existent and Caleb grew more worried as the clouds overhead grew more dimpled with deep, rippling crevices of grey and black.

With a loud crack of thunder, the trio hastened their step, looking feverishly for a stable structure to use as shelter from the impending storm. The thunder reverberated deeply throughout the river valley, across the lake, and through the trees before reverberating back in a seemingly endless quake of sound. Running across an intact bridge with shredded guardrails, Trina suddenly yelled out.

"Over there!"

She pointed to a quaint white farmhouse sitting on an oxbow lake carved out by the years of flooding and receding waters. It had an intact footbridge leading to it from the edge of the ravine they were approaching. To Caleb, the black roof of the two-story house looked unmarred, and most of the windows were still in place. With another deafening crackle and boom of thunder, the trio ran headlong into the falling rain toward the house, as the water pelted them in sheets with the arrival of gale-force winds

They crossed the footbridge single file as it was only wide enough accommodate one person. It was slippery with fresh rain, and Caleb was glad to be on more solid and less slippery land as he dashed toward the nearest white door of the house. He grabbed the knob and it turned with ease, opening wide to allow them all through. Inside, the house was bare, save for a few pieces of random furniture. There was no stove, or refrigerator, or even a dining room table. Strangely, white, lacey triangle-shaped curtains still hung in the windows, though they were dingy from years of neglect. The reddish-brown wood floors were warped from humidity. Some were splintered and grooved, and a thin film of ash-colored dust covered the wood. Except there was a noticeable path clearing the dust in the doorway that Caleb followed out of the kitchen. Along the far wall was a white brick fireplace in the next room, with dry wood stacked next to it. A yellow blanket was laid out on the floor in front of the fireplace, and a black pack lay open on one corner of the blanket. Caleb jumped slightly as thunder crashed outside, accompanied by fierce flashes of lightning, and the rain pelted the numerous windows with heavy clinks and splats.

Caleb's turned to face Trina, who had followed him through the doorway, but his words were lost in another crash of thunder as the wind tossed the rain against the glass. "Someone else is already here."

CHAPTER 11 — TRINA

Trina was proud of herself for finding shelter from the storm up until the point Caleb turned to look at her with beady-eyed caution, as she noticed the backpack on the floor. Durbin stepped up beside her and placed a hand on her shoulder, motioning for her to step into the corner. He pointed to Caleb to go up the wooden stairs to his left. He held a finger to his lips, indicating to them to be quiet.

She stepped softly into the corner, every creak in the wooden would have been heard had it not been drowned out by the torrential rains outside. The house groaned against the whipping winds. Durbin made his way to the far side of the fireplace room, as Caleb climbed the wooden stairs. Trina's breath caught in her throat as Durbin did something unexpected.

"Anyone here?" he called loudly to be heard over the rain and rumbling thunder. "We just came in looking for shelter from the storm. We aren't here to salvage."

The next few seconds were a blur to Trina as lightning flashed and thunder shook the house. A door flew off the wall toward Durbin, knocking him to the floor with a crack and a slide. There was a man on top of the door pinning Durbin down, he was screaming something at him that Trina couldn't understand through the waves of rain and wind knocking at the wall of windows. But she unknowingly grabbed the revolver from her coat pocket, pulled back the hammer with a click and pressed the barrel into the man's head adorned with blazing red hair.

"Get off of him if you want to live," She said to him coldly.

Caleb was seen frozen in motion on the bottom step. Lightning flashed once more. The man slid off the door and pushed himself to his feet slowly, but gracefully. He looked Trina up and down with a confused look as she kept her firearm aimed at him, her two hands firmly wrapped around the grip stock. Thunder crashed around the house and the windows again. Durbin pushed the door off his body and rolled to his feet.

"You— you aren't from the Spire," said the man with curly red hair. Trina dared not take her eyes off him despite the frequent distractions from lightning flashes alternating with rumbling and crashing thunder.

"Did they hire you to bring me back in?" he asked holding up his hands in surrender as he looked over to his black backpack unzipped on the yellow blanket in front of the fireplace. He shook his head. "I am NOT going back."

Trina relaxed slightly, keeping her gun trained on the man. He showed no fear of her. His green eyes matched his tightly curled mop of red hair, but his chocolate toned skin did not. His nose and cheeks were adorned with dark freckles. The palms of his wide strong hands were pinkish, but his arms were a rich brown color. He wore a black bandolier-style holster belt across his chest from his right shoulder, and her eyes moved to the red circle with the red crosshair sight through it displayed on his black shirt. It was the same insignia that had been on the sign they'd surveyed before being shot at from the Spire. His jeans were dirty, much like hers, and each thigh showcased another holster with a small silver pistol in each. *He is armed and didn't draw a weapon on me?*

"We aren't from the Spire," Durbin spoke suddenly. And at the sound of his voice, Caleb walked into the room to join everyone, the final stairs creaking under his boots. He held his hunting knife readily in his hand. "And we aren't here to bring you anywhere."

"You aren't dressed like you are from the Country, either. And you don't act like Marauders from the Glass City. And Loners would have shot me on sight for being in their house" The man acknowledged Caleb with a glance. "I'll be glad to share this house with you if you point that piece somewhere else, miss." He directed his words at Trina.

She weighed his words with his actions. Trina took note of the fact that he was clearly armed, but he'd also made no move to draw his weapons. He'd attacked Durbin with the door but hadn't intended to seriously harm him. He seemed much more afraid of returning to the Spire than he was of the people in the house with him. She lowered her gun.

"Thank you, miss," he said with a slight smile forming on his brown lips as lightning crashed once again. It wasn't yet evening, but the storm had darkened the room. "The name is Darius. This is my… halfway house, if you will. Too far north for the Spire, too far east for those zealots in the Country."

Darius sat down cross-legged on the yellow blanket on the floor next to the black backpack. He reached inside and grabbed a small box that produced a metallic rattle, similar to the sound of the rain hitting the windows. He put the box back inside the pack and reached for another one. He gave it shake and handed it to Trina, .45 was marked on the top.

"These will come in handy for that lovely piece you have there, miss." he said, but he held onto the box even as she placed her fingers on it. He looked at her with his green eyes, expectantly.

"I'm Trina," she said finally, and Darius released his grip on the box as she gave him her name.

"Your friends?" he asked, gesturing to Durbin and Caleb.

"I am her brother, Caleb." He jumped down to the floor, offering a hand to Darius. He sat beside him, moving his bow to allow him a seat.

"Yes, you are," Darius said excitedly. " —I like you already." Trina was glad that Darius was a far better person to encounter than Lassity.

Durbin was stacking firewood in the hearth, checking to make certain the flue was open before producing a flint striking rod from one of the many pockets on his vest. "I am Michael Durbin," he said, pausing to see if sparks were catching flame on the string tinder between the logs. "I apologize for us invading your home."

"It's fine, really, Michael Durbin. And I am sorry for assaulting you with a door. I had to make sure I could run if you were from the Spire. They— …did not take too well to my departure."

The sparks grew into flames and began to wrap their orange fingers around the stacked logs in the hearth. The thunder echoed off in the distance, the storm moving on. It grew darker, the sun setting behind the gloom of passing storm clouds, the fire the only source of light.

"And I am sorry for holding my gun to you, Darius," Trina spoke as sincerely as she could in light of the ups and downs of their journey so far.

"No, No. In this world, one can never be too careful, Trina. And don't you apologize for something now, Caleb," Darius said shaking a finger at him. "Truth is, as soon as I realized that you really weren't here for me, I felt awful about attacking you through the door. But, if I showed myself, and you were here to take me back to the Spire, I was as good as dead."

Trina sat down across from Darius, and Durbin sat between her and Darius' black backpack, his back to the fire. The light cast a soft glow on the shiplap siding on the walls, and the warmth was a welcome contrast to the cold, wet tendrils of black hair that clung to her neck.

"What happened with the Spire, Darius?" asked Durbin. He rubbed his bald head; Trina was uncertain if he hit it on the floor, or if he was exhausted from the day's travels. She could feel her own fatigue setting in now that she was on the floor, relatively safe and at rest, and she stifled a yawn as Darius began talking about the Spire.

"They are a...special group of people. They know their guns, that's for sure. And a whole mess of 'em are sharpshooters."

We were lucky to have a dull one, Trina thought.

"They sit all perched up there on that bridge in the name of protecting what's left of the Glass City, but Marauders have cruised around those flooded streets in their trolling boats with their machine guns for years. The Spire's leader is some pretty boy isolationist named Rapunzel—yeah, long blond hair and all—but he has been MIA for a few weeks. Some say that Suede had something to do with it."

Trina watched his green eyes dance in the fire. He was very energetic with his voice and talked with hands. His red hair burned like the embers in the hearth.

"But that was too much drama for me. Plus, they wouldn't form parties to scavenge, even if supplies were running low. And supplies were running low. Ammo, food. Clothing. But it isn't just the Spire either. Word has it that the Refinery is out of fuel, too. No fuel for the boats for the Marauders. That means no fuel for generators. And everyone's been firing guns like bullets ain't finite."

"And we can't even find potable water or useable farmland to build a new home," interjected Caleb.

"Right? Right." Darius's voice became more hushed and he leaned in like he was going to tell a big secret to the group. "But it isn't just water, and fuel, and food, and bullets that are dwindling. It's everything. Clothes, salvageable metal, the land itself. You been out there, right? Compared to the solid bridge of the Spire, the ground feels like a wet rag. Everything is falling apart."

Trina knew this. She'd noticed that the caravans coming through Bridgetown had fewer goods to trade over the last few years. Even the caravans themselves were fewer. Food and ammunition were worth more in barter and grew even more scarce each year.

"Michael, surely, you've seen how things have been. At the Collapse, no one had any clue 'bout conservation. Those fools acted like the shelves would be full the next time they raided the store, just like they was when money ruled the world. But now," Darius reached into his backpack and retrieved a couple of red and blue boxes of bullets and shells and shook them beside his head, "at least for the short term, these rule the world."

"Is that whole bag full of ammo?" asked Caleb. His eyes grew wide in amazement.

Darius smiled big, revealing a glow of pearl-colored teeth behind his dark lips.

"No wonder the Spire wants you back," laughed Durbin. "Too bad you didn't take all the caliber from the one who was shooting at us today."

"Got too close, did you?" Darius asked, far too excited about an incident that could have resulted in Trina's death. "And no one got hit? Man... Musta been Stambaugh. He's so trigger happy, but couldn't hit the Spire itself if armed with a tripod."

Trina could feel the group relax. It helped that Darius was easygoing. It even felt like the confusing hostile meeting and self-defense never really happened. She was grateful for how forthcoming he was with information. Durbin was able to only give accounts based on his past in regard to the Glass City and the surrounding areas. But Darius, who looked to be younger than Durbin, and older than Trina, was able to provide real-time knowledge about how things in the Black Swamp were functioning. She heard things that Durbin had never mentioned—like the Country. And Paul had only mentioned the Refinery in passing.

And just as with Paul, she felt a sense of warmth from Darius, a sense of ease and genuine kindness that made her glad to be with him. It wasn't that she found Durbin uncomfortable, or mean, or even unapproachable. Durbin was just not warm. In fact, he was even a little cold. Trina could not tell if his coldness was protection to keep him from getting too close to other people, or if he was innately stand-offish with people in general. *He sure was warm with Paul, though. But how could you* not *be?* Durbin's laughter toward Darius gave her unexpected courage.

"Where are you going after the storm clears, Darius?" she asked him boldly. Durbin skeptically raised an eyebrow at her.

"I don't know yet," he said rubbing his cheek and stroking his chin. The freckles danced on his nose in the firelight as his skin scrunched under his hand. "But I DO know that I need a sustainable home — and this ain't it. There is a hole in the roof upstairs. No farmland. Can't defend it. And you know this water is nasty, too."

"Well," Trina continued despite Durbin's dismissing looks and negative nods, "we were told to make way to the Windfields if our surveillance of Erie Lake shoreline didn't pan out."

"Shoreline? On Erie Lake?" Darius laughed. "The closest you will get to a shoreline on Erie Lake is at either of the old nuclear power plants—like The Core—and even that ain't really a shoreline. More like a concrete break wall."

Trina didn't appreciate being laughed at, but she did not let that discourage her. This man had much knowledge about their surroundings that could be invaluable to their survival.

"You have a better plan?" she asked.

"What do you plan to find in the Windfields, Trina?" Darius continued.

"We are heading to a settlement called Windy Well. A friend asked us to find him there if things don't go as planned. Are you familiar with the place?"

"Sadly, no," he replied. He had a confused and pained look on his face as if he were uncomfortable with not having information on a topic. But his eyes lit up quickly and he smiled his big toothy smile. "Sounds like it could be an adventure."

CHAPTER 12 — DURBIN

And now we have four to our ranks of mishappening adventurers. We have our grizzled veteran. We have our young scout in Caleb. We have our fighter in Trina. And now we have our weapons master in Darius.

Durbin laughed quietly to himself as he lay on the wood floor in the farmhouse, his backpack acting as a makeshift pillow. He was mostly dry. He was mostly warm. And he had a destination for himself and the Hurst children. *I can include Darius in that too, I suppose.* The fire crackled quietly in the stone and brick hearth beside him. Rain dripped with a light steady rapping from the bent gutter outside the window beyond his head as he lay. He knew he should be sleeping, resting for their endeavor towards the Windfields tomorrow —*who knows when we will have a roof over our heads again*— but the day's events played out in his mind repeatedly. From the sniper attack near the Spire, to crazed hermit Lassity, to the disappointment on Trash Hill, the sudden thunderstorm, and the mad rush that led to the meeting of Darius —it had been quite a day. *And I lost my hat.* He rubbed his bald head with a wave of disappointment and sighed.

Durbin tried to piece together the current social climate from Darius's information. He determined that the days of having any gasoline were nearly over —if they weren't already, which meant that Marauders in the Glass City may be moving elsewhere if they have no fuel to power their boats. And if fuel couldn't be processed, then the Refinery was a mass of useless aging steel —just another crumbling shell of a factory from a bygone age. The firearm fanatics in the Spire were running out of ammunition. And if they were running low on ammunition, then everyone else in the area would be soon, as well. The water quality all over the Glass City and Black Swamp area was poor and possibly dangerous. The vision of orange, purple, and green swirls in the churning lake water below Trash Hill flashed in his mind. Therefore, food was also growing scarce, so few things could grow and lure wild game to the area of the Erie Lake shoreline. The murky mires of rising swampland caused the roads to fall in on themselves, sinkholes were commonly swallowing potential shelters, rendering all urban areas potential and unforeseen hazards. *We thought this place was a dying hole before the Collapse?*

Darius was adamant about informing Durbin that his presence with them could be a liability if the Spire were to track him. As such, he recommended that they travel along the relatively dry northern suburbs of the Black Swamp, staying far from the Glass City and Spire territory. It would add days to their journey to the Windfields, but the risk of Loners, or raving lunatics like Lassity, holed up in abandoned dwellings they may happen upon was far more welcome than organized search parties. So, with a begrudging change in plans, come morning they would be heading south into the farmlands away from the Black Swamp. The farmland were primarily flat, and spider-webbed with creekbeds that shifted between flooded and dry with even small changes in the weather. Over a decade of unchecked trees and other vegetation hid sudden dropping ravines, inhabited by badgers and deer and snakes. Durbin planned to take the old superhighway that encircled the Glass City area and take it south. As much as he would prefer to travel under concealment, traveling with Darius and his knowledge and skill gave Durbin confidence to take a primary route. Durbin tried very hard to force from his thoughts the fact their path would take them near the remnants of Camp Moon.

But gnawing even further into the back of Durbin's mind was the idea of diminishing resources. He feared that most settlements in the greater Glass City area would be suffering from decreased food supplies, or capacity to produce food. He was certain that word of any community that was able to produce technology to create clothing and tools would be renowned —but he had heard of no such place during his recent travels. Though, if Durbin were being honest with himself, he often avoided most human contact. In swelling and unexpected moments of sadness, he had begun to wonder if they were at the end. He even asked himself if humanity had finally used up the last of its ingenuity, spoiled by decades of technological coddling and pampering, healthcare that protected so well that once absent even minor illnesses became deadly. Had years of codependence and interdependence on technology and medicine neutered humankind's ability to adapt and fend for itself? It seemed improbable to Durbin, as humanity had survived coups, and revolutions, and holocausts, and wars, and plagues, and famines for thousands of years. *Something to talk about with Paul.*

He propped up onto his elbow and looked around at his traveling party asleep on the floor. Trina's long black hair was still drying in the subtle warmth of the fire. She had one wrist on her forehead as she lay her head on her backpack. Caleb was curled up in a ball, one hand under his cheek between his pack and face. As he glanced at Darius, he was surprised to see him facedown on the floor, but under a palm above his head was one of his guns. His back rose and fell rhythmically with the breath of comfortable sleep. But eyeing his companions as they peacefully slept did little to calm his mind. Durbin rolled onto his side, facing the softly glowing embers of the fire, his backpack under his head. He wiggled his head to move one of the cans of food to a softer position under his ear, his mind a racing mess of past, present, and future —thoughts of his failures as a father, as a leader. With the thoughts of all the survivors whose lives he had ended over the years. With thoughts of how to salvage what dwindling resources of food, tools, shelter, and weaponry would be available in the coming years. Even more thoughts of how to handle the new challenges of Trina and Caleb came to him —felt as though he owed them more than he could have given to his perished family. He sighed softly, hoping for sleep to join him soon.

CHAPTER 13 — CALEB

With the early morning light came the whistling song of birds. Faint whispers of wind blew the water off the trees whose water-soaked buds seemed to triple in size overnight. The breeze blown water droplets rapped the windows above Caleb's head and he was the first to rise. Rubbing the sleep from his eyes and stretching, he cracked his youthful back and jumped up, fetching his backpack, bow, and quiver as he had every morning recently. He tip-toed across the creaky wood floor and peeked out the windows, observing the fresh grass sprouting between the house and the water surrounding it. He felt energetic and refreshed as though the stresses of yesterday were a distant memory. He was uncertain as to why. Perhaps it was the sunshine pouring into the windows after last night's storm. Perhaps it was the warmth radiating through the windows. Perhaps it was the visible green shoots on the various trees and plants outside indicating new life.

Regardless of the actual reason, Caleb looked down to see his three companions sleeping on the floor in front of the white brick fireplace; their bodies slowly rising and falling with breaths of deep sleep, and he smiled. He felt there was strength in numbers, despite being easier to see; and four in a traveling party is a far cry from his solo venture that led to him tracking Durbin.

They had discussed last night the plan for their journey towards the Windfields and Windy Well. They had agreed on caution and vigilance and on sticking together, taking a longer course that would leave them more exposed, but keep them far from Marauder territory. Darius gave Caleb the impression that he was worried about being tracked dutifully by members of the Spire, but Caleb wasn't moved.

"We all agreed to stick together, Darius," Caleb reassured him as they sat in a circle bathed in the glow from the fireplace. Night had fallen outside.

"You underestimate their tenacity, my man," said Darius pointing a finger at Caleb. "In these bags may be only bullets to you. But to them, it is a large amount of protection, coercion, currency, and bargaining materials. You are looking at the richest man from the Spire."

He looked directly at Trina and winked while making a sharp clicking sound with his tongue against his teeth.

"They won't take you back with all of us together. We won't let it happen." Caleb tried to sound authoritative.

"Oh, I trust your intentions, Caleb, but some of them Spire guys are bad mamma-jammas. Don't go getting' yourself killed for me, man. I'm prolly not worth it."

"You say that like it matters. Seriously, we are a team now." said Caleb.

At that, Darius nodded in agreement and offered his hand to Caleb, both men wearing smiles that glowed warmly in the firelight.

Caleb smiled once more as he stepped outside into the soft morning light with new greenery and softly dripping rainwater smelling fresh and crisp. Caleb breathed deeply, taking in the clean scent, a stark change from the putrid chemical and sewage smell from Trash Hill. He was amazed at the difference in the terrain only a few kilometers away. He heard water dripping along with a bent and split downspout splattering onto the rickety wooden stoop, the white paint peeling and curling while the boards warped and crooked, pulling rusty nails from their wooden moors. He approached the dripping water and opened his mouth, catching the cascading freshwater, feeling it cool his throat.

After quenching his thirst, he slowly turned around and viewed the land they'd rushed through in order to escape the thunderstorm last night. Bright green grass glistened with water droplets in the rising sun, piercing the rich dark soil below. A derelict garden lay off the porch to his right, its trellis cracked and bent with the choking pull of woody vines. In front of him was the narrow footbridge, with rough, brown metal rails and the wooden decking streaked wet with rain. Under the bridge sat still water so dark that it looked nearly black. It was impossible to determine how deep the water was or where it flowed, as the surface sat as still and smooth as ebony glass. Birds whistled and chattered overhead with song and squawks. *The air was definitely warmer today; spring is finally here to stay.*

Caleb heard heavy footsteps come across the wooden floor in the house and felt the door open behind him. He expected Durbin but was greeted by Darius's bright smile and striking green eyes, the chocolate freckles dancing over his nose and cheeks. He patted Caleb firmly on his back as he passed him and leaned on the porch rail. Brittle white paint peeled under Darius's dark hands as he took in a deep breath.

"Trina and Durbin will be out in a moment," he said to Caleb as he shifted his weight and leaned over the porch rail to the dripping gutter and drank. He sighed with pleasure as the water dripped into his mouth. He swiped his lips with the back of his wrist. "He asked us to be ready soon."

Caleb nodded and went back inside to fetch his backpack and bow. He found Trina and Durbin stretching away their sleepiness, then placing their packs on their backs. They looked tired as if the weight of yesterday's stress had not left them as easily as it had Caleb. He also wondered if travel was taking a toll on Trina, as she hadn't before journeyed more than a day away from Bridgetown. They were going on five days, now and while Trina wore a strong face, he could tell something was bringing her down. *Maybe it is Mom and Dad?* he thought. And he growled in his mind at himself refusing to entertain any thoughts of sadness lest he find himself less vigilant and a risk to his traveling partners.

"Darius said you wanted to be ready to leave soon?" he asked of Durbin who was strapping on his pack and patting each of his pockets as he did every morning.

"Yes," said Durbin reaching to straighten the hat on his head that was no longer there and he frowned as his hands held empty air. "We need to find our way to the old expressway corridor that runs along with the northern suburbs. It will take some time to find it from here —the foliage will be thick; pitfalls can be numerous— and I don't know how safe it will be. Neither does Darius. But he is adamant about not cutting across the city for fear of a search party out for him. And as I said last night, I am not too fond of stumbling into Marauder territory, or dealing with crazy Loners. We will take a long way, but it still guarantees no safety."

"I am not sure there is anything more dangerous than being shot at by an enemy you cannot see," said Trina. She had rolled up the sleeves of her red, white, and blue flannel shirt, and woven her long leather jacket through the straps of her black backpack. The silver revolver that was pocketed inside the jacket was now tucked into her jeans. She pulled out her shirt to conceal the grip.

"Sometimes, the enemy before you in plain sight can be more dangerous." Durbin retorted.

Caleb wondered if Durbin was thinking about the men who'd attacked him on the road the day they met. But Durbin made such quick work of dispatching them that it appeared he was in little danger, or even no danger at all. *Not like that sniper.*

Darius had also retrieved his gear and reattached his dual pistols to their thigh holsters. He strapped his large red hiking bag on his back and clicked the black nylon cheststrap over the red target-sight insignia on his black shirt as best as he could to try and hide his affiliation with the Spire.

"Let's be on the lookout for a new shirt for me, 'kay? Size large. No blood and no holes, though. I am a man of style." He outstretched his hands and bade everyone look at him. "Ha! Who am I kidding? I would wear a sundress to get out of this trash."

The foursome shared a short, timid laugh and exited Darius's self-proclaimed halfway house together. Across the footbridge, they walked single file, and Durbin led them away from the low morning sun. They made small talk, led primarily by Trina at first, as she talked about caring for the denizens of Bridgetown during the epidemic. Caleb shared the details of tracking Durbin several days prior. Their stories were interrupted occasionally by Durbin and Darius discussing landmarks and determining that they were staying on course. They had an occasional disagreement about how to traverse paths that were blocked by rubble or overgrown by foliage that erupted from chasms within the roads.

Then Darius spoke candidly to Durbin.

"A'right, man. I have heard from these youthful souls. Now, I wanna hear from you. Where does the man known as Michael Durbin come from? You gotta vengeance story? A family? You secretly waiting to murder us all in our sleep?"

Caleb's eyes shot open wide with shock. His mouth hung open slightly, perplexed by Darius's forward nature and the possibility of truth in his last statement. Darius hadn't seen the ferocity Durbin displayed against the scavengers.

"I'm kidding, Caleb," he apologized with a playful punch to Caleb's shoulder as they relaxed. "If he were going to do that, he'd have done it by now!"

Even Durbin laughed.

Caleb found Darius's humor quite odd. He was not accustomed to jokes and teasing or rapid-fire wit. Bridgetown was far too serious for that type of interaction. Every day was work and survival. As children, they studied their fatigued textbooks with yellowed and musty and torn pages a few days a week. They farmed the nearby hills, then waited for the lowlands to dry before farming them as well. They tried to pot water from the temperamental river that held both life and death. They hunted deer and goose, and rabbit, and tried to raise cattle and goats —then protect said livestock from scavengers and bandits. No, humor was not a common trait, and Caleb found it hard to keep up with Darius's wanton personality. But still, he greatly appreciated his company. It was refreshing in a certain way.

"You know Durbin," Darius continued, "in all those old fantasy stories, the adventuring party was just some haphazard mish-mash of character-arc-types. They all get together by happenstance and such, not really knowing who each other were. Right now, I peg you as the old brooding one who knows just about everything, carries some prophecy about a chosen one, and is recruiting us younger, more talented folks to take on some ancient evil."

Durbin laughed again; a bit harder this time.

"I have had several of those same thoughts, Darius," Durbin responded.

Darius smiled his bright toothy smile. They walked four-wide having finally reached the highway that bordered the northern suburbs of The Glass City. The late morning sun warmed their backs. Their roadway path sat below two steep embankments. Generally constructed of the formed concrete that ruts and wear chiseled by water. At times, the concrete gave way to soft earth, allowing budding life of springtime greenery to block their path. Overpasses of stained concrete crossed overhead intermittently, some of them collapsed into heaps of rubble that blocked their path, others creating makeshift ramps out of the highway corridor. They dodged boulders and twisted sculptures of exposed reinforcement metal, and weaved around abandoned vehicles and overturned tractor-trailers.

"Honestly," Durbin continued, "my knowledge about this area as it stands is nil compared to yours, Darius. So much has changed in the last decade or so, that much of what I recall doesn't exist. I have avoided the metro Glass City area for a long time. For a lot of reasons."

Caleb was interested, but he always feared to ask the grizzled, stone-faced man any probing questions. His stoic aura bled of a man who had seen much trouble in his life, and Caleb dared not to ask him to relive those troubles, for fear of what he might here.

"One of those reasons is only a few kilometers from here… Camp Moon," he continued without a change in his voice.

None of the others asked anything further. They waited patiently for Durbin to divulge information in his own time. They were curious but also reserved.

"Another reason," he sighed deeply, "is because I am a coward."

Caleb twisted his face in confusion. There was nothing this man could be afraid of. "No, that can't—"

Trina firmly gripped Caleb's arm and gave him a sharp sideways nod, only once, while looking him in the eyes.

Durbin continued as though he hadn't heard Caleb. "My family was murdered in Camp Moon about ten winters ago. So I left. I roamed the Irish Hills north of here while the Black

Swamp swallowed The Glass City. I made false friendships. Everything was for my gain because with my family gone, I had nothing to lose. I stole from people who trusted me. I killed people who crossed me. I ran away from settlements that wanted a commitment from me as a hunter or a gatherer."

Darius spoke in a tone much softer than Caleb had heard from him before. "But that was after we all fell from society…"

Durbin nodded, showing no other emotion.

"I want to know what Michael Durbin was like before all that."

Durbin turned up the corners of his lips in a forced smile. But as Caleb studied Durbin's face, that smile became larger, wider, and more genuine. His cheeks rose above his auburn and silver beard, slightly muddy, with small beads of sweat clinging to the coarse hairs.

"We used to have movie theaters," he said looking directly at Caleb. He then craned his neck and looked directly at Trina. "They were huge rooms where a visual story would be displayed on a screen. Sometimes, stories of love, sometimes of survival, or some to scare us. Some would be about a hero with magical powers, some were made just to make us laugh. We would go there as large groups together. Sometimes, hundreds of people in a large room watching a story on the screen. We didn't kill each other —well most of the time we didn't— and we didn't look over our backs every few minutes."

Caleb spied more droplets on Durbin's cheeks and thought they looked more like tears than sweat.

"I worked as a shipping manager for a sportsman outfitter. I drove a nice sport utility vehicle. I had the most amazing family. We gardened, we played baseball and soccer. Abbot was my little man, Celine was my baby girl, and Erin was my heart. My wife. My partner. My grounding. I worked hard for them."

Durbin kicked a rock that skipped across the rifted pavement, bounced high, and smacked a twisted metal sign with a tinny hollow-sounding crack that reverberated around them.

"We ate tacos once a week, and ham or turkey sandwiches for lunch. We had plumbing and heat, and lawns to mow. I loved reading fantasy novels and playing video games with my nieces and nephews, reading books to my kids…"

Durbin sniffed deeply and rubbed his sleeve across his nose before he continued. "Life was boring and fun all at the same time. We took all of it for granted."

Caleb didn't know what to think. So much of what Durbin told failed to make sense to him. He realized that Durbin truly did come from another world, from another time, when everything was a far cry from what it was now. He could only imagine people getting together for entertainment. In Bridgetown, the whole village gathered to discuss the state of the settlement —often poor— or regarding bad news or a call to arms to help harvest the gardens and farms.

"Those truly were the good ol' days, man," Darius responded, sounding lost in his own recollections of the past. The path climbed gradually upward, met by a crossing junction of several highway overpasses —a gnarled mess of concrete and steel overgrown by trees and shrubbery regaining their hold on the world around them. They walked in mutual silence for a short distance before Trina finally spoke up.

"So, Darius, what was your life before the Collapse?"

Darius shook his hands and his head simultaneously. "No one wants to hear that mess."

"Sure I do," she replied.

"I want to know you a little better as well," Caleb spoke up. He looked at Darius earnestly.

"I'm nothing special you guys," Darius started, gesturing into the air. "I was a teenager when the Collapse occurred. So, my formative years happened in this world that you know. I grew up in the Glass City. My dad was an Irishman who worked the docks. My momma was a school teacher in the poorest parts of the city. She had this cute, tightly curled mop of black hair that complimented her dark skin so nice, a little gap in her two front teeth. A lot of folks had moved past the stigma of a white man and a black woman being together. But there were some folks who had not."

Caleb listened intently to Darius as he hung his head and continued his story, his lips tight and turned downward in an effort to stifle emotion. Caleb struggled to understand some of it. The foreign nature of hate was lost on him. He tried to grasp the horror as Darius described his parents being murdered in front of him a few months after the Collapse.

Darius had been holed up with his parents in their downtown apartment as violent gangs prowled the streets, stealing, killing, raping for no reason other than terrorism and savagery. They were planning an escape for sunrise to the northern or western suburbs. But as they were readying to retire for the night, five men burst through their apartment door, shouting, screaming and firing guns with deafening blasts. They threw Darius by his red hair into a corner and screamed words about race and color and abominations while one of them held a pistol to his father's head. Another shoved his father down to his knees. Darius's mother screamed as two others grabbed her and ripped her clothes to shreds and the fifth man with a black swastika tattooed on the back of bare head undid his belt. Darius's father yelled obscenities and climbed to a stand after biting the hand of the man who held a gun to his head. His dad lunged at the man with the tattoo as he began to mount Darius's mother. But another gun blast went off, louder than all the rest. Darius covered his ears to stop the ringing and watched in terror as his father's head exploded in a splash of red. His mother writhed and kicked in pain but he heard no sound other than the ringing in his skull. The man who shot his father came up very close to him and pointed the pistol in his face. Darius shook with fear. The barrel of the gun looked to be several meters long and the voices of the men sounded as if they were kilometers away and underwater. The voice of the man holding the gun on Darius slowly grew clearer.

"He said to me, 'I don't kill kids no matter how ugly they are. But I can't say the same for Joe over there. You better run, mutt.' And so I ran out of that apartment as fast as I could. When my feet hit the street below, I heard the gunshot that killed my mother."

The bright afternoon sun was irony for such a dark story. The silence during pauses in Darius's narrative, accompanied by boots scuffing gravel and pavement, was a fitting soundtrack.

"I played lone wolf for a little while. I bounced in and out of a few settlements. I even tried to join the Country at one point. But wouldn't you know it? They don't much like half-colored men either. I was with the Refinery for a short time before the Marauder menace took over the Glass City after it permanently flooded. They taught me about engines, but we can't use them much now. About five winters ago I managed to get into the Spire. Learned everything I know about guns from there. I also learned about commerce from the caravans that came near. But reading was always my thing. You can learn a ton of info from books."

Caleb felt the sting of sadness in their group's common thread of tragedy. Durbin had lost his wife and children. Darius had lost his parents. And he and Trina had lost theirs. Caleb was beginning to think all of life was filled with only loss and despair, and as warm as the sun was on his back, inside he felt chilled and empty. The stresses of adventure were finally taking their toll on him.

CHAPTER 14 — TRINA

The four of them walked cautiously for days, avoiding pitfalls in the deteriorated highway, slowly navigating overgrowth that concealed ravines where the road disappeared. Sometimes, the solid concrete and asphalt gave away under her boots. Sometimes, the jagged edges of asphalt revealed a flowing river of brown water, flushing back toward Glass City, taking with it any loose earth and debris. At other times, the road buckled so badly she climbed the upward sloping embankments of earth, grabbing for saplings and bracing against rippled metal guardrails tossed about like strips of aluminum foil.

The hiking pack on her back grew heavy as the sun warmed her coat. The moisture in the air becoming thick and more oppressive from recent rains. Spring was in full swing feeling more like summer now, with the surprise last snow a few weeks back a distant memory. She began to sweat under her coat and considered shedding it, but lack of desire to carry it bade her keep wearing the leather.

She listened to Darius and Durbin discuss ways to hunt and field dress deer to make the carry lighter, techniques for avoiding badgers and how to spot swamp snakes. Darius insisted that black bears were making their way from the Northern Lakes, even though he had never personally spotted one.

The terrain eventually settled and became flat and level, the former highway a mosaic of grass and dirt, with islands of concrete in between. She spied a large green sign streaked black with age, the only visible letters were U-2 then 3 and S-O followed by T-H. Someone had somehow climbed up there to paint a white U to spell "south" and an arrow pointed to the highway. Underneath in fuzzy spray paint was written Windy Well, Sunfield, TreeTop, and Woodstock. Each had a crudely painted arrow behind it, indicating the direction one should travel to reach each settlement. It was foreign to her, to think that out in the middle of nowhere, this towering piece of stained and painted metal insisted that life abounded. The sign told her that settlements alive and well still existed. *It even gave directions*. With that, Trina dared to think that she and Caleb *could* have found a new home on their own. But as she looked about the deserted highway, and the towering sycamore trees with their pasty white tops and the densely packed spring foliage concealing their path, she realized that their chances of safely finding a beacon such as this were very slim. She quickly dismissed the thought and glanced at Durbin, silently thanking him for his selflessness and assistance.

"Sunfield is an awfully odd name for a settlement," said Trina, looking to the sign as they passed under it. Old crooked vines hung from it, dried and cracking, broken at unusual angles and dangling by threads. "You cannot grow sun in a field. Or is it referring to sunflowers?"

Darius quipped, all too eager to share knowledge with her, "Naw, nah, Trina. That place gathers the sun in giant flat panels. It uses that sunlight to create energy for the bunker which is under the hill where those panels are placed. But what they use that energy for? I don't know. I hear the people are a little… -odd." Darius made an unknown gesture to her as he pointed to his ear and drew an imaginary circle around it while sticking out a fleshy pink tongue.

As with so many things in the areas outside of Bridgetown, Trina was fascinated by the unique diversity of the settlements, their given names, and the resourcefulness of humans. If the last few weeks had taught her anything, it was that she had so much more of the world to see —as desolate and decaying as the world of man was. Something about that sign, its age, its meaning of direction to places that actually exist, its leading to human ingenuity and survival awakened something inside of her. A sense of adventure. A sense of purpose. She shifted her bow to her other shoulder and made a mental reminder to herself to go find Sunfield someday.

The foursome passed under the road sign and continued on a highway that was beginning to look more like a tunnel, with trees towering and curving overhead to form a loose canopy of twiggy fingers grasping desperately for a companion.

A day later, their environment changed drastically.

Gone were the towering sycamores and creeping vines of ivy. Little of the vegetation around them was taller than a couple meters, with wild vegetation of cattails, wheat, and unkempt mulberry trees, as well as occasional cherry trees with pink blossoms nearing the end of their bloom. The land flattened out significantly, and though they were now several kilometers away from the floodplains of the river, the land beneath their feet would randomly alternate between solid turf mixed with rubbled concrete to the squishy marsh that made sloppy wet noises as their boots escaped its suction grip. Small clusters of trees could be spied away from the trampled and cracked carcass of main roads, but it was clear they were now traveling in long, uncultivated farmland, untended by machine or irrigation for fifteen years.

The breeze picked up strongly around her, and Trina thought about the swelling gusts that hit her when she was on top of Trash Hill. She hadn't felt wind like that since. And now, with few trees to slow down its pursuit, the wind whipped the spring vegetation with a fervor, firm blades of wild grass clicking in chatter amongst each other. Geese and sparrows glided into the wind as several buzzards flew in concentric circles off in the distance, their black wings as sails catching the moving air. And then she saw it.

Far beyond the buzzards, she saw the slow-motion of silvery-white windmill blades turning against the wind.

"I think I see the Windfields!" she called out in excitement, pointing to a spot of reflected light below the buzzards' circular paths.

"Indeed you do," agreed Durbin.

"Should we pick up the pace?" she asked, motivated by seeing a destination.

"Not at all," replied Durbin, "The old farmlands here are crisscrossed with deep irrigation ditches. And those are well hidden by this tall foliage. Let us stick to the road, even if it briefly turns us away from the windmill. The Windfields is a large place, by my understanding. And I am not certain where Windy Well actually lies in all of it."

Trina looked at Darius for a rebuttal.

He shrugged his shoulders in surrender, "We waaaay outside my stomping grounds, girl. I'm trustin' the old man, here. Fallin' in ditches don't sound like much fun."

With that, they continued to follow what was left of the road as it wound ever closer toward the windmills, sometimes obscured by tall brown and yellow grasses and cottonwood saplings. The grinding chirps of crickets and grasshoppers greeted them at every turn, with an occasional surprise splashing sound as bullfrogs lept into waterlogged ditches away from the scuff of their advancing boots.

The paths were beginning to look more worn, with fewer heroic plants making a final stand in the dirt-filled cracks of the pavement. In some places, it appeared as though the weeds and foliage had been cut intentionally. Trina even identified grooves in the dirt that could belong to the wheels of caravan wagons. She smiled. It had been months since she had seen a caravan wagon. But she quickly realized she had nothing on her she was willing to trade.

Gently winding, the path became less pavement and more earth between the quickly growing springtime weeds. Some of the flatland grasses were trampled and bent as if by people or animals or cart. The wind caused the cattails to bustle against each other with frequent short gusts, producing a hollow wooden clicking. A woodpecker rapped against a tree trunk behind them in response.

Around the next bend of tall field grasses, they were greeted by a small group of sheds and ramshackle structures, pole barns, and tractors lying about like fossilized dinosaurs of a lost era. Windmills spaced a hundred meters apart looked down upon them, silent and unmoving. Few people bustled about, carrying sacks, or wood, or baskets of berries and greens. The settlers paid no attention to the foursome as they continued on their path, winding through the random structures and under towering windmills.

"Is this Windy Well?" Caleb finally asked Durbin. He looked confused and sounded doubtful. Trina was confused as well, as the randomness of the people and the layout of the buildings didn't give her the impression of an established settlement. She was further confused that people continued to act as if Trina and her companions were not there.

They passed another still windmill. It was heavily modified with objects of plastic and steel that funneled hoses down to the base of the windmill. Around the foundation were blue plastic barrels full of water. The hoses dripped water into barrels, catching the water from the funnels above. A man with greasy black hair, wearing soiled brown and yellow sheets of poorly tailored cloth that resembled robes, stood at the barrels holding a tin ladle. He scooped water from a barrel and slurped it noisily. He looked at them as they passed, glaring at them distrustfully as he bowed his head to hide his face.

Darius approached him, and the robed man froze with the ladle suspended near his lips.

"We are looking for Windy Well," he said calmly, looking directly at the robed man, "Perhaps you can kindly help us find it?"

The robed man slowly poured the water from the ladle back into the barrel, his eyes darting all over Darius, from his thigh holstered guns, to the Spire icon barely visible on his chest, to his open hands and ginger-red hair.

"You look like you belong there," the robed man said cryptically his voice as oily as his hair. Trina stepped up beside Darius. "You keep following this path through the Windfields. After the shacks is a clearing. After that, you see what you're looking for."

"Thank you," Trina said touching Darius's arm to pull him away from the robed man, then feeling the parch of her mouth, she asked, "Could we have a drink of water before we go?"

"You can," the greasy robed man rasped, "but he can't."

He pointed the ladle weakly at Darius, crooked boney fingers with round white knuckles wound around the handle. Darius, in turn, tightened his lips thinly, his arm tensing under Trina's grip.

"It's probably poisoned anyway," she growled at the robed man, pulling Darius away and moving down the path. Darius resisted only briefly before following her.

Caleb, in turn, walked up to the robed man who began slurping water from the ladle again.

"What's your issue?" Trina heard Caleb ask. And she slowed her pace. "Darius has never been around here. What has he done to you?"

"They are all the same," the robed man hissed. "You all go to your precious Windy Well. We have our own water here." He splashed water upward, pointing the ladle at the modifications on the windmill. "We don't need their water or their energy. We are doing just fine on our own out here."

Caleb shook his head and walked away. A small group of people stopped gathering and transporting goods long enough to watch what was happening with the travelers, but they kept their distance. Trina looked at the robed man one last time and imagined holding his head underwater in one of the barrels with his arms and legs flailing as he struggled in vain for breath, her face reddening with anger. *Who hates someone they have never met?* Then, feeling hypocritical for her own rage, she turned back to Darius. "We are not welcome here," she said to him. He nodded, then Caleb and Durbin followed.

The travelers walked briskly through the rest of the Windfields in silence. They passed dozens of windmills, most standing still against the breezes overhead. Several had groups of shacks and sheds at their bases, some boasted a water gathering setup similar to the one guarded by the greasy robed man. Trina stole glances at Darius, watching him slowly relax as the frustration of being insulted passed with the growing distance from the water barrels. Darius and she walked in step, which slowed as they left the makeshift settlement. Caleb and Durbin walked together a short distance behind them. Caleb implored Durbin for answers for the way Darius had been treated by the man at the water barrels. Much of it was unintelligible, but she saw Darius smile his bright toothy smile when Caleb clearly exclaimed: "That's not right!"

Any further conversation was interrupted by the slow droning thump of the next windmill, protected by colorful walls that sprawled away from and encircled its base. A large forest sat beyond, and fenced in, expertly tended farmland lay before it.

Trina knew without question that this massive lone fortified settlement was Windy Well.

CHAPTER 15 — DARIUS

Darius had seen many settlements in his days. Some were metal bastions of repurposed shipping containers. Some were heavy metal highway signs bolted together to keep out uninvited guests. Some were boarded up warehouses and retail centers serviced by the creative piping of water sills and water storage solutions. Even solar-powered bunkers like Sunfield were not foreign to him —one was a series of school busses half-buried in earth and concrete. But he had never witnessed a large settlement such as Windy Well, in the middle of nowhere, with a giant wind turbine as its source of energy.

Windy Well rose out of the budding greenery with walls and parapets of corrugated red and blue and green and yellow steel smattered with random swaths of coarsely weathered brown rust, faded green and blue highway signs patched together with wrought iron and chain-link fencing, oxidized by the elements and bolted together solidly with crude but intuitive engineering. To Darius, the walls were a masterwork in resourcefulness, and he wondered how long it had taken to deliver the scrap to this remote area.

Over the protective three-meter wall, Darius could see pipe framed scaffolding that created another higher level to the settlement. Settlers could be seen walking on the mezzanine between rooms, taking makeshift stairways down to the ground level, or the roofs above the quarters on the second level. Thick braided steel cables ran in every direction, some moving with baskets attached carrying supplies, some holding light fixtures to illuminate the catwalk mezzanine. The windmill turbine itself stood above the settlement, aluminum gleaming in the sun, the broad blades spanning the width of the settlement like a guardian angel's wings. Though the windmill could be seen from kilometers away, nothing prepared Darius for its sheer size. He could feel the droning thump of its movement in his chest as they approached even closer to the front gate of Windy Well.

From up high on the catwalk, someone in dirty clothes shouted down to an unseen person who called back as two large white plates of steel were beginning to raise up from their lower outside corners. Chains clinked along gears and steel squealed as a man in greasy denim overalls worn over a stained red shirt walked up to the chain-link fence remained as a barrier between them. Meanwhile the white steel doors thundered loudly into place, forming a triangle shape above them as metal slammed into metal. Darius saw Trina and Caleb jump slightly at the sound as Durbin walked up to greet the greasy man standing behind the chain-link fence where the white gate previously sat quietly.

The man wearing the stained red shirt and overalls stood at the chain-link fence, he rubbed a soiled rag in his hands and placed it in the center pouch of his overalls. He looked at his visitors with mild suspicion, the rough features of his face softening as stern lips turned to a very small smile.

"Welcome to the Windy Well, travelers. We boast safety in exchange for fair treatment and equal work by our members. I am the 'Mechanic'. Though most folks here have just taken to calling me Nick."

Darius spied Trina ducking and moving in order to get a better view of the settlers working behind Nick. Durbin walked up to the fence and addressed their greeter.

"I am Durbin. The skinny one is Caleb, the young woman is Trina, and our master at arms here is Darius. Paul asked us to meet him here a few weeks ago. Has he been here?"

Nodding in agreement, Nick again surveyed Darius, Caleb, and Trina briefly, as if to ascertain his judgement of them. Then he looked intently at Durbin, searching for something in his blank bearded face. "Paul. Short guy. Long white ponytail. Glasses. That your Paul?" He stated features like he was checking off a list in his mind. Darius briefly wondered how Nick would describe him. *Mostly black. Wild red hair. Big teeth. Flashy guns.* He laughed quietly at himself.

Durbin's blank face eroded and a big smile cracked across his cheeks, "Yeah, that's my Paul."

Satisfied, Nick smiled in return. He let out a sharp whistle and made a big hand gesture as he stepped back from the chain-link fence. Suddenly, an ear-piercing squeal rang out and the fence shifted to the right, sliding across the ground on course metal rollers to allow Darius and company to finally walk into Windy Well.

Darius noted how well he could hear despite the slow low-frequency thrumming of the windmill overhead. Everywhere in the settlement, people were moving and organizing supplies. Men were seen carrying clear blue plastic jugs, dirty with age, with water sloshing inside. Women were seen carrying crates of wood or plastic with a myriad of cables, junk, fasteners, tools or clothing materials. Still, others carried sacks of dried meat or dried fruits from the previous harvest. Kids carried logs and sacks of edible plants and roots. He thought he heard a combustion engine grumbling somewhere behind the central windmill. Darius marveled at the motivation and teamwork. If this were the Spire, bored men would be sitting on empty wooden crates, twitching for their guns at every seagull call or distant Marauder's gunshot. They would be grumbling with complaints if not sitting in silence, wasting away their pitiful, dutiless days.

"Paul should be in talking with Kimwu," Nick informed them as he led the group through denizens of busy settlers. "I will take you to his quarters."

"We don't mean to interrupt anything," Durbin responded apologetically. They kept pace with Nick while receiving an abbreviated tour of the settlement.

"You most likely will not be," replied Nick. He patted a child on the head as she passed carrying root vegetables in a faded orange-colored plastic milk crate. "Kimwu and Paul seem to enjoy each other's company. They will sit and chat for hours about nothing if they aren't engaged in any settlement duties. I have had to remind them to bed down twice this week."

Darius did not know Kimwu or Paul, but already he felt he liked them more than anyone at the Spire. Certainly, he liked them more than anyone they had passed in the Windfields.

Windy Well encircled the central windmill, the settlement's interior guarded by makeshift walls. Along the wall were shelter and shops, fabricated dwellings with walls and doors and windows. Catwalks and ladders and stairs made a passage to an upper level where there more were homes, and porches hosting miss-matched, decrepit lawn furniture. But there were also strategically designed parapets and portholes cut into the tall steel walls. Below some of the tiny openings were crates of bolts or arrows with traditional bows and crossbows hung nearby.

Nick led them toward a twisted metal staircase that resembled a fire escape from downtown in the Glass City. It was bolted and tied to hodgepodge support framing hastily welded to the top of a wheel-less semi-trailer. On top of the semi-trailer was a small shipping container, yellow with rusty crust formed on its outer edges. An awning of dirty green and white vinyl hung over a roughly cut, doorless threshold adorned by a brightly colored blanket of broad red and yellow vertical lines with sharp green diamonds spaced over them.

"I will check on Kimwu and Paul for you. Hold tight for a minute." Then Nick disappeared behind the colorful blanket. Darius heard Nick descend a metal ladder, his heavy boots clubbing each rung with a muffled clank of rubber on metal. The foursome stood patiently on top of the semi-trailer and continued to absorb the cohesive business of the crowded settlement. Men worked in groups of two and three to hang thick black cables, ropes and braided steel wires. Shops were clean and organizing supplies in preparation for shuttering for the evening. Some kids helped carry crates of food and wood to women or men waiting to fill baskets that were pulled up to the higher mezzanine with pulleys and ropes and yet more braided steel cables. Other children stacked empty crates near the front gate, which had been closed again. Guards walked the parapet built upon shipping containers and semi-trailers, two were armed with Carbine rifles and watched the settlers working down below, but also watched the overgrown farmlands outside the settlement's protective walls. *This is a good place*, Darius thought.

"Ah, my friends, my friends!" Darius heard a soft and cheerful voice exclaim behind him. He turned around to see a short box-shaped man, just as Nick had described. The square black-framed glasses gave him a scholarly look, but his short, muscled arms gave an impression of resilience and strength. His thick arms struggled to embrace Durbin in a brotherly hug as they bulged slightly under the cut off sleeves of an old grey and red flannel shirt. After hugging Caleb, then Trina, the short white-haired man offered a square meaty hand with calloused, sausage-like fingers to Darius.

"I am Paul," he said, looking up to Darius with a soft, fatherly smile.

"Darius." He smiled back, as Paul then pulled him closer for a brotherly squeeze.

"And my friends have taken good care of you?" Paul asked with a small wink of his eye.

Darius thought for a minute feigning indecision. "It's been a two-way street," he said finally. "These three be good people."

Paul and the others were sharing warm-hearted small talk when the colorful blanket in the doorway moved, and a tall dark figure came forth. He bent forward to keep from hitting his head on the threshold, then stood to full height, towering over Durbin and even Darius. Paul looked to be a white-haired child next to him. The tall man's skin was the color of roasted coffee beans, dark, and rich. His bald head still gave a slight sheen in the late afternoon sun. His smile revealed bright pearly teeth behind thick, purple lips and sat above a chiseled chin that hung over several necklaces of beads along with purple and green polished stones from another land. Covering his long and narrow frame was a short-sleeved shirt faded red with abstract yellow patterns randomly placed about it. His extremely long arms snaked out of the sleeves and were decorated with various bracelets of leather and beads. His long legs were covered with cream-colored linen pants tied on by a vibrant green rope, the loop of the knot hanging down one thigh. His feet were protected by brown leather sandals, worn and dusty from many miles of walking.

"Welcome to de' Windy Well," he said pleasantly. Darius recognized his thick accent on *W*'s, short, and oddly pronounced vowel sounds, and hard *D*'s in place of *th*'s, as Kenyan. "I am Kimwu. De' organiza' of dis place."

Kimwu greeted each of them with a firm handshake, learning their names, repeating each one quietly with a nod and smile. He made a point to look each in the eye, and inspected their face briefly before approaching the next person. Darius was in awe. He had not had the company of a Kenyan in several years, and to be greeted by Kimwu so warmly was enough to bring Darius to tears. He now understood more of the bitter bigotry spat at him in the Windfields by that greasy robed man at the water barrel. And suddenly, Darius was okay with it. Kimwu's large hand smothered his in genuine salutations, the contrast of dark and light brown skin reminded Darius so much of being a child and holding onto his mother's hand… Darius immediately decided that he was going to be in the service of Windy Well, and of Kimwu, for whatever they both shall need.

CHAPTER 16 — CALEB

Caleb struggled to keep pace with the flowing water.

Sully was pumping water so fast, but Caleb was not moving the buckets quickly enough under the well's mouth. Precious water soaked the earth when he failed to get the next empty bucket under the flow. Caleb did not have time to marvel at the fact that clean, clear, potable water flowed in the middle of this settlement.

The pump sounded out with high and low squeaks, timed to a splash of water in faded, clear blue buckets with dirty metal handles. The yellow paint had chipped away on the pump's head, revealing ancient rusted steel underneath.

"You gotta keep up, Caleb!" Sully said, his mellow voice barely heard over the noise of the pump.

Caleb had to fill a bucket, run it over to what Sully had called the water carriage —a short trailer of steel and wood that held a large white dome-shaped tank with a hole in the top. Caleb then had to climb a rickety ladder that leaned slightly right and pour the bucket into the opening of the dome. But before running with a full bucket, he had to place an empty one under the flowing spigot so it could fill while emptying the other. Twenty liters at a time he did this, up the ladder, down the ladder, stumbling as the ladder shifted further to the right, spilling water down the side of the tank, slamming the buckets together and knocking over the full one when he lost his footing to approach the pump again…

Then the rhythmic squeaking of the pump handle stopped. Caleb fell to the ground, huffing and puffing, as Sully came to sit next to him.

"You know I was just messing with you, right?" he said, pushing his elbow into Caleb's.

Caleb turned his head sharply to look Sully in the eyes. "What? What do you mean?"

"We don't need to fill the water carriage so quickly," Sully said with a smile. "What would be the point? We still have a three-day journey to get it to Woodstock!"

Caleb scowled immaturely at Sully, rubbing his sore shoulders and arms. He then looked up to see the water carriage half full. The water still sloshed against the sides of the rounded tank in soothing waves. His arms felt heavy and weak. His spirit bruised by Sully's prank.

"And don't worry about the water level. We actually have several teams that help with the filling. Lots of people benefit from the medicine from Woodstock. There are a lot of people willing to help get water to them in return."

Sully had an earnest tone to his voice, as though he personally at one time had benefited from this partnership with the settlement of Woodstock. He described the hidden settlement consisting of makers of poultices and tinctures, of farmers who cultivated the land. Sully said that they were "earthy folk" and had specific rules for animal uses, and only ate what produce they grew.

"But, aren't we leaving today?" Caleb asked. He recalled

the urgency in Sully's tone when he met him two days previous, during a meeting in the Windy Well council room.

He had only been a resident of Windy Well for two days but volunteered eagerly to take on a meaningful job to help the settlement. The decision was hastily made in a room where Kimwu was introducing the new residents to other leaders of Windy Well. It was a dark room, lit by softly glowing light bulbs, powered just enough to burn, barely enough to illuminate. The air was a bit stuffy in the dark shipping container, with Darius, Durbin, Trina, Paul, Nick, Kimwu, Caleb, two serious-looking women whose names Caleb couldn't recall, and a middle-aged olive-skinned man named Omar. The makeshift room had no windows and the air was stifling hot, the metal heated by the full day of sun. Everyone sat at a long table with three plastic pitchers of clean water spaced around it. As Kimwu was describing several available jobs in the settlement, Sully appeared after rapping quickly at the wooden door that didn't fit snuggly in its opening. He stepped into the room and looked at Caleb, pointing a wiggly finger.

Durbin cast a dismissive look at Caleb as Caleb shrugged with uncertainty.

"I need a new young man to help out with the water carriage, Davide says he is getting too old to travel that far all the time," Sully said finally, clearing the air of tension. "Can I have him, Kimwu? At least for the Woodstock runs? It would be great acclamation for him to Windy Well and the surrounding areas."

Kimwu looked at Sully calmly, sitting tall and regal at the head of the rectangular table, his bright yellow shirt with green sleeves seeming to give off its own light in the darkened room.

"Dat decision is not mine to make. I am not his commanda'. He can choose his own place in dis' community." Kimwu looked permissively at Caleb.

Caleb, in turn, looked at Durbin for direction, feeling his face redden with embarrassment for being made the center of attention. He shifted uncomfortably in his wooden chair that creaked achily under his movements. He finally twisted in his seat to look directly at Sully, his long, sandy brown hair darkened with water and sweat.

"I get to travel to other settlements with this job?" Caleb finally broke his silence.

Sully nodded in affirmation, the shadows cast from the dim lightbulbs dancing on his sharp-featured face.

But now, Caleb looked at that sharply chiseled face in brighter midday light. Sweat and water beaded along his cheeks and jawline —cut like a rock sculpture— and dripped off of his pointed nose. He wiped it roughly with his shoulder and snorted.

"Not today, I will have others finish filling the water carriage, then, we will leave at first light tomorrow. We will get Shiva and Hercules from the stable and hitch them to the water carriage after packing rations for the road," Sully said, serious again.

Caleb knew they boarded a few horses at Windy Well, but he had yet to meet Shiva or Hercules. When Sully was explaining the job to Caleb, he mentioned they were permanently on loan to Windy Well from Woodstock, so long as they were well nourished and only used to haul the water carriage. Sully then mumbled something about harmony and all creatures followed by something that sounded like he wouldn't hurt them anyway.

"Can I meet them, now?" Caleb stood from his crouching post beside the well's pump apparatus.

"Sure, why not," Sully said, rising with him before calling out to someone in the shelter behind the water carriage. "Adam! Can you and Mora finish filling the water carriage? I'm taking Caleb to the stable."

From the hollow darkness within the opened shipping container sounded a voice of affirmation, but Caleb could not tell if it were Adam or Mora.

Caleb and Sully left the well's area, even farther away from the front gate, the windmill, and the town square. They were deeper into the residential zone with more and more stacked and modified shipping containers and makeshift shelters. They walked past an alignment of numerous portable generators, all humming idly, with heavy gauged cables snaking out of each and slithering into another alignment of shelter and shipping containers. Light brown and grey smoke danced out of oddly shaped tin boxes and pipes that appeared to fuel the generators.

"That's Nick's motorized shop," Sully informed Caleb. "He is always working on something in there. And Windy Well is always better for it. The lightbulbs and wiring, the water tank and flow system for showering…the gate lift systems, and even the layout of the settlement —all engineered by him."

They had used one or two generators in Bridgetown,

but Caleb could not recall the fuel used. He had never been in charge of the generators. These generators outside of Nick's shop were attached to fabricated steel and tin hoppers that seemed to burn some material while condensing then funneling the smoke into the fuel canisters of the generators.

Still, Sully dragged Caleb along, over the flat earth and trampled grass, up and down short scaffolding and along narrow, grated steel catwalks that connected the tops of ramshackle structures. Sully would call out what specific places were, throwing out names of people who Caleb had not yet met, hinting to their role in the settlement. Caleb stood in the middle of a catwalk, questioning how a horse would navigate it when it dawned on him that Sully was taking this route as a means of introducing Caleb to other areas of Windy Well. The horses would obviously take a more practical route around the settlement to the well proper before being hitched and bridled to the water carriage.

Back again on solid earth, they rounded a corner. The invasive smell of natural waste permeated Caleb's senses, the hair-curling rank sweetness of decay and partially digested foods made him shake his head. Sully laughed lightly.

"Sorry. I forgot to warn you that we also keep all of the human waste back here. Together with the horses' dung, we can fertilize the fields around the well. Nothing truly wasted, I guess."

The stables sat near a gate similar in construction to the massive metal gate Caleb had entered with his friends a few days ago —heavy corrugated steel behind chain link fencing— powered by cables and gears and muscle. Shiva and Hercules were content in their stables, eating straw and mushy fruits and vegetables tossed into a mounted trough. A blond stable hand with his hair pulled back in a tight ponytail hung iron shoes from a wooden crate as the horses ate, uncaring of Caleb's presence.

Shiva was the smaller horse, a pale blue-white color that showcased her muscled shoulders and flanks, her cone-shaped head dressed with a simmering silver mane which a teenaged copper-haired stable hand not much younger than Caleb brushed as she fed on the trough. Hercules was larger than Shiva and just as radiant with a golden coat that reflected light like still water at sunset. He was sculpted perfectly, majestic and powerful; Caleb was certain Hercules could pull the water carriage by himself. He finally noticed Caleb, his pear sized brown eye tilting to track him. Hercules finished chewing his fruit and raised his long head out of the trough to look directly at Caleb.

"Can I touch him?" Caleb asked Sully. Sully combed his fingers through his own locks of hair, pushing them away from his smiling eyes.

"So long as he lets you. Just like caravan horses, approach slowly, make sure they see you. Feel free to talk to them, before you know they can see you." Sully leaned against a post that held up the roof of the stable and smiled at Caleb just as he turned to approach Hercules. Caleb thought that Hercules was smiling too, showing his large, dull ivory and brown teeth, licking the smashed apples from his lips.

Caleb brought his hand between his and Hercules' eyes, before gently stroking his nose. "You are handsome, aren't you, Hercules," he said calmly as he ran his fingers through the horse's golden mane. Hercules snorted and seemed to nod in acceptance, then he seemed to notice Sully. Hercules pranced in place and backed away slightly from Caleb.

"No, no. We leave tomorrow, buddy," said Sully as he softly dragged his hand along Hercules' back towards his lightly flailing tail. Once at Hercules' backside, Sully said to the blond long-haired stable hand, "Can you two bring the water carriage and hitch them tandem tomorrow morning?"

"Sure thing," responded the stable hand managing horseshoes. "We will re-shoe them shortly, and saddle them with the travel bags after bringing back the water carriage."

"Thanks, my friend," said Sully before he turned back to Caleb. "Let's go to the windmill. I want to show you something."

Again, Caleb found himself being dragged by the hand through Windy Well. Though the path was different this time, they still traversed narrow dirt paths, rickety ladders, and tilted mezzanines. Behind a conglomeration construct of metal and wood at the base of the wind turbine, they climbed a hidden ladder. It led them to a square balcony that only had a view of the forest beside the settlement. But the back end of the balcony butted up to the main pillar that supported the wind turbine. A metal stairway began at the juncture and wound up the mast of the turbine.

The stairs were bolted into the mast, though they still felt less stable than Caleb was comfortable with. The thin railing to his right was far too low for a secure hold, and far too thin to grip with any confidence. The ground level of Windy Well was far below them —growing further away— as Sully lead the way up the spiral stairs.

Then, the climbing stopped, as they reached another balcony. It sat as a lookout point high above the settlement. They were very close to the slowly spinning blades of the turbine, still below them enough to be safe. The droning and thumping of their motion was stronger here, but Caleb had grown used to it over the last few days.

Caleb spied another ladder attached to the main pillar of the turbine, vertically rising to the engine component of the turbine. The height was dizzying, and thankfully, Sully made no motion for the ladder. Looking down into settlement below, Caleb determined they were about halfway up the mast of the turbine, guessing the height to be about fifty meters. The settlers below were tiny, bustling about the settlement with daily tasks and responsibilities. The wind picked up, blowing his hair from his face and Sully let out a sound of relief that led into restrained laughter.

"I love it up here," he said joyfully. "My favorite place in all the Well."

Caleb could understand why. The lookout post allowed for a view of the forests below, the farm fields —both tended and unkempt— of corn and wheat. He could see the edge of the Windfields. The sun illuminated the earth all around them, casting the caravan trails of dirt in tones of brown and orange. *It truly is beautiful. It is also peaceful.*

Sully took hold of Caleb's hand again, as he did when he led him wildly through the settlement. Caleb braced for being pulled again and led speedily to places unknown. But Sully just looked at him. His gaze was gentle, but with an intensity that Caleb couldn't understand.

"I don't bring just anyone up here, Caleb," he said. "I am often up here alone. Reflecting. Taking in the world. This place is special to me. I want it to be special to you, too."

Caleb was at a loss. Sully's words made sense. But his tone was all wrong. The touch of his hand was not uncomfortable, but it seemed to imply more than Caleb understood. It seemed that Sully meant more than he said, that he wanted more than to just show this secret lookout to Caleb, but his mind was not able to grasp any meaning. He felt he was doing a poor job of hiding the confusion on his face.

Sully let go of his hand. "Ah, too much. Too soon. I'm sorry, Caleb."

Caleb was still confused about Sully's intentions, but answered honestly. "Thanks for bringing me up here, Sully. This place *is* special. I appreciate it. And I appreciate you."

Sully placed his hand on Caleb's shoulder and leaned close as they looked out over the surrounding wilderness.

CHAPTER 17 — TRINA

Raelynn insisted on Trina trying every bow in her arsenal before they ventured into the lands around Windy Well. The two women were in Raelynn's lodging, built high on one corner of Windy Well, nestled along the tallest wall facing south. Her lodging was a blue shipping container that sat on the corner like the guardhouse of an old log fort. There was a catwalk that surrounded her home that allowed for surveillance of the settlement and the farmlands beyond the walls. Inside was dimly lit, like most of the dwelling within the Well, but the lighting was sufficient.

"But I like my bow," Trina told her as Raelynn grabbed a camouflage-patterned crossbow, a matte black recurve bow with a silver line along the center length and a brown and grey compound bow with a series of moving pulleys and complex alignments of bowstrings. Raelynn sat them all gently on the table, displayed caringly, showcasing their cleanliness and emptiness.

"Of course you do. But have you ever hunted anything with it?" Raelynn asked. Her long, faded auburn hair hung in a thick braid past her shoulder and a stray strand of hair hung in front of her eye. She continued to question Trina in silence, her eyes judging and thoughtful.

"Not really," Trina responded sheepishly, "Caleb did most of the hunting. His bow was faster than mine. Mine has a very long draw."

"Exactly why you should try something else. Your bow is a shortened style of the longbow, designed for long-distance and aerial assaults. Not the best hunting tool, honestly." Raelynn moved the strands of hair from her face, tucking them temporarily behind her ear.

Trina felt somewhat embarrassed. Much like her revolver, she carried her bow around more for peace of mind rather than to be used as a tool. She had only pointed the gun at Darius as a threat and for leverage, though she never had any intention of firing it. Her finger was not even on the trigger. But she realized also that she had rarely nocked her bow as Raelynn continued to educate her on the differences between short bows and longbows, and how she was using shorter shafted arrows instead of the longer ones more appropriate for her draw…

"This is a bolt —not an arrow," Raelynn continued, holding a fat short arrow that appeared rigid and lined, lacking colored fletchings, boasting a broad metal head of vicious angles designed for rending flesh. She turned to load it into the camouflaged crossbow.

"Crossbow really isn't my style. Too heavy, and too slow to reload," Trina said. She was slightly bored but slightly anxious. She had been told that she was going to be hunting with Raelynn —a stern woman several years older than herself— exploring the forests and farmlands for meat and skins so that the settlement could tan some leather for trading and cure meat in preparation for next winter. She was not anticipating a mundane, step-by-step tutorial on arms.

"It may not be," Raelynn continued, "but a huntress of Windy Well will be well-versed in all instruments of hunting — so long as I have the ability to teach. The men can keep their guns. A huntress will stalk her mark silently, loosing arrows with wordless malice... Our prey never knows we were there."

Raelynn unloaded the crossbow and picked up the recurve bow, it's silver line gleaming in even the soft yellow glow of dim lightbulbs. She drew the string empty, bending the bow slightly, all of the muscles in her arm becoming rigid, bulging with strength and muscular definition momentarily under the force of the flexing bow. As she panned the room with the drawn bow, Trina flinched as the silver line flashed once more. She contemplated briefly what her prey would think if they were instantly blinded by the bow before being impaled by its mortiferous shot.

"You will find this bow much easier to handle in short and long distances with vicious accuracy," Raelynn said, relaxing the drawstring, flipping the bow around with a deft flourish and handing it to Trina. "This one is yours now, Huntress. Do amazing things with it."

As Trina touched the smooth bow handle, she saw in her mind's eye the flash of the silver line before the black shaft of an arrow whizzed into view. She shook her head to clear it and placed the other hand on the bow, looking over its soft dark curves, running her fingers along with the rough but tidy drawstring, her heart settling from her vision. "Its name is Panic," she said slyly.

"It is now, Huntress." Raelynn smiled at her in approval.

"Let's prepare for our journey.

Later that afternoon, Trina and Raelynn left Windy Well, turning their backs to the heavy steel gates, heading northwest across the swamp farmland hybrid, avoiding standing water and mushy grounds. Each woman wore her bow across her back proudly, along with a leather quiver full of arrows, and rucksack with supplies of parachute cord, striking flints, dried meats, chicory stalks and flowers, small plastic canteens full of clean well water, and small hand-woven sacks of dried fruits. The springtime air had given way to an early summer day, the heat finding Trina and Raelynn shedding their jackets. The ladies bared their shoulders in colorful flannel shirts that had the sleeves cut off.

They trekked the land towards large forests that did not seem to get closer. Up gentle slopes, they hiked. Soon they came to a low point in the earth spongy beneath their boots with the steady flow of a river ahead of them. Upon arrival to the riverbed, Trina saw it to be quite shallow, and they hopped flat grey rocks to reach the other side. They hiked up another slope, and then across another field of golds and greens, with intermittent cottonwood trees growing like woody weeds amongst the long-abandoned farming fields.

Trina was grateful for the opportunity to provide for Windy Well, to be useful for the settlement, and to be taught by Raelynn. She appreciated how welcome they'd made her feel in such a short time. But she missed the camaraderie of Durbin and Darius and Caleb. Their bonds were forged strong in the brief time of travel while sharing tragic stories of loss. She attempted to make personal conversation with Raelynn.

"How long have you been in Windy Well, Raelynn?" Trina began.

"Since about the beginning," she said, still surveying the land, listening for the movement of prey. "Probably twelve winters, now. Kimwu and Nick had begun construction shortly before I arrived. We still had small reserves of gasoline available back then, could still use trucks and powered equipment to move the heavy stuff. Kimwu accepted me without question, requiring only that I am accepting of all who seek the safety of the Well. And that I pull my own weight, of course."

The women entered a wooded area that Raelynn stated could be a haven for prey, doe mothers nursing their fawns were easy targets, but the cover of the trees could offer them a rare option to hunt a buck.

"How did you become a Huntress?" asked Trina quietly as they scouted the area for an ideal camouflaged covering from which to ambuscade.

Satisfied with a perch on the long, thick, horizontal limb of an oak tree, easily climbed by way of a smooth, grey boulder underneath, the women sat about three meters off the ground. They straddled the tree branch, sitting tandem with Trina in front, facing the direction of the shallow river they had walked through earlier.

"I had a skill. And they had a need. My husband was former military, and a sportsman hunter. He taught me plenty of hunting skills after the Collapse, as we hid from the violence. So, I learned how to hunt. I just began calling all the female hunters in the Well Huntress. Some are better than me. I just happen to be the first. But we all embrace the title of Huntress."

Trina mused on her words momentarily and turned her head to look at Raelynn. "I know I may have been standoffish initially, but I do thank you for welcoming me, Raelynn."

"It is always a pleasure to welcome someone who wants to have the best for the settlement, Trina. Having you and your friends will be good for Windy Well. Strength in numbers is good." Raelynn nodded, looking lost in her thoughts for a moment. "Trustworthy people are in short supply anymore."

"Have you found people meaning to do harm to Windy Well? It seems quite defensible. Nick did not even let us in without a fair amount of consideration."

"Over the years," Raelynn replied, "Nick has become quite discerning regarding people's character. And having Kimwu as our unofficial leader puts things into perspective. If someone is not agreeable to Kimwu being from Africa, then they aren't welcome at the Well. It's simple really. And quite disheartening the number of people who are turned away because they cannot handle taking instruction from him because of the color of his skin."

"For you to have such a strong and thriving settlement for all these years... Kimwu must be quite the leader."

Raelynn laughed quietly. "He would never agree to being called a leader. He feels that no person should have true power over another. He is full of wisdom, he mentors effectively, and he is the glue that holds the Well together. But he will tell you it is Nick who is the glue."

"Where do you fall in all of this?" asked Trina.

"Me? I merely find the best fit for new settlers. As I told you before, I get to know new people. I make bonds. I find out what job would benefit most from their skills. You were a practicing healer back in Bridgetown? Don't be surprised if I call on you for some medical needs and assisting Doctor Soma, as well as hunts."

"I wasn't very good at healing…" Trina remorsefully recalled the many people who died at Bridgetown as she tried to learn medicine from tattered books with yellowed pages that often fell from their bindings, her clumsy fingers mixing and grinding herbs.

"That isn't the point, Huntress." Raelynn said encouragingly, "We receive medicine from Woodstock, made by the herbalists there. All we do is administer the medicine as needed for illness. They have done all the work in creating it. I only need a person with a heart for healing the sick. And that is something you have."

Trina did know in her heart that she longed to heal sick people. Perhaps it was a pang of sorrowful guilt from not being able to save her friends and family in Bridgetown, or perhaps it was something deeper—a calling from the earth or her soul. But her failure to save even one soul from the water-borne illness demonstrated to her that she lacked the knowledge required to be a useful healer. *Maybe I can meet up with some of the herbalists from Woodstock and they can teach the ways of making medicine? Or maybe this Doctor Soma?*

"Eyes peeled; a deer approaches," Raelynn whispered. And both women quietly slid their bows from their shoulders.

Moving smoothly and stealthily they each drew an arrow from their quivers. The deer was walking along the edge of the woods, dropping its head to the ground in search of fresh green shoots to eat. It looked to be a young doe with no fawns following, not a large buck as they were hoping. The doe moved gracefully, each limb being placed gingerly before lifting and stepping with another, presenting as a type of dance. The doe would then drop its snout low to the ground for a few seconds before raising her head high above her shoulders and looking around. Then she would begin her dance sequence again.

Trina was nervous about the distance. She feared the mark was too far away for her to cleanly take it down. She longed for the deer to enter the woods and approach them, desiring a guaranteed shot and no risk of the mark escaping.

"Patience, Huntress," Raelynn whispered from behind her. "Wait for your shot. You will know it to be the right time. Now is not it. Relax the draw. Let the mark come to us today."

The tension in her arm faded, and Trina relaxed the draw of her bowstring while keeping the arrow nocked and ready. She breathed in deeply, quieting her mind, trying to become one with the woods, absorbing its air, its smells, its balance, and its tranquility. She felt the coarse bark of the oak tree bough under her thighs. The whistles and chirps of the birds up in the leafy canopy became clear. The smell of the moist soil below them filled her senses with images of dirt, and seeds, and leaves leftover from winter. She exhaled slowly, her vision homing in on the slowly dancing doe, casually entering the tree line, then prancing in the sunlit grass. She relaxed even further, trying to imagine herself as the doe, bending low to eat tender sprouts of dandelions and new grass, prancing wispily amongst the roots and molehills, oblivious to any humans nearby.

And that was when they all heard it.

It was a shrill but guttural wailing. Seemingly both high and low pitched, not a scream, not a groan but somehow both. The sound was painful. Not that Trina had to cover her ears, but whatever was making the sound was clearly in pain. The doe lifted her head in alert, ears upright and twitching against the sounds and the breeze. Trina looked at Raelynn, "Is that human?" she whispered.

"I am not sure," she whispered back.

They continued to whisper even though the doe had bolted away from the origin of the wailing, somewhere far to Trina's right, running feverishly instead of dancing as it had moments before, its vertical white tail signaling danger.

The wail sounded again, and Raelynn signaled to Trina to descend the tree. The women dismounted the large tree limb, their coarse pants scraping the bark as the wailing sounded out intermittently. It remained incoherent as the women walked quietly through the underbrush lining the floor of the woods, rays of sunlight beaming through the branches of the trees becoming more densely packed with young leaves of maple and locust and oak. Outside of the wooded circle, the wailing grew louder, drawing the women toward a mass of mulberry shrubs. As they drew even closer, they noticed that shrubs concealed the steep drop of a rocky ravine that reverberated the wailing off the earthy walls.

At the bottom of the ravine, they found it. Nestled in

a crumpled mess of green and white linen robes was a person, only their cleanly shorn head visible within the mass of robes. The figure was blocked from falling into the creek at the bottom of the ravine by outcroppings of grey and white rocks that cradled the broken body like stoney hands. Trina and Raelynn watched for several minutes, waiting for the figure to move, but it never did, despite infrequent groans and wails. They began to make their way cautiously down the ravine's edge.

"Do you need help?" Trina called out. The robed figure was on the opposite side of the ravine, and Trina noticed Raelynn surveying the steep embankments and rocky outcroppings for the safest path. Young trees grew at sharp angles and rose from the steeply banked earth.

"Are you all right?" Trina called out again to the person lying near the bottom of the ravine.

More groans bellowed from the mass of robes, painful sounds of distress and injury. The women swiftly slid down the muddy edge of the ravine, digging the edges of their boots into the earth and gingerly catching tiny rocky ledges to slow their descent and avoid flipping headfirst into the swirling muddy water below. They made small splashes in the water as they crossed the ravine's flowing current, hopping rocks that broke the surface. They approached the stone cradle where the injured person lay —quickly but cautiously— hands on the hilts of their knives that hung from their belts.

"Are you injured? Can we help you?" Raelynn spoke out this time, her voice deeper than Trina's, with a silky undertone of comfort and trust. The person in the mass of robes attempted to move but only groaned once more. No audible words were heard, and Trina decided to take a risk in approaching the mangled figure.

Trina reached down and pulled back some of the crumpled robes to reveal the figure's soft face. She was bruised around her nose and eyes, her bald head revealing split skin and dried blood. Upon movement, her eyes fluttered open, green but empty, looking through Trina as though she were not there hovering over the broken woman.

"S—Sun...fff." The robed woman attempted a coherent sound, she grabbed Trina's shirt weakly, trying to pull her close. Her eyes narrowed, seeing Trina for the first time. "Sunfield." she said plainly and she collapsed her arms onto her chest and closed her eyes again, still breathing heavily.

Trina turned to Raelynn while trying to cradle the robed woman's head to avoid further injury on the rocks underneath her. "Are you from Sunfield? Or were you going to Sunfield?" Raelynn asked as she yanked a canteen from her pack, unscrewed the chrome cap, and drew the opening to the robed woman's lips. The clean water splashed on her chin and ran across her lips, she sucked some into her mouth and sputtered softly. She then made another non-descript sound.

"Can you direct us to Sunfield?" Raelynn asked, but she did not wait for an answer. She scanned the embankments of the ravine once more. Trina did the same, attempting to identify where the young woman had fallen from to indicate a direction of travel. She spied several rough and muddy marks where it appeared feet had dragged a short distance before being thrown airborne, only to drag and gouge the soft earth again a meter or so farther down the slope. The marks were in line that led to their current location on the rocky outcropping suspended over the water.

"I think she fell from there," Trina said, pointing to her observations.

"Wait here with her. I am going to survey from the top of the gorge." And Raelynn made her way up the steep embankment made of rock and mud, uprooting saplings that lacked the strength to stand stoic against the angle of the earth. At the top, Raelynn stood several meters above them. She shielded her eyes from sunlight and pointed.

"I see the reflective panels!" she shouted down to Trina. "We can carry her along the ravine bottom out that way, and climb up to where the gorge is less steep." Raelynn then slid cautiously back down the ravine — a much quicker journey than climbing —and aided Trina in lifting the young woman who groaned deeply.

Clumsily navigating the entangled roots and rocks along the ravine's edge, Trina and Raelynn carried the young woman till the embankments became less tall and steep, allowing them to rise out of the creek bed with less difficulty. They carried her, walking side by side supporting her robed torso, her broken legs hanging off of Raelynn's forearms as Trina supported her shoulders and head. Only rarely would the young woman cry out, and even less frequently would she open her eyes. Her skin became blotchy with a pink rash.

Clear of the ravine's confines, Trina saw rows of sparking light in the distance lining the cusp of a too perfectly formed hill. Large rectangles of shimmering black and silver panels stood on firm pillars of concrete and aluminum, tilting the panels at an angle toward the sun and facing south. "Those glowing panels are Sunfield?" Trina asked. The women began walking that direction as if in answer.

"The actual settlement is said to be a bunker underneath that hill, powered by those solar panels. But I have never seen it," Raelynn answered.

Still, they marched on, carefully cradling their injured infirmity as they encircled the solar panels, searching for an entryway. The spring grass gave way to a narrow dirt path that cut along to the dark side of the solar panel covered hill, carving a very short tunnel that was walled by grey iron and a vault-like door. "Do we knock?" asked Trina.

Suddenly the door thudded, its weighty thickness revealed, accompanied by both a high-and-low pitched squeal of metal on metal. It opened to reveal another bald woman wearing green and white robes. Trina and Raelynn stood holding their injured young woman. The greeter gasped and called to someone out of sight, "They have found Demetra. Tell the Matriarch she is injured."

Footsteps were heard as another woman in robes ran from the heavy vault-like door. The robed greeter stared at the broken woman in Trina's arms, then looked up to Trina and Raelynn studying their faces intently.

"Please, bring Demetra inside."

CHAPTER 18 — DURBIN

"Can I offer you tea?" Nick asked Durbin earnestly.

Durbin was lost in thought, perusing the walls of machinations and inventive creativeness in Nick's shop. One entire wall was lined floor to ceiling with books that featured titles such as "Alternative Energy: A Guide.", and "Small to Large Engine Repair.", and "Something from Nothing: The Necessity of Invention.", and "How it Works: Volume 23." Another wall was piecemealed together with various shelving solutions designed to hold slightly oxidized hand tools and crudely modified power tools with cracked plastic shells and frayed brush motors. Durbin turned slowly, taking in the varied content of the walls, tables and shelves, their homely nature, their crude rapport, and salvaged ingenuity. He felt that he was in the presence of an intelligent man who had forgotten more than Durbin would ever know.

"Tea, Durbin?" Nick asked again, placing a hand gently on Durbin's shoulder, gaining his attention once more.

"Yeah. Sure. I would like that, Nick. Thanks."

Nick then disappeared into another room; its threshold covered by a tattered red blanket. The hum of makeshift generators resounded outside; dimly lit lights hung from the ceiling of the semi-trailer over Durbin's head. The past few days had been a bit of a blur for Durbin. The kids, Caleb and Trina, had set out almost immediately to assimilate into Windy Well culture, with Caleb being recruited by Sully for water caravan duties, and Trina being stolen away by Raelynn to become a Huntress for the Well. Raelynn was quick to add that she valued Trina for her healing skills rather than her use of a bow, but insisted that the latter would come about in time. Durbin, on the other hand, had been left to relish the "old guys" and sit in on important deliberations with Kimwu and Nick and Paul and Omar Hussein at Paul's request. Durbin failed to understand what a post-Collapse settlement could be enduring that would require regular governing, but he was quickly enlightened to the fluid inner workings of Windy Well. Each person had specific duties designed and implemented for assurance of settlement survival. People to maintain human wastes. People to manage the distribution and use of water. People were assigned to hunting and foraging, and livestock, and storage and preservation of foods. Still, others were in charge of fabric creation and usage, garment sewing, shoe repair, housewares construction, and designs. Others had more specialized tasks such as child delivery (on the rare occasions when it happened) and medicine administration — though Dr. Soma held the reigns on healthcare. A small number of men and women made up a special salvage team that would disappear for days or weeks on end to urban areas in search of scrap and scavenge materials that could be repurposed at the Well. And yet the amount of work did not stop there, as people assisted in the operation of stables, and the windmill turbine, and the power lines that trollied modest amounts of electricity to the settlements scores of living quarters. The amount of management taking place in Windy Well was more than observation would warrant, and Kimwu insisted that it was a team effort. He refused to be called a leader —though most of Windy

Well heralded him as one— and preferred to be referred to as a 'facilitator' rather than a 'governor.'

Returning with a dented tin mug of steaming floral tea that smelled of chamomile and lavender, Nick pulled a wooden stool out from under a cluttered table and offered Durbin a seat. "I found the least dented mug I have. It should not leak on you, but it will pour funny."

Durbin smiled genuinely and breathed in heavily the aroma of the tea, its sweet softness a reminder of a comfort he had forgotten. Nick sat on a similar stool across from Durbin, cupping his own dented tin mug. He took a sip of it loudly, slurping childishly. "I don't know about you, Durbin, but I miss coffee."

Laughing heartily, Nick's eyes twinkled with a glimmer that Durbin recognized from years past —from the old world. Nick's face was one of genuine hospitality, which was a luxury that not just anyone could afford to offer any longer. Durbin smiled to himself. *Such joy from a cup of tea.*

"It has been years since I have had coffee," Durbin replied. "Blast us for living in the wrong part of the world."

"I even tried to get Sully to scrounge some from Woodstock. But it turns out they can't grow coffee either." The guys laughed sadly at their farce plight, the dimly lit room a stark contrast to their momentous joy and humor.

"I was a bit awestruck by your collection of goods here in your shop, Nick. There are many items that remind me of our old world —when we had coffee." Smiles touched the men's lips.

Nick set down his mug of steaming tea on a metal workbench and rested his chin on his fist, looking longingly at his library of books as if for the first time. "It wasn't easy to acquire most of this stuff. But it has been worth it." Nick changed positions and reclined his body on the stool leaning back against the workshop table. "The stupidity of people amazes me."

Durbin rolled his eyes at Nick's comment, "You don't say." He agreed with his tone.

"I mean it. Man, in the months after the Collapse, I was working hard to gather resources. When it became obvious that the America we knew was not coming back, I searched for knowledge along with physical resources. Durbin, I watched society collapsing long before it fell into the hole we know it as now. The kids knew how to do nothing. Even the adults... They couldn't cook. They couldn't farm or garden. They couldn't repair an engine. They scarcely knew how to write. When the rolling blackouts started occurring, and all the technology-based infrastructures started failing, that's when I knew I had to start looking for books. But wouldn't you know it? These people who lacked all the common sense to boil water started burning down libraries. Libraries! The houses of the knowledge that wasn't dependent on electricity or online connections... And they burned them down. Fools." Nick shook his head shamingly. "So many more of them would have lived. We would have been able to recover so much more technology."

Durbin felt everything Nick said about the pre-Collapse population to be true. They had no resourcefulness. To him, they were beings of energy, constantly tied to an electronic device that force-fed them information while teaching them nothing at all. Many of Durbin's coworkers had become accustomed to not having to *know* anything. If pressed at all, they responded with, "wait, let me look that up" without retaining any of the information. Whatever had to be looked up was regurgitated into the appropriate situation with the information subsequently discarded. And when that technology failed, millions of people were left blind and powerless, feeling in the dark for answers they had never bothered to keep in their minds.

But many of them were gone now. So much of the generation that had grown soft had been rid of this world. The lazy ones too. One hard winter and they all starved or froze to death, unable to bear the elements —unable to muster the will and know-how to survive. It seemed to Durbin the only ones remaining were those who could adapt and those who were violent. Of course, Darius did mention something about a group referred to as "The Country"; supposed zealots who had long adopted a life devoid of technology...

"Hey, Nick?" Durbin started. "What do you know about the people outside of the Glass City? Outside of Windy Well?"

"Well, I haven't been on a scavenging team in years. And we only communicate with trade caravans and Woodstock for the most part. They all are decent folks for the most part. A few of the caravan merchants can be swindlers if you aren't savvy enough. Woodstock is full of the nicest group of hippies, and they make some right good medicine. Sunfield keeps to themselves. There are many small settlements around, just like that Bridgetown those Hurst children are from. But I don't know how many still stand. To be honest, I get a fair amount of news from the radio..." Nick turned to look at a silver box with a series of dials and switches on its face, a clear rectangle lined the top of the case, numbered and etched with a thin white and red needle pointed at a worn number.

"Someone is broadcasting radio?" Durbin exclaimed. *Radio!* He couldn't believe that. It was a dying form of media before the Collapse, and amazing that anyone still alive would remember how the archaic technology worked.

"Just one that I have found so far, but there could be more across the country, I suppose. One station I found by accident. Broadcast by a man calls himself 'Spectre.' Says he is in the heart of the Glass City, but who knows for sure. Radio broadcast is on at different times from day to day. Sometimes he broadcasts a loop of the same info for hours. Sometimes it is live. He has even done music at times."

Durbin was equal parts intrigued and excited. He had turned on radios in the past. About Camp Moon days, maybe occasionally later. But he was always met with hissing and static or dead air. No radio broadcasts could be found.

"Can we check to see if he is on currently?" Durbin asked him, an excitement that he had not felt in years showing on his face.

"Sure," Nick obliged, walking over to flip a switch on the silver box. It clicked loudly, then the men were greeted by a rich, low voice, smooth and silky, but powerful, its richness identifiable through the buzzing static and flared hisses.

"*—nd for the first time in years it is being reported that the Country is opening its doors — gates — to any who want to join. The entry fee is a promise to accept their ways. I am not usually one to judge, Glass City, but that doesn't sound like a deal I would be rush-*

ing to. If anyone wants your conformity in that fashion? You may just want to leave well enough alone. And speaking of looking for people, the Spire reports that a thief made off with mass amounts of ammunition from their bridge top base. They are looking for a black male with red hair going by the name of Darius. They also state that he may have been complicit in the death of their former leader, Rapunzel. But when the news comes from their new leader, Suede, this host is raising a red flag..."

Nick and Durbin looked at each other. "That your Darius?" asked Nick, his eyes wide.

Durbin was quick to calm his concerns. "He stole the ammo before going AWOL, but he had nothing to do with that death. In fact, he said that Rapunzel had not been seen nor heard from in some time. He was suspicious of something as well."

Nodding, Nick relaxed his face. "It wouldn't do well to have a killer in Windy Well."

Holding his tongue, Durbin rubbed his bald head and scratched behind his ear, then ran his hand along his thick auburn and silver beard in contemplation. "I have killed people before," he finally said, shamefully. He surprised himself with his honesty.

Nick answered with a spitting sound from his teeth. "We *all* have, Durbin, but not in cold blood. Not with malice. Not as a savage."

Durbin nodded and chose to let it be as Nick had said. The radio had begun to play music: tinny saxophone over piano and bass guitar that Durbin recognized as smooth jazz. Light snare drum taps popped to an inconsistent rhythm with the flirty highs and lows of the piano. He leaned back, cupping the dented mug once more, inhaling the floral scent of the tea and pretended for just a moment that he was thirty years old again—and the world was right once more. The music was suddenly interrupted by a rapping on the metal wall of the shipping container turned home.

"Nick? Durbin?" spoke a man with an accent that reminded Durbin of his Lebanese friends from years ago.

"In here, Omar."

"Kimwu would like the group to meet in his place about the new well. Can you be there soon, friends?" His voice was dulled and echoed by the steel, somehow sounding miles away while reverberating close by.

"We shall be there in a few," Nick answered. "No need to wait." He switched off the radio, ending the beautiful instrumental music with an obnoxious click. "Caleb told me about your run-in with the Spire. He told me that you made a great sacrifice in order to save them and yourself." He produced a wide brimmed, brown leather cattleman's hat with a flat frumpy top. He handed it to Durbin.

Durbin's mouth was open in surprise. "I don't know what to say…"

"Paul also told me that you have been a vagabond of sorts in recent years. I think The Well could benefit from having someone such as you around. Consider this a bribe… —or a welcome gift."

"Thank you," Durbin responded genuinely, placing the hat atop his bald head, and smiling with comfort as the headband mysteriously held a perfect fit.

Then Nick beckoned for Durbin to follow him to Kimwu's shelter.

Durbin was once again inside of Kimwu's stuffy and cramped shipping crate, dimly lit and full of warm air. The large conference table again held plastic pitchers of clean water, and mismatched plastic cups long past their usefulness, faded and warped, with frayed rims. The group was missing Raelynn and Trina, along with Sully and Caleb from the other night. But the rest of the group was present, including Paul who sat with his head resting on clasped hands, and Omar with small beads of sweat already forming on his brow and dripping along his cheeks to his thick black beard. Durbin and Nick opted to stand, allowing chairs for the women present. Dr. Soma kindly accepted a seat.

"I will not take mooch of your time, as we all have tings of import to finish. But I tink it best for us all to be on da same page." Kimwu spoke stately, his Kenyan accent noticeable, but his English strong. "Omar?"

Omar rose from his seat, wiping his brow with a blue rag and tucking it into his brown pants front pocket. Stains of sweat ran rings around the collar of his yellowed T-shirt.

"As many of you know, we have been discussing the process of drilling another well to keep up with settlement demands and the demands of settlement trade deliveries. As such, we have decided to drill the new well near the west side of Windy Well by the stables. This gate is closest to the pastures, and the horses, where it would be of substantial use and ease.

We will, however, be moving the water carriage house and supplies closer to the stables as a result."

The table murmured and nodded, in acceptance of Omar's logic.

"We will need manpower to move the drill truck into position, to clean and ready the augers, and to carry wood to the wood gasification generators to power the drill truck," Omar continued.

Nick moved forward from his leaning position on the wall next to Durbin and raised his hand. "I will need someone to help me grease the joints on the auger arm too. It needs to be able to articulate freely and handle any jolts from any rocky earth it may encounter. Just lettin' you know, I am low on engine grease. I'll do the best I can with what I got."

Kimwu spoke up, "You always do, Nick, an' for dat, Windy Well is always grateful."

Omar nodded in agreement. "We would like to begin tomorrow with prepping the drill truck and the generators. If we have the well dug in a few days' time, we can have the water carriage house moved out and reorganized before Sully gets back from Woodstock."

Nick continued on, stating that after the drilling of the Well, they could then lend the drill truck to a settlement to the south. Durbin lost focus in the formality of it all, and his mind wandered away from the conversation.

Durbin was not certain why he was involved in this group, why he was privileged to sit in on the settlement meetings and be given the opportunity to provide input —*which he wouldn't do*— or even aid in this operation of building a well. But, he looked at Paul and recalled his words spoken at Media Hospital. *I feel they are going to need me soon...* And Durbin questioned if this was what he meant. Obviously, the only reason Durbin was a guest in Windy Well, let alone on this council, was purely Paul's influence. Durbin lost himself in thoughts about purpose and flowing water as the council mentioned last-minute requests and agreed on timings and recruiting volunteers and helping hands from various zones of the settlement. Then the council suddenly dismissed and were leaving Kimwu's hotbox of a shelter and conference room, an aura of excitement now present for the coming project. Honestly, despite his intentional self-distancing, Durbin was a bit excited to watch a well being built, too. But, he decided he was going to give them distance to act as a community. He would be out scavenging for supplies that day.

CHAPTER 19 — RAELYNN

Raelynn had only heard mention of the hermit-like all-female settlement of Sunfield. Caravans talked about the great sweeping hill covered in black and silver solar panels that channeled electricity into the bunker. The underground facility was described as a technologically advanced shelter where the monastic women hydroponically grew herbs for medicines and vegetables for trade and consumption, all while writing scriptures that honored their Matriarch. They were quirky and eccentric, with their robes and shaved heads and Buddhist qualities that are driven by a female-centric slant. Finding one of these women in the wilderness was a rare circumstance indeed, but to then be invited inside the underground facility that they called home? Raelynn was nervous and excited, uncertain of how she and Trina would be received by these women of solitude and piety.

The massive vault door closed behind them, the heavy sound was both ominous and crushing as it closed off the natural world that Raelynn had lived in and grown accustomed to. She found herself in a long blue and grey corridor lined with round plastic and metal conduit and bulky square switch boxes. Soft white tubes of light ran along the top edge of the walls humming quietly, illuminating the ceiling and hallway to its distant end. It had an unearthly feel to it, cold and sterile, unfeeling and also unwelcoming. There, the young woman who was ordered to retrieve the Matriarch was talking hurriedly to another woman, both wearing the same green robes as the vault door greeter and Demetra. Two more shorn-headed women donning green and white robes ran down the hall towards them, their light feet clicking on the unmarred concrete floor. When they reached Raelynn and Trina still holding the broken and groaning Demetra, they offered quiet thanks and took Demetra's body from them. Raelynn felt lighter and stood up, stretching and rubbing her shoulders; Trina did the same.

The greeter spoke again, "Apologies. My name is Ciera. We will treat her injuries and return her to her sister. The Matriarch will want to meet you and show gratitude for saving Demetra. If you would follow me, we can make our way to the Matriarch's quarters."

Trina glanced at Raelynn. She nodded in approval and the women were led down the hallway, quiet save for their clicking footfalls. They passed several doors that each held a tiny square glass window with rounded corners. They were moving too quickly to glimpse what was inside, but Raelynn assumed they were individual quarters for the residents of Sunfield. The corridors made sharp square turns that led them down pristine steel grate steps that funneled to more sterile corridors lined with rooms. Raelynn hadn't seen such cleanliness since before the Collapse and the immaculate nature of the bunker was unsettling to her. The dirt, grime, odors, and daily soil of life had become customary for her. *It's too clean* was a nagging thought in her mind. She found it strange that the hallways felt both cold and warm concurrently.

Amongst the crisp, almost intrusive sound of footfalls in the hallway, Raelynn could hear something else. A grunting sound, rhythmic and forceful —nothing like the painful wails of Demetra in the ravine. Sometimes the sounds were masculine, other times they were the sound of two or even three voices; Raelynn's huntress-trained ears deciphered different voice qualities. She was perplexed, as no other voices were heard throughout the facility. No women conversed, not even Ciera as she led them toward the quarters of Sunfield's Matriarch.

"I thought this settlement was inhabited by women only," Trina whispered to Raelynn as she touched her hand, still walking side by side.

"I, too, thought—"

"We have a few domesticates here. They are to help us procreate and encourage the continuation of Sunfield in the name of the Matriarch. They are cared for as most livestock is cared for: fed, watered, permitted to exercise, they are given safety and warmth. They are even played with," Ciera said. She stopped and turned to face Raelynn and Trina. "Our whole purpose is to give feminine glory to the Matriarch by way of worship and the provision of sisters. Once we give birth to a sister, we shave our locks. A sign of a true sister and honoree of the Matriarch. None are truly worthy of the Matriarch's glory until they are shorn..."

Trina spoke up as Ciera's words trailed off while she turned away and resumed leading them down the hall. "What do you do if a boy is born?"

Ciera turned her head to look at Trina, a confused look wrinkled in her hairless brow. Thinking quickly, Raelynn rephrased the question for her. "What happens if one doesn't give birth to a sister?"

The confusion on Ciera's face dissipated. She nodded and then pragmatically stated, "All anomalies are discarded."

Trina stifled a gasp as Raelynn squeezed her hand to quiet her. "Our apologies, Ciera. This is Trina's first time outside of our settlement. We are still attempting to teach her the ways of the world." Raelynn hoped it was enough to stave off any offense Ciera may have felt.

But Ciera seemed unphased. "Which settlement is that?"

Raelynn asserted herself slightly even though Ciera had resumed leading them down the corridors. "We are from Windy Well." She felt a compliment was in order to dissipate any tension. "Our electricity capacity pales in comparison to your facility here."

"Indeed, we are blessed by the Matriarch and the sun, as they both bathe us in the light required for life. She empowers each of us as she empowers these hallways with light and sound."

The sycophantic meter with which Ciera spoke was starting to aggravate Raelynn. She wanted to be done with the Matriarch and leave the rigid uncomfortableness of the bunker. It all felt so counterfeit and austere. Despite its sprawling corridors that lingered on forever, the underground chambers felt claustrophobic. She wanted to be free of the Sunfield bunker, and quickly. Raelynn was not worried about being taken captive, as she and Trina were not stripped of their weapons upon entering, but she wanted to be released of the uneasy feeling none-the-less.

Finally, Ciera stopped in front of a metal double door adorned with the same square windows with rounded corners. There was a slight fog on the bottoms of the windows. Ciera knocked twice with the base of her fist, then flipped a latch that clicked loudly and seemed to pull both doors open simultaneously. Inside were several large tabletop gardens lit by orange and white lamps that heated a variety of herbs and leafy greens. There was a plain steel desk in one corner, where a bald woman sat with a feather quill in hand as she poured over crinkling papers and handmade leatherbound books. She was adorned in white and orange robes, instead of the typical white and green that all the previous women had been wearing. She wore a necklace with a large silver sun-shaped pendant that dangled between her robe covered breasts, swinging above the books and unbound papers. Standing to her right was another pale young woman, nearly Trina's age, dressed in green and white, but also with long, brilliant, red hair half-tied in a pristine braid pulled behind her head, where it met the loose hair that draped over her shoulder and fell past the middle of her robes. She was quite short in stature—so much so that as the woman in orange quietly placed her quill down on the cold steel desk, she looked up at Raelynn and Trina, and her shorn head reached shoulder height of the red-haired young woman.

The woman in white and orange robes smiled and rose from her desk; the red-haired girl bowed and stepped away. Ciera stepped forward to greet the woman and bowed. "Matriarch, these women hail from Windy Well, it is they who returned Demetra to us."

Trina and Raelynn stood nervously in the middle of the

room as Ciera closed the steel doors behind them, trapping in the scents of chamomile, lavender, frankincense, and other medicinal aromatic herbs in the room.

Matriarch stood tall in her robes —much taller than Raelynn or Trina— the orange and white swirling around her long and narrow frame. Raelynn was reminded of Kimwu by the manner in which she moved silently, holding herself in a way that was poised, yet commanded attention. She had startling green eyes that were sharp yet somehow also distant as if her mind were simultaneously entrenched in an elsewhere thought and wandering aimlessly.

"I am pleased to have daughters in Sunfield. Two who understand the flowering sanctity of a woman's life. I owe you many thanks for returning our sister to us, aiding in her recovery. She set out in the later afternoon yesterday, searching for herbs and roots to transplant. We will find out what happened to her. Where did you find her exactly?"

Raelynn cleared her throat and stepped forward still holding Trina's hand. "We found her at the bottom of a ravine just south of here, just past the forest. The brush was thick nearby. It is possible she didn't see the drop-off at the ravine's edge."

Matriarch looked over Raelynn's head. "Demetra knows our lands fairly well. I would sooner believe that something was chasing her."

Her tone was not accusatory, but Raelynn felt Trina grip her harder, fingernails pressing deeply into her flesh. Raelynn spoke again. "While we were hunting, we saw little other than deer, and certainly nothing dangerous."

"No...certainly not..." Matriarch spoke more quietly, lost in thought, or preoccupied with some other pressing matter. She swirled her orange and white robes, trying to remove something from them like shooing a fluttering moth. "You are from Windy Well, I am told? Would the Well be interested in establishing a trade route? We are well versed in hydroponics. We produce fresh herbs for medicine, and fresh vegetables for nourishment all year long. The weather does not affect our growing seasons here. Please, upon your return, give word to your leader. But, if you do decide to seek trade, please send only your women. It will be better for our relationship going forward."

Matriarch's tone was a haunting drone of monotone, with her inflections not quite matching statements or questions, the rhythm of her words broken and bumpy with emphasis oddly placed. Raelynn wondered how the Matriarch had been able to convince other women to join her cause. But, having a solid shelter was by itself inviting to most people, regardless of the leadership within.

"Kristina, my child, can you fetch these ladies a few vials for clear heads and wound treatments? Women in the wilderness must be prepared."

The young red-head with the long braid named Kristina nodded while bowing deeply and, in a flourish of green and white cloth, turned to one of the tables lined with garden boxes. There was the light clinking of glass and whisking of cloth as she floated silently toward Raelynn. She bowed deeply and handed her two vials, one with a pastel purple fluid, the other with a clear fluid, both corked. She handed two more to Trina. "The clear one is for clear heads —to reduce stuffiness that occurs at various times of year," she said faintly, almost breathy and seductive. "Use it sparingly though."

After relieving herself of the gifts, Kristina floated backward, returning to Matriarch. Trina slid her vials into a small pocket in the side of her rucksack.

"Perhaps you should also see them out. I have need to dispose of a failed domesticate, and should probably do so before tending to Demetra."

"Yes, Matriarch," Kristina replied obediently, rubbing her long flaming locks down her chest. Then she floated past Trina and opened the double doors. "I bid you follow me."

Back to the entrance the ladies marched, past noisy barracks-style rooms that Raelynn now understood to be the rooms of the 'domesticates', though she could not tell how many there were, and they still encountered very few women as they continued up the grated stairs. Down a distant hall, a manly scream sounded in protest, but the scratchy shrillness dissipated quickly as they climbed the stairs. And that is when Kristina's demeanor suddenly changed.

She turned to face Trina, her robes settling quickly as she spun. And she quickly whipped her head around to ensure no others were around. She grabbed Trina's forearms earnestly.

"I need you to get me out of here," she hissed.

Trina was frozen in shock. The look of uncertainty on her face caused Raelynn to speak.

"You don't look to be in danger here," she said calmly.

"You don't understand. I have not been able to produce a

sister. And domesticates ...men—are dying as a result. She kills them if they don't help to produce sisters." She was panicked, but quiet, nervously looking over her shoulders in case another sister was coming down the hall.

"The Matriarch?" asked Trina, finally unfrozen.

"Yes. My mother," Kristina said coldly.

Raelynn shook her head and began walking toward the vault door exit once more. *No, I don't want any part of this.*

"I am only alive still because she is my mother. She would have had any other sister disposed of if they could not produce more sisters—but not me. So, she gets rid of the men instead."

"How do you come by these men?" Raelynn asked. "Are they so foolish to see no other men here?"

Kristina swallowed, "We are ordered to seduce men who come along trade caravans, to ensnare them with lusts, and lead them to their pens."

In disbelief, Raelynn sped up her steps, unable to find the exit quickly enough. Trina followed Raelynn's hurried pace as Kristina pleaded while trailing them. They turned the corner and entered the hallway where the vault door lay in wait. Ciera had resumed her post at the door, in view of a monitor screen that Raelynn had not observed before. Its grainy blue-grey image showed the empty area just outside of the vault door.

"I beg of you. Please help me to leave Sunfield."

Raelynn turned to Kristina and pulled her ear close. "I will not risk sour relations—before they even get started—between Sunfield and Windy Well by kidnapping the Matriarch's daughter. I am also unwilling and unable to do anything to change what happens here. So long as they keep to themselves, what each settlement does is their own business."

"But..." Kristina whimpered, her youthfulness on display.

"However," Raelynn hush-yelled into Kristina's red hair, "I will send the next trade caravan that tends Windy Well to you here. They will call for you. What you do at that point is on you"

Kristina's shoulders sank. She bit her upper lip and held back her frustration, regaining the composure of servitude she'd possessed in the Matriarch's quarters. "I accept," she responded, unruffled.

Ciera had not once looked in their direction, her eyes reflecting the bluish display of the security monitor. And Trina, Kristina, and Raelynn closed the final distance to the exit door.

"Thank you again for retrieving our sister, Demetra," Ciera said before the vault screeched open. Insanely bright sunlight blasted through the door, blinding Raelynn and Trina. They shielded their eyes with their hands.

"You're welcome," Trina responded first to Ciera, then turned to Kristina, "and thank you for the elixirs."

Kristina nodded, as if the exchange in the previous moments had never happened, and she replied, "Mercy to you from the Matriarch. You have served one of her daughters, our sister, and shall you be served as well."

Raelynn relayed her intent to establish a route of trade from Windy Well upon their return and thanked Ciera and Kristina for seeing them out of Sunfield. As the vault door loudly sealed behind them, they continued out of sight of the security camera, walking in silence until they came to another thicket of woods for hunting.

"Are you really going to send someone to her?" Trina asked.

"I will direct a caravan to her, yes. But what she does in order to leave is firmly dependent on her."

Trina nodded in acknowledgment, and began to ready her bow as they approached the woods farther north and west of Sunfield.

Raelynn finally released Trina's hand. "Let's make camp when we get to the woods. I am too frazzled by that insanity to track marks at the moment, Huntress."

CHAPTER 20 — CALEB

Woodstock was a light-hearted Bridgetown, alive with sounds and laughter, music from acoustic guitars and goatskin djembes, the smell of dried and fresh flowers, and burning herbs, sage, and lavender. The perimeter of the circular commons area was a cloth rainbow of tents and yurts, with a few permanent dwellings created from old rubber tires and mud, mosaics of green and brown beer bottles creating windows to allow sunlight to enter. The meager homes surrounded shops and a large central bonfire pit, dug deep, serving as a source of heat, light, and food preparation, with several rotisserie spits fashioned from charred wood and forked conduit pipes. Lanterns hung on posts, lighting various paths through the commune gathering around the pit, with a trail of lanterns leading towards an empty stable.

Caleb and Sully were leading Shiva and Hercules with the water carriage toward that stable, carefully forging a route through the sea of dirty people singing and chanting, dancing barefoot, hugging and kissing, sharing ornately carved pipes while blowing plumes of blue and purple smoke from their lips. The horses maintained their composure through the crowd and noise, unphased by the disjointed tribal rhythms and the sounds of several different songs being played simultaneously. The crowd would part casually, allowing enough space for the mighty animals and their load. They would then fill the space behind them, continuing with their dancing and songs, and

Caleb wondered just what exactly they were celebrating. Sure, the winter had finally said goodbye and spring was fiercely arriving with summer-like heat, slingshotting tree buds into leaves and grass shoots into golden fields of dandelions and violet and indigo crocuses, but Caleb heard nothing in their songs about the seasons or reasons to celebrate anything but love.

The ebb and flow of the people along with the steady drone of strumming strings and pounding drums became hypnotic to Caleb, mesmerizing him while the commune seemed to sway as one, but they would blindly sidestep and make space for the carriage without a word. The haze stung his eyes slightly, but it became tolerable, as they went on, his head feeling lighter as the smell of burning leaves and skunk stink began to creep into his nose. He stumbled slightly, shook his head, and continued to lead the horses and carriage to their destination.

A dancing man appeared beside Caleb and Sully, jester-like in appearance with a brightly swirled tie-dyed shirt and loosely woven shawl worn over torn denim jeans, crowned by a head of long, wild, grey and brown hair. Mud caked his toes as he pranced happily about, playing soft and then shrill notes on a flute. He would stand on one foo, and rotate his body slowly, aiming his flute toward the sky blocked by trees, then spin again pointing the flute toward the ground before stomping his other foot into the mud and jumping in the air, his jester-like caricature on full display. He jovially danced a path before them and their shipment, leading them effortlessly through the celebrating inhabitants of Woodstock.

It occurred to Caleb that perhaps they were only celebrating the arrival of the water they were delivering, and a large smile emerged on Caleb's face. He felt needed and important with that thought, and suddenly he too had the urge to dance.

Sully stepped in time with Caleb, approaching his right side while the jester fellow continued to dance. "When was the last time you brought water to them?" Caleb asked over the cacophony of musical sounds.

"We were here last month during those several days when it felt like spring was returning." Sully explained. "But the water carriage was only about three-quarers full, so they have been operating on less water than usual. We had to transport less water because it could freeze at night, and we didn't want to rupture the carriage tank. In the winter, it is hard. The water freezes during transport, then we have to wait for the water to thaw in one of the heated yurts before we can transfer it to their vessels. The rest of the year is much easier."

The steeds were unphased by the music but still appeared relieved when they entered the stable joining a small number of other horses. The yokes and hitches were undone, and the water carriage was removed, rolled back into an adjoining yurt by five Woodstock settlers. The axles creaked and groaned as they carved ruts in the mud and earthen floor. The horses snorted and twitched their heads, shaking off tension and showing excitement about the baskets of soft apples and stalks of leftover wheat and straw hung before them in the stable.

The dancing flute player approached them, his hand gently grazing the faces of Shiva and Hercules as they pushed their noses into him. He slid the silver flute into a brown leather satchel hung about his waist. He stepped with muddy feet towards Caleb and Sully with outstretched arms.

"The water bearers from the Well have arrived, man."

His thin arms reached as wide as his pale forehead was tall, his untamed hair complimented by wild blue eyes that were alive with fervor and love. He was a jester and a wildman together, his brightly colored clothes clashing boldly with muddy feet and an unkempt appearance. But it was all brought together in a unique way by his, and all of Woodstock's, conviviality.

Sully and the jester shared a brotherly hug. "Sully from the Well. I have missed you, man." After a few strong back pats, the jester turned to Caleb. He offered a pale, bony hand in greeting.

"Caleb, please meet Jerry Gee. He is the mayor of Woodstock. Has been for as long as there has been a Woodstock."

"Mayor? Naw, man. I am, like, more of a...-facilitator of this wonderful commune. Every woman, man, and beast are of equal value here."

Caleb reached for Jerry's hand, and as they touched, Jerry pulled him close for a hug. He was surprisingly strong given his thin, almost frail appearance. "I am pleased to have met you Caleb, man. Welcome to Woodstock!" Then he released Caleb. "And like, thanks so much for helping Sully bring this month's supply. It has been a rough month, man! We were able to capture some rain and snow melt over the last few weeks, but you know, gotta be conservative. I haven't washed, in like, weeks."

Caleb admitted that he could only smell the skunky air and Jerry chuckled childishly. "Make yourselves at home, Sully and Caleb from the Well. The water will get drained into our casks, and then we feast, man."

Later that night they filled their bellies on bread and honey, thick sweet apple butter, and salad made of tender green shoots and winter onions and shelled walnuts. Caleb was impressed with how well they ate and expressed his gratitude for the delicious meal. Sully, Jerry, and a few other Woodstock residents were sitting comfortably at a round table in Jerry's yurt, discussing the ups and downs of the weather during the last month, exclaiming that "Mother nature was crazy, man.", and they all hoped to get their planting in soon as their cold season stores were running quite low. Then Caleb felt something cold and wet touch his hand. Then, just as suddenly, he felt something rough, hot, and wet touch his hand. He recoiled quickly, taken by surprise and looked underneath the table to see two golden eyes. A grey and black dog looked up at him, panting lightly, as if talking to Caleb. The canine's face was grey with markings that resembled a black beard. His black ears were pointed and folded over themselves, twitching occasionally to the sounds of others' voices. Caleb reached slowly for the fluffy black scruff of the dog's cheeks, petting him lightly. Then the dog pressed his face into Caleb's hands, nuzzling him back, before turning and sitting down on the floor beside Caleb's chair.

"Such a sweet dog you have here, Jerry. He is so friendly." Caleb said from across the table. He let him rest at his side, and the dog would occasionally tap its nose on his pinky to remind him it was there.

"Oh, Flint? Yeah, he is a good dog, man. Too bad his man-friend passed this winter. He has had no one to call his since then. We have all been just taking care of him. He, like, just comes and goes, and whoever's place he lands is whoever feeds him that day."

Caleb noticed Flint was quite skinny and wondered if they had fed him much at all. His shoulder blades protruded slightly from his back, and his fur was more coarse and seedy than the hair of either Shiva or Hercules. Flint sighed lowly with a throaty growl of contentment and reservation —almost as if to answer Caleb's thought about food. Then he placed his muzzle on Caleb's boots.

"He lost someone important to him as well?" Caleb said as the weight of Flint's snout rested heavily but comfortably on his boot. He looked down at the shaggy dog once more, their eyes meeting. Sadness was held in Flint's black and golden eyes. Caleb understood that sadness; it was not a sensation of loneliness, having been cared for and surrounded by people, but more a sensation of longing. A feeling of grasping deeply for something that vanishes in a mist of time, shadow, and disappointment. For Caleb, it was reaching for his parents, even their memory, but their images in his mind were quickly fading. And Caleb knew that Flint was longing for his owner, his lifelong friend. The winter had taken from both Caleb and Flint the only things they had known since birth.

"I think it is high time we toasted our friends and their glorious delivery." Jerry had stood up suddenly and held his rainbow-colored cup over his head with a skinny pale arm. Gatherers on the floor pulled their feet under them as they sat on colorful floor rugs, looking upward at Jerry. Some raised their own rainbow cups, some held up smoking pipes, others raised outstretched hands with splayed fingers as high as their bodies allowed. "These fine dudes traveled from the Well, bearing clean and delicious water," Jerry crooned and the crowded yurt cheered. "They have cared for our steeds and have employed them dutifully. Nearly every month, they cart the water carriage here, and quite frankly, man, we wouldn't be alive if it weren't for them and the Well!"

The yurt cheered more, whistling, and whooping, while others sang short jingles of praise and thanksgiving. Plumes of smoke were blown into the air, clapping of hands together and on bare thighs. Flint's ears perked up as he lifted his snout from Caleb's boot. He looked around at the excitement, then back up to Caleb who was certain he saw the dog smile before laying down once more on his boot. The dog sighed heavily as the crowd cheered again, and placed his square furry grey and brown paw on Caleb's other boot.

In minstrel-like fashion, a woman and man both with sandy brown hair piling on their shoulders, began singing about the virtues of water, one lyric at a time. Others would join the chorus at various points, as though they knew the song from a long-forgotten memory. Sully leaned over to Caleb, "They do this every couple of months. Davide found it annoying, but I don't mind. If I can be celebrated like a king just for doing my job, I'll take it."

The feasting continued, with music and drink, and smoking pipes, with couples dancing with their bodies pressed so close together they moved as one being. Caleb was growing weary of the unending celebration, and frankly, he did not understand the need for it. He stood up to retire to his cot in the darkened yurt next door. Flint rose too, following Caleb outside. He panted and pranced along at Caleb's heels, his tongue flapping loosely from his maw, giving the dog a youthful and careless look. Caleb turned into his yurt, buttoning the door flap after letting Flint inside. He sat on his wooden framed, muslin sling cot. Flint placed a paw on Caleb's knee then rubbed his cool, wet nose against the fabric of his tan cargo pants.

"You really like me, don't you boy?" Caleb acknowledged as he bent forward and ruffled Flint's grey-brown fur, just between the turned-down ears. "I'm sorry about your man friend." Caleb continued as he rubbed Flint's cheeks, shoulders, and chest. He thought he heard the dog whimper in response.

Caleb then lay back on the cot, while Flint curled himself up underneath it, and they both slept peacefully.

CHAPTER 21 — DARIUS

The noise of the generators was louder than anything that Darius had heard in years. Automatic machine guns, high-powered sniper rifles. Their blasts were mere puffs of sound compared to the thundering roar of the half dozen or so generators that were powering the drill truck. It rumbled with the force of an earthquake as it rolled into position near the empty horse stables. The generators were modified by Nick to utilize wood gasification, in order to provide the truck's diesel engine with ignitable fuel. The generators were stacked on the black flatbed of the drill truck where the auger typically rested. As a result, the auger and articulating arm were elevated, and Darius —along with several other Windy Well settlers—were hoisting cables out of its way as Omar slowly drove the truck through Windy Well. They would pull on their own ropes and cables, assisted by pulleys anchored high above the settlement, raise the cables that housed the electric lanterns, bulbs, and diodes that illuminated the catwalks and mezzanines. Then as the truck passed under, they would lower their ropes, and race to the next set of cables to be elevated.

Darius grunted as he heaved, his feet struggling to find traction on the grated catwalk as the vibrations in the metal disoriented him. Sweat soaked his flaming red hair and darkened brow. He shook his head in an attempt to clear it of the resonance and fuzz.

"Why couldn't we have driven the truck *around* the

settlement and come in the backside near the stables?" Darius yelled over the noise of the generators to the man assisting him.

"The terrain is too rough with deep grooves and ridges on the north side, and the tangled growth is too thick on the south side. It takes too much fuel to go around on flatter ground," he shouted back to him. Some syllables were lost in the raucous sound of the truck, but Darius was following what he said. *Naw, y'all shoulda thought this through a little more. There had to be an easier way.*

A chorus of wild shouts sounded out, barely audible over the engine roars. The auger arm had hit one of the metal shelters atop the middle mezzanine. Settlers scrambled, some to check on the truck, some to observe the shelter. The home now housed a large gouge through the corrugated metal of the blue shipping container wall, bent and rippled, but it did not seem to be dislodged from its foundation on the mezzanine. Omar maneuvered the drill truck, adjusted the auger arm, and continued slowly around the tight corner towards the stables. There were no more lighting cables overhead in the drill truck's path, so Darius returned to the front gate to resume his entrance guard duties.

With the noise of the new project far behind him, the quiet allowed Darius to regain some peace. From his perch atop the heavy white steel gate, cables, chains, and fencing, he looked about the Windy Well, taking in the picture of a settlement that was so unlike the Spire, so unlike any settlement he had ever called home. Of course, it wasn't home like when he was a kid, complete with his mother and father, with a furnace providing heat and pipes and flowing water with powered plumbing. Or even with his daily school life, his handful of electronic devices that helped him stave off boredom after he had finished with composition homework. It wasn't quite like having a couch to sit on, complaining to his mother about the black kids in the community center making fun of him for his red hair, or the white kids making fun of him for his chocolate-colored skin. No, it wasn't like that at all, because he felt included here. He felt like he belonged. The walls of the Well offered protection from the outside dangers of treacherous people, but inside —it offered sanctity of the individual, it welcomed those who desired peace, who had grown weary of the settlement infighting and the wilderness' unaccountable savagery; and it was home to those who had been victimized.

But in the Well, Kimwu's leadership was also a refreshing change for Darius. The Marauders, even the Spire, frequently had leadership that—no matter when or how it was overthrown—was always depicted as a power-hungry despot who ruled his settlement with an iron fist. They demanded fealty and loyalty —always in exchange for some morbid form of protection. But Kimwu was different. He insisted that Windy Well leadership be communal, that no man or woman held governance directly over another, and for survival, the settlers of the Well worked as a team not driven by needs as an individual.

A few days back, after Trina had left with Raelynn on a hunt, Darius was in Kimwu's quarters. They were discussing Darius's occupation responsibilities within the settlement when he questioned Kimwu's devotion to collective governance instead of taking a more executive role.

Kimwu leaned back in his chair, crossing and uncrossing

his long, bony arms. He talked with his hands when he was relaxed, Darius noticed, and moved more than his stateliness would typically allow. "Many years ago, back in Kenya, we wa' ovarun by a maniac claiming to be da' savya' of our lands. He talked sweetly, earning trust from da' masses. He was one man. And tru' conniving and false policy, he rose to lead all of Kenya. And den... he decided dat da' people of Kenya —who granted him his power— were no longer needed."

He changed positions while he told his story, looking more at the floor as the tale grew darker, avoiding Darius's eyes. "Many of my people died as he began a culling. Dare seemed to be no reason. He would murda' some, and spare udda's, only to set dem to da firing line lata'. He burned half of our capital of Nairobi to da' ground before claiming it for his own seat of powa. He let in only dose who agreed to do his bidding wit'out question. Den he sent out extermination squads to eliminate da rest of us."

Darius could hear the sadness and oppression in Kimwu's voice. He pieced together in his head the unspoken things in Kimwu's story: the blood, the torture, the disregard for life and humanity. Because of his own youth in the Glass City in the months following the Collapse, he knew well about the orphaned children crying in the streets before becoming victims themselves, or kidnapped and groomed to follow in the heinous footsteps of their captors.

"Somalia and Et'iopia had fallen to pirates. Several of my people fled to Uganda, uddas' ran furder to find protection in da jungles of da Congo. Afta my family was kidnapped and most likely killed, I fled to Tanzania. Zanzibar airports wa' still operating, and I was able to negotiate travel to America. I taut my troubles wa' behind me. Perhaps, I only brought dem here."

Kimwu then lowered his shoulders and sank further into his chair, his long, thin frame closing in on itself till he looked the size of a child. He sniffed deeply and wiped his face with long, dark hands. "When dis new well is drilled, I desia' for Windy Well to fosta new trade with more settlements, building a larga' community of peace. Da Glass City may be lost to us, but perhaps we can move our coalition towards da west. We must continue to rebuild dis nation with peace in mind."

"What if some of them others out there don't want peace Kimwu? You know, my experience, there are more people who be willing to shoot me than welcome me into their scrap-built home."

"Der be people who want peace. Der be people who do not desire to have powa' ova' what is left of dis land."

Darius turned away from the settlement commons and scanned the poorly tended farm fields to the south, the forest to his right was budding fully with young leaves, the greenery increasing daily, shadowing the moist, earthy floor that was beginning to harbor an abundance of button and morel mushrooms. The trade route leaving the Well split south and north, lined by wild grasses and cat-tails that stood taller than most men, but off in the distance, perhaps a kilometer or two away, Darius could see a cadre of men dressed in black and grey. As they neared Windy Well, he could see they were equipped with tactical armor and vests, some with small firearms holstered, others carrying long-arm rifles and carbines. Darius counted ten men. He signaled to another watchman, who signaled to another, and down the watchmen's line, the message traveled. It was possible that the soldiers would pass beyond Windy Well, or they would have to turn left along with the split and deliberately come to the front gate below Darius.

They turned left.

Their march was asymmetrical, they were off-beat and mismatched, almost jangly in their movements. Some were looking toward The Well, some distracted by the vegetation growing past their shoulders, others observed the ruts in the path carved by trading caravans. One man of the pack picked his nose and kicked rocks. *They certainly don't look harmful,* Darius thought, bemused by their rag-tag nature. Other than being heavily armed, Darius didn't find the military presentation particularly threatening, and he gave the signal to the guards below that ten men were approaching.

The front gates let out their defiant, skull-piercing screech as each metal barricade was tilted into the sky. Darius remained perched at his post to let the ground guards manage the visitors. The air was calm today, and the turbine on the windmill remained silent and still, allowing Darius to overhear parts of the conversation.

"Water? Yeah, we got clean water…leader here…they… back….new drill site…yeah, *they*… no… different 'round here…"

There were more indecipherable words. The speaker of the soldier-looking men spoke with a bone-in-the-throat smoky voice.

"Yeah, we'll have them come up when they can. Davide! Can you relieve Nick and Kimwu? Tell them we have the diplomat from down south —and we have his boss!"

Davide ran off towards the back of the settlement, through the same path the drill truck had chugged along earlier in the day. Darius watched him zip through man-made alleyways to the far side of the settlement, where the rumble of generators and roar of the diesel engine could be heard faintly. Darius decided to follow, staying to the mezzanine in order to look down onto the settlement and survey their guests. He rounded the corner that the drill truck had hit when Omar was threading the truck through the narrowest passage. The wood gasification generators were roaring loudly now, the sound unblocked by the dwelling structures. Kimwu and Nick passed by on the ground level beneath him. Darius rounded another corner and could see the drill truck in action, loudly working on the new well.

The men and women around the drill truck were carefully clearing earth away as the auger lifted out of the ground. Another group arrived with a long steel tube to extend the length of the auger which had stopped spinning. Four men held the auger with leather-gloved hands while two others unfastened a cinching collar to detach the auger. Like a well-timed dance, the steel tube was placed into the coupling of the auger, and both were lowered into the hole. The collar was cinched on once more, and arm attached again, and the spinning drill was forced deeper into the earth. Then the teams prepared their tools once again for an exchange of steel. Omar checked the generators on the flatbed of the truck under the suspended auger arm. Paul was close by, near the passenger door of the cab of the truck. Davide, standing on the back ledge of the truck bed, had assumed the controls of the auger as it plunged into the ground, erupting black and copper soil upward along the length of the steel tubing.

Satisfied, Darius turned to peer around the corner to check on Kimwu and Nick greeting their visitors. As he turned to the corner, from behind him there came a terrible squeal of metal on rock, so loud it drowned out the generators, then a powerful crack followed by screams. A generator popped like cannon fire, the truck went silent, then as Darius bolted back towards the gathering at the drill truck, each generator went silent in turn as Omar approached each one. The auger stood twisted and spiraling out of its hole, with the arm bent and jagged, covered in maroon gore and bits of bone, but the real tragedy was Davide being held by Paul. His chest was ripped open from armpit to armpit, eyes empty and unfocused, blood dripping from his gaping mouth of voiceless screaming. Paul held Davide's unmoving body, eyes closed, whispering quickly and loudly. Several settlers stood around lost, — unsure of what to do; others wept. One stumbled away from the group surrounding Davide's body and vomited. Darius jumped down a rickety stair to the ground with swift parkour motions, briefly touching feet to metal stairs before his boots hit the earth and he slid in next Paul.

"I turned for just a moment, what happened?"

Paul remained focused on his prayer over Davide's body. Omar spoke up. "I think we hit rock. The auger got lodged, and the torsion ripped the drill's driveshaft. Davide was up on the control panel. And the twisted shaft cut him down."

The silence that had fallen in Windy Well was creepy

after the droning roar of the machinery. Darius kneeled on the ground next to Davide's body, still cradled by Paul. The scuffling of boots on earth could be heard approaching the stable yard, and Darius wondered why the visitors would be interested in the Well's tragedy. Nick came to Darius's side.

"Good Lord…" he whispered, kneeling down next to Paul and Darius, "my friend." Nick, with wet eyes, looked into Darius's own. "I was manning those controls before he sent for me and Kimwu."

He observed fear in Nick's tearful eyes, a realization that he could have been the mangled body lying in the dirt.

Nick reached over the remains of Davide and gently closed his eyes. Paul ceased his prayer, and likewise, gently laid Davide's body on the ground. He pulled back strands of long salt and pepper hair from his frozen face. All three stood up from the ground and stood to face the visitors flanking Kimwu. The shortest one of the group, with ashen grey hair mixed with black hair, long greasy locks that hung past his chin, standing farthest from Kimwu, spoke with his smoky, bone –in-the-throat gravel.

"Gawd, another one…" His beady black eyes pierced into Darius with icy daggers, then the beady eyes looked at Davide. "Well, that's unsettling."

Darius was unsure what to make of this character, his snarky demeanor, and his coldness.

"We used to have an agreement, Kimwu, at least we did when our diplomats talked over the winter about our water situation…" The greasy man surveyed the Windy Well settlers who were still gathered around the drill truck with its shredded steel for an auger arm. He tugged agitatedly at the tactical pads in his body armor. "I am starting to think you cannot hold up your end of it at the moment."

"As you can see, Balon, we ah suffering from an unforeseen setback," Kimwu responded, his courtesy and composure resolute.

"A setback?" Balon scoffed pointing at Davide's body "Setback? I think that poor sod over there would call it a bit *more* than a setback."

Darius, however, was not as composed as Kimwu, "Hey, you show some respect for the dead, you—" Nick and Paul grabbed him and pulled him back as he tried to advance on Balon.

"No," Nick commanded him, releasing Darius as he nodded reluctantly, tightly drawn lips showing his true desire and anger.

Balon glared at Darius. "You know, the Charles family, MY family has suffered a number of *setbacks* because of errors from people like you." He waved both of his hands like pointed guns at Darius and Kimwu. "And based on this mess of a truck, it looks like Gale Fortress will not be able to complete its well. This means the firearms that we brought —in good faith, mind you — will not be staying here. I should have known better. Really. And every time I try to give the benefit of the doubt, you stupid, dark-skinned miscreants just ruin everything you touch. History has shown me that you like killing—especially on accident."

Balon walked in a small circle as he continued ranting, then abruptly stopped and tilted his head to on side, not looking at anyone in particular. "Take the leaders," he said calmly.

There was a commotion of moving bodies with clicks and clacks of metal, then grunts and yells and suddenly the settlers of the Well were faced with ten semi-automatic rifles aimed at Nick at Kimwu.

CHAPTER 22 — BALON

Balon Charles cursed the heat. He cursed the tactical armor worn by him and his men as they traversed the fields and forests and ghosted highways northward. He cursed the walking and the discomfort and the lack of a soft chair or bed. But mostly, he cursed the purpose for it all. Gale Fortress had been suffering from poor water issues for nearly two years now. The reservoir was stagnant and full of algae, with only a mild reprieve during winter months before it would freeze. It was all Balon could do to get enough men motivated to collect a sufficient amount of water to store away in water barrels. But the truth was, it was never enough. Never enough acceptable manpower, never enough water, never enough food. Even with four functioning wind turbines, it was never enough electricity for the compound. Balon was getting desperate, and with fewer and fewer resources, his grip of power on the Gale Fortress was waning.

But last summer, a trader caravan made mention of a settlement farther north —but much farther west than the Glass City— that had built an inground well in the shadow of functioning wind turbine. Balon sent his right-hand man, Jarvey, to negotiate a water deal, or to acquire their equipment for drilling a well themselves. Jarvey was a good lap dog. He scurried the distance between settlements, a journey that took a couple of days in good weather on foot, more than once to make contact with Windy Well and broker an agreement.

Jarvey was oddly coy, stating that he would prefer to handle the dealings without Balon getting personally involved. Balon was fine with it. The less he had to focus on matters outside of the Fortress, the better, for he had to maintain his control of the settlement. He trusted Jarvey.

"They require a certain delicateness, Balon," Jarvey said to him last winter. They sat in his quarters deep in the belly of Gale Fortress, warm and comfortable. "They have an almost backwoods nature to them. And their leader is not someone you would see eye to eye with."

"All the better for you to deal with them then. Did you offer them the guns?" Balon inquired. He ran his thin but large-knuckled white fingers through his ashen grey and black hair, removing long greasy strands from his face.

"I did," said Jarvey, "but they were surprisingly privy to the fact that guns are worth much less without the ammunition. They negotiated increased rounds of ammo —which we don't have to spare— and informed me they would have the drill truck ready in the spring, after the last thaw, and after they dug their second well."

Balon sighed with a tone of botheration and waved his hands freely. "Sure, more ammo. The Fortress needs a sustainable water source. And we need their machinery in order to do it. Have some of your men search our supply stores for more tradable goods to offer the caravans to replenish our supply of ammunition. We will take other measures if necessary. And after the last thaw, head there to retrieve the equipment."

"But you will need to go with me when we pick up the

equipment. It would be a show of good faith to be face to face with the leadership of Windy Well as the leader of the Fortress," Jarvey said hesitantly.

Balon raised his eyes at Jarvey, "Both of us gone from the Fortress for several days? At this time? And who will assume leadership? You are to assume top dog when on those rare instances when I leave."

There was a pregnant pause before Jarvey spoke next. "Brody can take the helm—"

"Brody?!" Balon exclaimed. "Brody has been trying to usurp me from within since last summer's water shortage. He only ceased once I gave him the southern barracks to stay away from me."

"Exactly," Jarvey responded. "Let us give him a taste of manning the Fortress and see what he does. You still have enough grip of power over the Fortress; I have seen to that. And if he oversteps his bounds, you have reason to remove him permanently."

Satisfied, Balon conceded to Jarvey's counsel.

And so, after rounds of negotiations between the Fortress and the Well, Jarvey had arranged for the drill truck to be on loan in exchange for ten assault rifles with magazines initially and fourscore of ammunition cases to be delivered after the acquisition of the truck. Jarvey assured Balon that he was instructed on the truck's and its drill attachment's usage; even how to maintain the wood gasification generators. But now, Balon, Jarvey, and eight of the Fortress's men were navigating the springtime heat clad in tactical armor to exchange arms and equipment with Windy Well.

And Balon cursed the heat.

He vowed not to make any journey without protections. Tactical armor was a must, as Balon had been in the middle of some terribly brokered deals in the years since the Collapse. He always came out on top though. He learned early on that mercy was a profound weakness, and that an iron fist got a man much further than a soft heart in this dying world. Even though Balon trusted Jarvey with his life, he would not go to Windy Well unarmed and unprotected, no matter how cordial Jarvey stated the settlers were. To break the monotony of the several days' hike, Jarvey led the men in marching chants and songs. Each man, except Balon of course, took turns carrying the camp supplies in massive canvas hiking backpacks. Balon was looking forward to driving the drill truck back to Gale Fortress and to being rid of all the hiking. He considered leaving men behind to complete the return trip on foot if there was not enough room for them all.

They traversed the Windfields, the sprawling acreage of wind turbines after wind turbines; many dormant and defunct, or missing their massive metallic white fins. Scores of electricity-generating windmills filled the scores of kilometers between Gale Fortress and Windy Well, with trade caravan routes carving the best paths that snaked about the pearlescent obelisk-like machines.

"There is a windmill that rises above a small, dense forest. It is surrounded by battlements and ramparts of steel and fence rising about two stories or so in the air. That will be Windy Well." Jarvey spoke loudly so that all the men could hear, but Balon knew that he was really only talking to him. The other men knew their roles of following orders and protecting their Gale Master.

The conglomerate of re-purposed tractor-trailers and shipping containers, held together by spindles of steel and cable, piecemealed stair frames, and shoddily welded scaffolding finally came into view. As they approached ever closer, weaving between the grasses and cattails as tall as he, Balon found their fortifications to be scant and easily broken. Only the massive gate of white steel haloed by a well-designed parapet offered a suitable defense. Balon cared little about the settlement itself but found himself getting excited by the thought that in a mere week they would have clean well water and finally be free of the roulette game of drinking from the reservoir.

A shadowy figure, with details lost in the early afternoon sunlight, made motions from their position on the parapet and the white·gate sections squealed as they lifted up away from each other. Jarvey took the front position of the pack after a vague hand motion from Balon, and the guard on the other side of the chain-link fence identified Jarvey. Welcoming words were exchanged, and the fence groaned on its resistant casters as it opened to allow Balon's men entry. They were greeted by a couple of unarmed guardsmen, dressed in shabby flannel shirts —one green, one blue— both with cut-off sleeves and worn denim pants over tan weather-beaten work boots.

Jarvey and the guardsman in green talked briefly; Balon couldn't be bothered to follow the details. Instead, he looked around at the ramshackle appearance of Windy Well. More incongruent than Gale Fortress, it seemed built over time, adding sections and levels and growing taller with each passing year. Each section seemed to take on a new look, be it semi tractor-trailer, shipping container, railroad car, wooden hovel, or canvas tents. The network of cables and ropes, some as thick as Balon's arms, fascinated him as it was plain to see they were used for transporting goods between levels of the dwellings. Gale Fortress was just blocks of warehouses and defunct machinery, repurposed and powered by whatever wind turbine was closest to the need. In the early days, they had transported steel planks, truck trailers, and railcars to create a perimeter of defense, further fortifying the settlement. Everything had its place. There was no need for intricate networks of cables and ropes to deliver goods. All distribution of resources had to be authorized by Balon anyway...

"I'll go get them," the man in green plaid said, as Balon only paid half attention to him and Jarvey.

"Them?" Balon asked. "We are only dealing with the top in command today. To get this truck."

"Yes, them." said the man in green plaid, shaking his head and heavily sighing in elucidation. "We do things differently around here." Then he shouted out to someone unseen as Balon turned to Jarvey.

"What do they have here? Parliament? How does a settlement this size have need of a council? Is this what you have been dealing with?" Balon hissed at Jarvey, fearing that maybe he should have handled this venture himself starting months ago in order to streamline things from the very beginning. He didn't like haggling. He didn't want to clear things with a council.

He wanted the drill truck. And he didn't like others pretending they were in control of situations in which he was certainly in control.

Balon fumed while he and his men waited at the open gate for some time before two men came into view, rounding a corner and walking beside the ramshackle construction surrounding the base of the wind turbine, oddly quiet in the calm springtime heat. One man was shorter, with broad shoulders and thick forearms, grease-stained overalls clung to his massive shoulders covered by an oil marked, red T-shirt. He wiped the sweat from his brow with a massive forearm, the sweat matting his coarse black hair. The other man was extremely tall and slender, adorned with bright patterns of yellow, red, and green, with black bones for arms and legs that stretched far beyond his torso. His skin was dark, but Balon was not sure if was because of the shadows cast by the walls or not.

As the two men that Balon assumed were leaders approached even closer, he noticed that the tall slender one had skin the color of roasted coffee, made to look darker by the bright color arrangement of his clothes. Balon writhed his fingers in vexation. The two men offered handshakes in greeting to Jarvey, greeting him with welcome and smiles. Balon twitched slightly at the sound of Kimwu's accent. His jaw clenched in silence; lips tight with nervous energy.

"I am Kimwu," he said as he stretched an abnormally long arm to Balon with long fingers like black snakes with pink bellies. Balon kept his hands away from the snakes and instead tucked them into a pocket of his pants. The snakes recoiled back to the patterned shirt. Then the shorter man with strong forearms waved a red bandana handkerchief in his direction.

"I am Nick, the 'Mechanic'," he said, wiping off his fingers with the handkerchief, leaving black oily smudges across the bandana pattern. Balon removed his hand from his pocket, but Nick kept his tied within the red cloth. "You are Balon Charles, right?"

Balon grunted through tight lips, one eye on Kimwu.

"We have been meeting with your man for some time now. The new well will be ready today or tomorrow," Nick continued.

"You are welcome to stay in any location wit'in de Well dat you would like until de truck is available," Kimwu chimed in. It sounded like snake hissing to Balon.

Suddenly, a terrible screech of metal on metal sounded across the settlement, then a chorus of screams from the direction Nick and Kimwu had come from. Immediately, Nick and Kimwu turned to run toward the disturbance, Jarvey gave Balon a questioning look and, they too, made a lazy pursuit to see what had happened. The main courtyard of Windy Well narrowed to alleyways between steel and plastic, catwalks and salvaged fire-escapes rigged together. There was a commotion around the corner, sharp voices of shock and sadness. Balon knew those tones. They often accompanied unexpected and preventable death. His voice had mirrored those tones when his own father was murdered by African doctors before the Collapse. Then his mother...

The roaring generators quieted and the drill truck rumbled to a stop as Balon, Jarvey and their men turned the corner to see a mangled mess of a man on the ground held by Nick, a square white-haired fellow, and an abhorrent man of chocolate skin and flaming red hair. "Gawd, another one..." Balon muttered loudly, feeling the lines in his cheeks deepen as his face became even warmer. It wasn't just the sun. Then he paid more attention to the mangled body of the greying man on the ground. *Well, most of the body*. His chest was mightily ripped open, rib cage removed from its protective housing over fleshy, delicate organs. "Well that's unsettling..." Balon thought aloud.

Balon lost himself in his own words, trying to stay one step ahead of the situation while restraining the rage that was burning inside of him, embers fueled by the rubble of his plans. He droned on about agreements and bargains and how they had failed.

Then the anaconda-like Kimwu hissed some more in Balon's direction, the only word actually worth hearing was "set-back."

When the doctors were caring for Balon's parents all those years ago, they called all of their mistakes "set-backs." When the infection raged within his father's body, immune to all drug therapies, it was a "set-back." When his lungs shut down because of an adverse reaction to a procedure —it was a "set-back." When his mother did not respond to the cold therapy after a heart attack... when she had a stroke on the operating table —another "set-back."

"I think that poor sod over there would call it *more* than a setback," he growled indignantly.

The flaming haired black kid lunged toward him nonsensically but restrained quickly —*and intelligently*— by Nick the 'Mechanic.' Balon looked at the kid sideways. *Those types of outbursts will land you outside of my graces, kid*, he thought, not really caring whatever guttural utterances the kid bellowed. He began to pace in small circles, the rising anger forcing him to move.

"You know, the Charles family, MY family has suffered a number of setbacks because of errors by people like you." He pointed to Darius and Kimwu with a gun-shaped hand imagining their heads popping like blood-filled balloons. "And based on this mess of a truck, it looks like Gale Fortress will not be able to complete its well. Which means the firearms that we brought —in good faith, mind you— will not be staying here." He scoffed some more, his pacing circles becoming larger and larger and more erratic as his body failed to control the mounting rage. *No clean water for us, again.* "I should have known better. Really. And every time I try to give the benefit of the doubt, you stupid, dark-skinned miscreants just ruin everything you touch. History has shown me that you like killing — especially on accident."

He rambled on a short time more, spitting curses furiously, drool clinging to his lips and chin, and when he noticed that the Well settlers had let down their guard, he calmly and suddenly said, "Take the leaders."

His men were caught off-guard as well, clamoring to raise the holstered weapons at Kimwu and Nick, quickly circling in and closing the distance to eliminate their escape. Balon marched to another massive white gate that he identified on the other side of the drill truck, aimed his gun at the nearest person, and threatened, "Open the gate!" At this time, Balon's men were escorting Kimwu and Nick toward the screeching gate as it lifted into the air. Jarvey, *such a loyal lapdog,* brought up the rear of the marching line, his gun pointed toward Kimwu's head.

The red-haired kid regained his courage and raced toward the entourage. Balon raised his gun at him.

"No, Darius!" shouted the square white-bearded man, and Balon twitched his finger with a single pull of the trigger. A lone bullet cut the air and pierced Darius's thigh high above his knee with a bloody splash. He shouted and stumbled to the ground, where he punched the dirt in pain. He tried to stand, and stumbled again, unable to bear weight on the injured leg. The square white-bearded man scurried up to him, clumsy in his shape and size. "I'm okay, Paul. I'm sorry."

The entourage marched on with their captives, weapons at the ready, with an occasional muzzle push to Kimwu's shoulders. The rest of the settlement stood in shock, uncertain of what was going on or why.

"Take me!" Darius then yelled from his place in the dirt. "Leave Kimwu here and take me!" Paul helped him to his feet, and Darius hobbled forward as Balon's men crossed under the massive white gate. "Force me into servitude, since that's what you want. I know your type!"

Balon snorted. "You really are stupid, aren't you, blackie? What use to me is a man who cannot walk?" Without warning, he fired another round at Darius, this time the bullet grazing his other thigh, opening the flesh in another splash of blood as Darius fell to the ground again. Paul was unable to hold him.

"Shut the gate!" Balon yelled turning his gun toward the settler nearest the control switch. They scrambled in fear, fidgeting clumsily with levers while Balon let loose a warning shot and the gate squealed again. "I am taking with me the most important thing to your pathetic settlement!" he shouted as the gate lowered near their heads. Then he suddenly grabbed Kimwu and kicked him back into Windy Well as the gate crashed down behind him, closing off Balon from the Well once more.

Balon turned to his other captive, sneering in anger and morbid happiness. "You are my mechanic now, Nick."

CHAPTER 23 — RAELYNN

With the bizarre spectacle of Sunfield behind them, Raelynn and Trina made their way to Woodstock. With any luck, they would meet up with Sully and Caleb, along with any acquired game. If they happened upon enough marks, perhaps they could trade for preservation salt —they would need it to preserve their meat for next winter.

"But it is only spring," Trina said to Raelynn as they were discussing their objectives for the next few days before returning to Windy Well.

"Indeed, Huntress, but the winters have been getting ever worse. We have to start planning for the next as soon as one ends. When the settlement gets behind on resources, it is painfully difficult to recover. Surely, you experienced that in your home of Bridgetown?"

Raelynn found Trina to be quite intelligent, but was often caught off-guard by her naivety about the world. Many conversations reminded her that Trina had spent much of her life in post-Collapse society, but also in the relative comfort of a self-contained settlement.

"We... —always found a way to get by," Trina responded quietly. "Everyone always pitched in. We all had our place. Despite the yearly floods and occasional bandit raids on our crops or livestock, we recovered, replanted, rebuilt. Whatever it took. But we weren't very good at planning and preparation.

How could we have been? We were always at the mercy of the river."

They walked about the field grasses and wild shrubbery, greens and yellows and whites blossoming about them with sparse explosions of color. Even lilacs were beginning their showers with shades of violets and pinks.

"Yes, but at the Well, we have to be more proactive and take preventative measures. We are far from the old suburbs on purpose. We stay away from Loners and the Marauders, and the countless other factions that have popped up and then fizzled out over the years." Raelynn was an educator at heart, and never felt burdened when teaching. She never tired of sharing useful information. "Being farther away kept us a bit safer —brigands would have had to travel farther, but so did we when we had to gather and scavenge resources. It forced us to be more aware of everything in the settlement. Strong communal leadership was helpful."

She tried hard to impress upon her the balance of free-thinking and collaboration that Windy Well valued. If Trina were to be a part of the Well, she would have to adapt. Raelynn knew that Bridgetown was not too different in regard to philosophy and survival, but she couldn't help but think that their methods were more... —primitive. Not that The Well was a bastion of technology; not much of the modern world had survived the Collapse, and what did, barely ran on wind power or solar power, and scraping up just enough energy to get by.

And then there were settlements like Woodstock which, nestled in a thicket of woods that protected the farms and simple dwellings, held nearly no technology at all. But still, they held fast to making poultices, medicines, salves, panaceas, as well as providing enough smoking materials for all the old Glass City. They also excelled at raising crops, though Raelynn was unsure of where they learnt their herbology skills. On her best days, she would describe the residence as eccentric, lighthearted fools who loved only half of nature, and misunderstood the other half. They adored their plants and vegetation and refused to eat most meat, raising only goats for their milk. Their stance on hunting —or the lack of it— was at odds with Raelynn's occupation as a Huntress, who felt at one with the primal side of nature. She understood the balance of life and death, the spiritual aspects of hunting and letting certain marks go off into the field to be tracked another day.

She tried to instill that into Trina Hurst accordingly.

Trina missed her first goose. And her second. But soon, she nabbed three large geese in a row, as they hunted a gander in a field near a dry creek bed. From the branches overhead and some thin rope cord from their packs, they hastily made a litter for carrying their bounty. Then Trina regrouped and took down a small brown doe, an arrow straight through the neck. The deer ran a short distance, then dropped dead, Trina wrenched the arrow free gracelessly, but was excited for her success regardless. The women carried their prizes upon their handmade litter, taking turns pulling it along as they continued their route toward Woodstock.

Woodstock was one of those settlements that were usually smelled before it was seen, the aroma of burning herbs, the drying of plants, and a general scent of uncleanliness permeated the woods surrounding the tent-encircled camp. Then there was the smell of goat manure from mountains of compost. But sometimes, Woodstock would also boast bouquets of floral aromas, and the rich earthiness of fresh fruits or vegetables being produced by well-tended stalks and shrubs. This was not one of those times, as the winter had held its grip too long on the region, and the earth was sodden mud much too wet for planting just yet. But there was no doubt that the settlers of Woodstock would not postpone their planting much longer if they had not planted already.

The naturalist settlement could also often be heard before being seen, too. Especially during times of celebration. But if you asked Raelynn or even Sully, they would say that Woodstock was always celebrating something. They celebrated the completion of the season's planting, the beginning and end of harvesting, the flowering of certain trees, the arrival of new children, the deaths of important settlers, the first rain after a rare dry spell or drought. They were truly a carefree and happy people in Woodstock, if a bit whimsical in their methods, and Raelynn would be remiss to deny a tinge of jealousy for their enduring happiness even in dark times.

Windy Well was such a serious settlement compared to Woodstock, always putting business before anything else, always putting the survival of the camp ahead of any individual liberty, but never in an oppressive way. Everyone in The Well was of a similar mindset: —to live through the winters and survive as a community. Not that Woodstock lacked the survival mentality, but other than medicine and farming, they lacked the dedication to any further advancements in their settlement. They were much more laissez-faire in their motivation and upkeep. *Different settlements attract different types,* she thought.

Somewhere between the mentalities of settlements like Windy Well and Woodstock were the trader caravans. One such caravan was approaching Raelynn and Trina on the faded gravel path. Two mundane-looking brown horses with untamed black manes steadily hauled a yellow pickup truck bed adorned with a weathered wooden cap that rose a meter or so above the yellow walls of the truck bed. A seat was fixed to the front end of the truck bed, behind the horses, where a rider sat, armed with a rifle on their backside and shotgun mounted to the wooden cap. The rider wore a tattered tan cattleman hat, and layers of denim and yellow cotton clothes. The rider appeared female; a small figure perched on the mount behind the horses, but Raelynn could not be certain with the layers of clothing and the shade of the cattleman's hat.

"Are you going to stop them and tell about that Kristina girl at Sunfield?" Trina asked as the women carried their goose-filled litter off the path to allow the horses space.

"I will, as I promised, and I'll also see what wares they have," Raelynn answered responsibly. She then waved to the trader, who slowed the horses as they plodded to a heavy-hooved stop. Their makeshift yoke fashioned to the re-purposed truck bed groaned with the change in momentum. The rider doffed the cattleman's hat to reveal a tight bun of blond hair and dark eyebrows over blue eyes set in a slender, feminine face with a pointed chin.

"You in need of any supplies for trade, ladies?" she said, laying the hat on her knees and loosening the reins. "I'll give plenty of fabric or steel for some of that goose there. Those animal worshippers had not any ounce of meat there in Woodstock. And Sydney Mora does not shy away easily from any fair deal." She was not unfriendly, but her drawling accent and haughty disposition caused her to sound more caustic than she probably intended.

"I was wanting to get some salt blocks from you," Raelynn responded hopefully, "We will gladly trade some goose. Hunted just yesterday."

Sydney's lips tightened and curled disappointingly. "'Fraid those same animal worshippers took the last of my salt —not sure why, really. They got no meat needs pre-servin'. And salting all those plants can only make 'em taste so good."

Raelynn thought for a moment, defeated briefly by the lack of the one substance she felt she needed most. If they didn't start to recoup their meat stores at The Well now, next winter would be even worse than last. Preserving their meat was becoming more difficult, and keeping vegetables fresh through long winters was becoming impossible. It was going to get more difficult to keep the peace...

"You have any ammo to trade?" Raelynn finally said, looking up at Sydney.

"In fact, I do, missy." Sydney crowned her head with her hat, wiping her hand on the brim with an approving swipe as she jumped off her mount with a heavy—footed clunk. She opened the tailgate of the truckbed after fiddling with rusty and complicated lock hardware. The open space revealed a narrow area made up of an unfurled bedroll. The left side was built up with knotty wood shelving, stocked with random colored boxes, piles of fabric, whole articles of clothing, tactical armor, tools such as axes and small sledgehammers, boots, a couple of crossbows hung from the ceiling, and several small firearms mounted wherever there was space. Sydney heaved her small frame up into the truck bed with a metallic protest from the tailgate. "Most people lookin' for forty-five. You need forty-fives?" She continued to peruse her shelves, touching a few colored boxes that rattled and clinked.

"Actually, I need .22 caliber," Raelynn said. She wondered if Sydney was a part of a larger caravan, or if she'd decided to trade on her own. Her wares were as fully realized as Raelynn was accustomed to from more traditional caravans.

A loud, whistling sigh came from the truck bed. "I only got one box of twenny-twos. Fi'ty rounds in the box. I'll take three geese for it."

Raelynn was surprised by the grunt that resounded close behind her. Trina was there, her face wild with disbelief. Raelynn knew what she was thinking. All of the effort to take down three geese. The first two failures. All the spent patience and diligence. And it was worth only fifty rounds of ammo. She knew that to Trina, this was not a fair trade. But, in truth, the price of ammo had been going up significantly in recent years. What used to be one goose for one box of ammo two summers ago was now three geese for the same box of ammo. And it would probably get worse as time went on.

She shook her head defeatedly after looking at Trina and leaned against the crossbar of the roof of the trader's cart. "Are arrows more affordable?" She asked, trying to hide the irritation in her voice.

Sydney opened and closed a few drawers near the back of the cart. "I have thirteen total. Fiberglass. Three of those are broadheads, but they are used. One goose is the cost."

A better deal, it seemed —at least arrows were reusable. She looked to Trina to see if she approved. She held her head a bit low so that her black hair hid her chewing her lip in deliberation. Then she looked up at Raelynn and mouthed, "sure". Trina shook her shoulders and lifted her head before leaving Raelynn to go retrieve a goose from the litter.

Sydney crawled out of her cart with two handfuls of arrows of assorted colors and lengths; the three used broadheads looked dull and slightly bent. She then sat on the open tailgate waiting for her bartered goose. "Syndey?" Raelynn spoke up.

"Yes ma'am?" she said resting her pointed chin on her fist, propped up by a bent knee.

"Are you familiar with Sunfield?" she asked the trader quietly.

Sydney looked to think hard for a moment before speaking. "I reckon I have been there once or twice. Don't recall it being very profitable. Maybe I got a vial of elixir or something. Yeah, that sounds right. All ladies up in there, right?"

"Yeah, that's the place," Raelynn acknowledged. Thoughts of Sunfield's bizarre nature buzzed in the back of her mind. "Is it too much to ask you to go there for me?"

"Oh, I ain't got no room for a hitchhiker—"

"Not to take me there," Raelynn corrected. "I made a

promise to a woman there. Kristina is her name. Flaming red hair. Probably the only woman there with hair. She wants to leave...er, escape... Sunfield. I couldn't risk her coming with us for a number of reasons. I told her I would direct a trader caravan to her and what she chose to do at that point was her doing. Could you be that trader to help her leave whatever threatens her?"

Sydney had taken to chewing on her fingers. She nodded repeatedly but not in response to Raelynn's question.

"I still ain't got room, but I will see what I can do. Why is she the only one with hair?"

"Maybe that is why you have to help her leave," said Raelynn coldly.

Sydney nodded slowly, "Sure... I'll see what I can do..."

The women completed their barter, Trina eyeing the bent arrows suspiciously with sharply down-turned lips. Sydney affirmed that Woodstock was only an hour or so away by horse if they remained on the trade route. They carried their litter, less one goose, for another two hours before being greeted by the colorful yurts and tents of Woodstock surrounded by oak trees, large budding garden plots, and small farms. The only notable smell that Raelynn detected was the smell of mud, though the smell of smoke clung to oak leaves overhead. They arrived at an entry point —not quite a gate, but not quite open either— tended by a skinny man with long curly brown hair, sunken eyes, and scattered whiskers on his jawline. He wore a leather poncho over a colorful shirt and tattered blue denim jeans. He was barefoot, save for the caked mud covering his pale toes, and he smiled as he sucked on a brown wooden pipe that produced purple-grey smoke.

"Hello ladies," he coughed as he pulled the pipe from his lips. "You are more than welcome here at Woodstock, but I will have to ask you to place your game in the storage bin in the tent behind me. Some folks here are really put off by hunted animals."

Raelynn eyed the man's leather poncho incredulously. His hands flustered around his adornments. "No, not me. I don't mind using the tanned hide of a deceased goat. All things have a purpose, I say. We just don't want anyone put out. I assure you that your game is safe. You just missed the trader caravan by a few hours, but there may be one or two within Woodstock who would desire trade. They will cook the meat outside the settlement, of course…"

"Thank you for the offer of storage," Raelynn said with a forced apologetic tone. "Can you tell me if anyone from Windy Well is still here?"

"Sure! Yeah!" he said excitedly. "Sully and Caleb are here. First time meeting Caleb. Good kid that one."

"Caleb!" Trina exclaimed.

The pipe-smoking man looked at her as though seeing her for the first time. "You look a bit like him, you know."

"He is my little brother," she said sheepishly.

"Yes, yes, it makes sense now," he said rubbing the sparse whiskers on his face, "Caleb and Sully should be in Jerry Gee's yurt, preparing to leave with their empty water carriage. Taking off tonight or first thing tomorrow, I think." He pointed off past a large stone-lined fire pit, wagging his hand with less discretion than Raelynn would have preferred.

Raelynn and Trina crossed the humble public circle of Woodstock. Some settlers were tending to produce baskets of leaves and herbs. Others sat lazily on rocks or wood haphazardly stacked to resemble benches while they sucked on pipes and puffed purple smoke. They passed a tall tent with an open door flap. Inside, a woman and man stood over a table that held several sloppy lines of glassware. The man hurriedly manipulated a stone mortar and pestle as the woman poured an unidentified liquid into a glass with a round billowed bottom. She added green and brown powder from another stone mortar and swirled the solution in the glass. Satisfied, she firmly plugged the narrow neck of the bottle with a cork and went on to another billowed glass. Another tent made a shelter for drying herbs and plants, strung across the tent clipped to thin brown twine, frayed from use.

A wild man Raelynn recognized as Jerry Gee emerged from the flap of a colorful yurt. He was followed by Sully and Caleb with a grey mangy dog at his heels. Caleb exclaimed as he saw Trina, Sully gave them a timid wave. Jerry looked as alive as ever, hair wild about his face, boney arms flailing in an abstract but energetic greeting. Caleb ran to Trina and embraced her, with the dog prancing playfully on hind legs, lapping his tongue at both of them. Raelynn felt Sully nudge her arm with his elbow—his typical greeting.

"How is he doing? Acclimating to his responsibilities?" Raelynn asked him. "How is he acclimating to being *here?* I am not even accustomed to being here, and it isn't my first time."

She couldn't hide the annoyance on her face, though she tried.

"He is wonderful," Sully said with feigned drama to match Raelynn's agitation. "He has been helpful, cordial, understanding of their idiosyncrasies, and he even made a friend." Sully motioned toward the prancing mangy dog. Its coat was drab and unkempt, but its smile was notable despite its long boxy muzzle. Sully turned to face Raelynn directly. "And how fares your newest huntress, Huntress?"

She could feel the playful jest in his laugh, a sense of sarcasm long lost in this world. Raelynn knew that Sully was joking, because she never chose poorly when it came to grooming a new huntress, or healer, or craftsperson. She had a skill for placing people exactly where they worked best for Windy Well. She pursed her lips in a smile and shaped her eyes in an affirmative look to tell Sully that this time was no different.

"Trina tells me that these two have been through much in recent weeks. They are strong—hardy, even." She watched as Trina knelt down to ruffle the dog's coat and box his ears. "The dog is part of this month's trade?" Raelynn asked.

Sully laughed, genuinely this time. "That's Flint. He has not left Caleb's side since we arrived. Jerry jokingly mentioned that he could be traded for me." He pulled his long, blond hair behind his head into a ponytail before letting the locks fall back to his shoulders. "But really, Flint just latched onto Caleb. He recently lost someone, too. Maybe they have some sort of unseen bond of grief or something?"

"Maybe…" Raelynn mumbled. Personal or emotional bonds were not experiences she often had anymore. People called her cold. But in the end, she was driven towards her goals of The Well's prosperity and survival. Everything else was secondary, because from her perspective, if there was no Windy Well, then nothing else really mattered. The Well was a beacon of welcome and community — which wasn't found in many places, Woodstock notwithstanding. She ensured that anyone welcomed to Windy Well had a place of responsibility, and whatever they did when they were finished with those responsibilities was their own prerogative.

With a clatter of plastic, metal, and wood, Shiva and Hercules arrived with the empty water carriage. It's side packs were loaded with later-winter produce, nuts, hemp rope, and glass vials of medicine per a monthly agreement between the settlements. They were packed with supplies for the two-day journey back to Windy Well. Once out of sight from Woodstock, they would trade-off in pairs riding on the empty water carriage — the horses would not mind the load with no water aboard. They would hunt for game periodically, aiming for more deer if able, with the water carriage available to carry larger quarry.

The ride back to Windy Well was uneventful, if bumpy, with several deer being shot and dressed along the way. Trina took down a doe with one of the bent broadhead arrows acquired in the barter with Sydney; unsurprisingly, it snapped when she pulled it from the animal's throat. The field-dressed game lay under burlap cloth, covered and protected from insects and the increasing heat of the late-spring sun. Even with the game piling onto the water carriage, it was mostly empty, and creaked and bounced noisily along the gravel and pavement paths without the water weighing it down. With their hardened, unfeeling pallor, the massive white doors of Windy Well greeted the travelers, hiding the trouble that Balon Charles had caused two days prior.

Each of them had expected to find a new well installed near the horse stables. Instead, they found a settlement in shock. Davide was dead, Kimwu injured. Nick had been abducted. Durbin had disappeared and was feared to be on a revenge-fueled suicide mission to rescue Nick. The drill truck was damaged and sat motionless,s blocking their path to the stables. Despite being new to Windy Well, Paul delivered all the information to Raelynn with tact and respect —something she much admired about the man— and he, too, had tears in his eyes as he explained about Davide. When Trina heard that Darius had been shot, she burst out in exclamation, "Darius has been shot! How is he? Where is he? Please take me to him!" Caleb, on the other hand, had taken to sitting on a bench with one cracked slat in the back support. His lips were tight, and his eyes narrowed. He quickly developed a serious and quiet tone and looked at no one except for Flint, who crowded Caleb's feet in order to get as close as possible to him.

Raelynn, of course, was more worried about Kimwu's injuries and whether they would affect settlement operations. She told herself they would not affect much of the day-to-day, as Kimwu had designed the governance to function independently of one or two individuals. But, with Nick being out of the picture, and being held hostage by this Balon Charles, as he is called... —Raelynn did wonder if the Well would suffer a bit. Nick was easily the smartest person in the settlement —though not as refined as Dr. Soma. He possessed boundless knowledge about all things mechanical and mathematical, electrical, and regarding physics. He kept their moving parts moving and has had no prospects for a protégé to serve in his stead. That meant without Nick, there was no one to manage the electricity allotment for the cold stores to preserve their meat when there wasn't enough salt. It also meant that there was no one who understood the intricacies of the windmill and how it delivered the right amount of power to the various sections of the settlement. Raelynn had offered her hands and muscle once or twice over the years to assist in repairs and running cables and wires, but she was not adept at the technical aspects and had only been to the top of the windmill enough times to know about the power exchange system and the emergency evacuation belay system to be used in case of a fire.

Indeed, Nick Nathanson's absence would be a problem.

CHAPTER 24 — DURBIN

It had been one full day of hard travel. Loaded with wits and light weaponry and determined to rescue his friend Nick, Durbin —unencumbered by a party— traversed the darkened swampland without fear of pitfalls or sinkholes, or unseen ravines or even scavengers. Windy Well had come to feel like home rather quickly, with Nick and Durbin forming a solid friendship, —perhaps out of loneliness or perhaps out of necessity— but a friendship that Durbin was prepared to honor. But it was more than that. Nick Nathansen, the 'Mechanic' of Windy Well, the seeker of knowledge and proprietor of post-Collapse philanthropy was integral to the survival and flourishing of Windy Well. Durbin was not inclined to let the savagery and fickle disposition of Balon Charles take another friend from him, or remove a pillar of the Well, without a fight.

He traveled day and night, through soggy black marshes and scrubland hills, through forests of mighty oaks, majestic glowing sycamores weeping willows, and red-hued cypress, over battered and disused highways, and through long-forgotten farm fields —overgrown with midwestern ferns and soft mulberry trees. He shimmied unstable metal bones of dead bridges spanning muddy waters of unknown depths. He climbed ravines that held small trickles of clean water and had to find ways around others that had become murky mires full of leeches and putrid black liquid. He passed through small abandoned railyard towns, but with no time to scavenge for supplies, he pressed farther south towards Balon's Gale Fortress.

Much of the walk was spent with Durbin cursing himself for being absent from the Well during the drilling and upon Balon's arrival. Of course, he had no clue that Balon was approaching the Well, or that he was intending to borrow the drill truck. Despite being invited into the inner workings of Windy Well's council, that information was not given freely to Durbin. Or perhaps Balon's arrival was so soon in the Spring that it came as a surprise to Kimwu, and the Well's council may not have felt that that business was necessary for Durbin to know. Regardless, there was ought Durbin could do with the drill team. He was known to let settlements carry on as they always had, with him becoming only minimally involved in their affairs. The drilling was no different than a settlement-wide celebration of the harvest, or a fishing run, or a food preservation day where they salted their meats and fish in preparation for winter. On the day of the drill, Durbin gathered a few baskets and set out foraging for berries, roots, leaves and stems, and even the occasional morel mushroom. He had gone into a few abandoned farm houses to scavenge supplies. He let Windy Well be Windy Well, with the settlers' designated jobs and responsibilities, while he ran off to be Durbin, —solitary and nongregarious. In his several decades in life, he would have learned that his alone time too often came with a cost. A run-in with a badger, a missed opportunity. But this time, it had come at a cost of life, injured friends, and a hostage situation.

Upon arriving back at the Well, he found Darius injured with bullet wounds to his thighs, Davide ripped apart by the destroyed arm and auger of the drill truck, and Nick being taken prisoner by an angry and volatile man named Balon Charles. The settlement was in mental disarray, trying to clean up Davide's body and the mess left by the drill accident, Darius and Kimwu needing their injuries tended. Omar was tending to Kimwu, and Dr. Soma was dressing Darius' thigh wounds, Paul was trying to calm people in shock from witnessing Davide's brutal demise, with dried blood and bodily tissue still smattered across their faces. Kimwu eventually told Durbin of the deal with involving the truck and a shipment of armaments. With tears in his eyes, he told of Davide and Darius, and Balon beginning to kidnap him and Nick but only taking Nick at the last moment. Durbin fidgeted with the wide-brimmed hat upon his head —the hat that Nick had given to him only a few days before— anger clearly visible on his face as Kimwu pleaded with him not to do anything that would put himself or Nick in further danger.

Now he followed the path made of rails, remarkably intact, laying on deep blackish-brown cross-ties embedded in the ballast of white and grey, coarsely chunked granite. The technique for laying railroad ties was hundreds of years old, still tried and true, as well as effective, preserving the rail path with no perceivable destruction from the elements. *If we only had half of their engineering knowledge today, we might have a better world for ourselves.* Durbin thought. *They did so much more with fewer resources than we can manage with a century's worth of cheap technological garbage.* The rail ties were mostly undisturbed, save for chicory, wild asparagus, and miscellaneous woody weeds that had grown unchecked over the years. Durbin pocketed several stalks of the asparagus and the chicory, munched on some of the purple flowers and tender heads for nourishment.

Paul had instructed Durbin that the railroad would pass through several abandoned towns, and would continue south, where it would converge with several dozen rails in a yard that led directly to Gale Fortress. Paul said it was a massive fortification, a derelict appliance factory powered by several wind power generators. Before falling into his hate-driven tirade, Balon had bemoaned the reservoir which sat near the fortress, now stale and rank with stagnant water, ridden with disease. As he continued into a second straight day of fast paced hiking, he knew that he could not miss his destination, imagining the rumbling hum of several wind turbines, and the fetid smell of the useless reservoir.

The rails turned and led Durbin into a woodland of cottonwood trees, their softly rippled lumber reaching high into the sky, releasing white powder puffs that resembled snow. The cotton seeds gathered on the ground, forming a plush, fluffy carpet, but the darkened railties drew straight lines through the whiteness. The rails were met with others to the left and right, then even more rails farther down the path. The rails multiplied more, and the trees grew smaller and scarce, the white cotton flowing like waves crashing over the metal ties. Flowing amongst the rails, the white blanket of fluff continued on out of the woodlands, clearing away before revealing a colorful wall of organized junk protecting a giant boxy light blue structure streaked with trails of rust. Forced-air condensers, exhaust fans, and ports sat upon the top of the structure like metal sentries. Durbin pressed forward, the waves of cotton parting before him when a breeze picked up carrying the stench of stagnant water towards him. He had arrived at the Gale Fortress.

Durbin turned right toward the edge of the expanse of cottonwood trees, making his approach to the massive settlement. He would need their cover in order to scout the Gale Fortress and determine a portal of entry.

The fortification covered several acres, with a perimeter fence piecemeal from chain link, shipping containers, stacks of crushed automobiles, rusted sheet metal, and various scrap heaps of rubbled bricks, concrete panels, and twisted steel trusses mixed with remnant spools of razor wire. The makeshift walls prevented Durbin from seeing the grounds proper, but he could see at several points into the complex, wind turbines' silver-white blades towered high above the boxy blue appliance factory, but only a few thrummed in the air. Large, cylindrical searchlights sat unmanned on the corners of the factory, made of several dozen blocks conjoined together or attached by covered crossings. Impermanent guard boxes sat above the roof of the main structures behind the searchlights, nailed together with scrap wood, tied together with discarded lengths of rope, cable, and wire. Riggings of counter-ballasts and flatbed carts stood like sentries ready to lift loads from the ground to the upper levels of the complex, often placed on the roof over roughly cut openings in the blue steel walls. Durbin could not see into the darkness of those maws and scanned farther along the grounds.

The railyard opened into a wide expanse of open-air but was obstructed with more makeshift barricades, the switchyard leading to a gate, not unlike the giant white steel gate of Windy Well. A breeze blew the stench of the stagnant reservoir from somewhere beyond the trees to his right. He needed to gain a clearer line of sight into the compound, but dared not try to scale the long towering trunks of cottonwood trees. They lent no branches for climbing until ten meters into the air at least, their wood so soft and brittle that any limbs would collapse under Durbin's weight. The land around him was unbearably flat. He realized that the only way to improve his vantage point would be to climb a portion of the makeshift barricades and perimeter without losing a limb to the razor wire or shambled steel. But he also realized that he could only do that after the sun had fallen behind the trees, or the Fortress itself, or he would be spotted easily by any patrols or guards. He remained under the cover of trees and bush as he searched for any elevation and found himself longing for the Irish Hills up north. Upon the right hill with the proper line of sight, one could see for kilometers, with hills swooping underneath, giving birth to flowing creeks and abandoned American Indian war cemeteries. *Just one hill such as that now, and I could hide among the brush and stake out the Fortress without issue.*

    He sat at the base of a thick tree, the railyard to his left, a hot, putrid breeze blowing from the water pit to his right, out of sight. In front of him was the Gale Fortress, not as foreboding as the name would imply, but rather, just as derelict as every other warehouse and factory that Durbin had encountered in recent years. He spied patrols lazily climbing the sentry boxes that were hastily built on the corners of the roof of each blue block of the fortress. *Two sentries on patrol,* he noted. He timed them at about fifteen minutes per full perimeter march after they reappeared again. Durbin ascertained that there were more blue blocks to the warehouses and factory than he could see and became lost in trying to determine just how many men were housed in the Fortress. He was disappointed to realize that he saw no main entrance to the Fortress. He also saw no communication from the roof sentries to any ground patrols. He considered throwing a rock over the barricade but was wary about arising suspicion too early. Even though the shadows grew long, there was still plenty of daylight to reveal Durbin's position were he to climb any portion of the barricade. He half hoped the searchlights were operational, that they would enhance any shadows and give him blind cover to any patrols in the swaths of light.

  The cracking of sticks and branches and a scurry of dried leaves startled Durbin as he jerked awake from a sleep he had fallen into by accident. He caught a glimpse of a white stripe smothered by black fur, a skunk, as it hastily skittered away from Durbin lying with his back against a tree. He had instinctively grasped his bowie knife and his recently acquired pistol. *It is no replacement for Exodus,* he thought as he released his grip on the gun. The knife remained in his left hand as he peered through the darkness into the white beams of searchlights. They were unmoving, casting a bright glow in large circles upon the Fortress's blocky segments and upon the grounds below the barricades. Durbin stood from the base of the tree and searched for a portion of barricade between two searchlights, hoping for both the cover of darkness and the blinding of anyone within the aura of the lights. He found a spot far away from the main gate he had located at the railyard, but he found the barricade difficult to scale. It was no more than three meters high, but the razor-wire and bent steel —along with uneven scrap concrete chunks with protruding re-bar— made if difficult to climb without losing a limb or an eye. About two meters up, Durbin found a niche in which to rest. The smell of the reservoir was strong, stagnant, moldy water clinging to his nostrils, pungent and heavy. But he heard no flowing water. What he did hear was the sound of boots crunching on gravel. Durbin stopped his breathing and held very still. Voices accompanied the boots as two men were discussing a prisoner and orders.

"But Brody ordered us to step up patrols in case anyone from the Windy Well decided on some heroics," said a very average-sounding male voice.

"I doubt it," said the other man, his voice higher pitched, reminiscent of a small man with a short temper. "My buddy Luke was with Balon and Jarvey at Windy Well. He said they were scared stupid backwoods hicks. All except for the smart-mouthed blackie that Balon shot in the legs. Luke says that guy is going nowhere fast."

Durbin resisted the urge of anger that flared within him at the disrespectful mention of Darius. Crumbled concrete shifted under Durbin's boots and rolled away below him. He drew in more breath sharply. But the men continued walking, unaware of his presence, bickering about the potential onslaught of Well Rebels and whether the Fortress was ready for a war with another settlement when their water and food situation was so dire. Durbin tired of straining to hear their words when he noticed a pattern in the rebar to his left. It made a bit of a ladder as it protruded from the concrete chunks that rested heavily against a crumpled railcar. As the voices disappeared entirely, he silently climbed the ladder of metal hoisting himself to the top edge of the rail car. He perched atop it, positioned soundly between the fields of two white searchlights that illuminated the ground, safely secluded in shadows. He scanned the closest segments of the Fortress, spying the lookout towers for sentries on patrol of the high ground. There was one sentry up in the lookout near the searchlight to his left, though Durbin was not certain which direction the sentry could be looking. He only noticed his black silhouette against the deep dark blue of night. The white beam of the searchlight darkened all detail not bathed in its radiance. He cowered low against the roof of the railcar and watched the sentry.

But he didn't leave his post.

Durbin watched him turn occasionally, the brim of his cap pointing outward then disappearing, giving a slight indication of which direction he was looking. Durbin sighed quietly. Then he saw a patrol of two men, one average-sized and one smaller with a higher-pitched voice, approaching to his right. They walked side by side along the perimeter just inside the barricade —their path taking them below Durbin's perch. He crouched lower, silently.

"I don't think they have a plan for the water supply," said the man with the higher-pitched voice, "since this whole well thing went south, Brody and Balon have been at each other's throats. Brody threatens Balon telling him to watch his back. They aren't the least bit concerned with us grunts."

"You heard about the mutiny?" asked the average-sounding man. He had a rifle strapped to his back but looked disinterested in using it. "I might side with Brody." Both men wore black tactical gear, nondescript and protective. Durbin considered taking out the average looking man to take his gear but wasn't sure he could dispose of both guards silently. Both of them were out of sight below Durbin.

"Brody?!" the other guard's high-pitched voice cracked. "Brody has less of a plan for the Fortress than Balon. Both of them only care for power and themselves."

Durbin tried to count off time from the point when they had passed below him at the railcar. He needed to more precisely time their route and be ready for a window of opportunity to breach the Fortress without being seen. He peered up at the sentry in the lookout once more.

He remained there, moving slightly only occasionally, the silhouette of the bill of his hat pointing in the direction he was looking.

"But I never feared for my life since Brody was given the southern barracks. I was always afraid Balon would off me just for being me." said the average guard. The patrols' backs were to Durbin and he could see them once more.

"If you was black, maybe," said the high-pitched guard. There was something weaselly about him. Durbin wouldn't have much of any reservations disposing of these guards if the need or opportunity arose. They continued walking out of earshot and Durbin tried desperately to stay focused on how long before they approached again. He spied the sentry on the lookout frequently, noting that his viewing area included the grounds in front of Durbin, the light area to his left, and an undetermined area beyond the corner of the Fortress, toward the railyard gate. He suspiciously eyed the cavernous opening in the building directly ahead of him, trying to find light or shadow to indicate a guard there as well. He visually swept along the ground, taking note of each personal doorway and an overhead door that he could see. All of them were closed, and their number was great. No windows were evident on the walls of the building he could see. But there were no other identifying marks either. There were no signs indicating "prisoners" or "Balon's secret office", and any doubt that Durbin had been fighting off for the past two days was now catching up to him. He realized he had no idea where to go. The massive appliance factory was guarded, illuminated, and he had no clue where Nick was being held captive or where to begin his search, let alone how to keep from being caught himself. Based on Kimwu's opposition to Durbin rescuing Nick —a founder of Windy Well— he doubted that Kimwu would be willing to send a party for a lone man only recently accepted into The Well.

No, Durbin acknowledged, *I am in this one alone.*

While scanning as much of the Fortress he could see from his cloaked perch atop the railcar, Durbin assessed that he would benefit from moving away from the sentry in the lookout on the roof. He planned to make towards the wall of the Fortress ahead of him, between searchlight fields and then move right, and around the corner. With any luck, he could find a way to scale the Fortress; take out the sentries stationed there, scope out the complex more completely, and buy himself some time with fewer eyes to catch him.

The voices of the average guard and high-pitched guard were returning. It had been nearly twenty minutes. *About one and a half kilometers*, thought Durbin while calculating area in his head. *That is a lot of ground to cover without being seen.*

"You know," squeaked high-pitched guard, "there is a terrible lack of women in Gale Fortress. Maybe we need a female leader? Or maybe just recruit some women from some smaller settlements?"

"I heard that the Country has plenty of women. Not sure I'd be wanting to join their ranks just for the chance with a woman, though," the average guard muttered.

"Yeah, I heard those women were tainted with something anyway. Weird folks up there in the Country." High-pitch guard's voice went cold at the mention of being weird.

As the patrol guards moved further, Durbin once more timed the patrols perimeter march, he estimated about twelve to fifteen minutes were all he had to find another hiding spot before the guards were within view. He planned to be alongside the walls of the main buildings of the Fortress and hoped that the darkness would be his friend. He observed the sentry one final time, the silhouette of his hat indicating he was not looking in Durbin's direction.

As nimbly as his age could muster, Durbin slid along the slanted roof of the railcar and jumped to the earth below. His boots crunched the ground and he rolled softly, raised to a crouch, and moved quickly towards the nearest wall between searchlight fields. At about 150 meters, his legs burned from crouch-running. He looked up the roof to his left and could no longer see the lookout post of the sentry. He stood and ran the remaining distance, pressing his back to the wall concealed in darkness. Bright auras still illuminated the yard to his left and right, and he could see the perimeter barricade upon which he had perched for what seemed like hours. The darkness felt deeper here, or perhaps he was only telling himself that. He turned in the direction opposite of the sentry that had taken so much of Durbin's attention as he hugged the wall of the Fortress. He could feel the cold of the steel through his shirt and vest. Average guard and high-pitched guard appeared at the end of the wall, still beating their perimeter, though they were too far for Durbin to make out their words. Only murmurs and short bleats of sound reached his ears as he clung low to the ground in the darkness. After the patrol passed once more, Durbin stealthily moved to the far corner of the current wall and poked his head to peer around the corner. He lay very low to the ground, shrouded in darkness, but he moved slowly, taking no chances.

There was another series of buildings, all the same, blue color, greyer in the darkness. Only one searchlight shone in the yard here, and Durbin realized he could see no lookouts or sentries from his vantage point. That worried him. But he also noticed something relieving. There was a mass of vines climbing up a darkened portion of the next building, well secluded from the light or any possible rooftop lookouts. It slithered partway up the wall, where it gripped scaffolding that resembled a fire escape. *Getting to the roof will be good for my view. I can remove any sentries, and find out where Nick is or is not.*

Elusively, he covered the ground between the corner and the vine wall with silent speed. His eyes darted left and right as he scanned for potential guards. Lunging forward, he grabbed for the highest portion of vine he could reach, clutching cold, woody vines in his grip. The broad leaves rustled loudly, and he hastily pulled himself upward, his boots finding footholds in the bramble. The racket he made was like a rock concert in his ears; he was certain he was drawing the attention of every guard, sentry, patrol in the Fortress. He found the cold, hard steel of the ladder of the retracted fire escape and hoisted himself through the rungs onto the rigging platform. He pressed himself prone into the bars of steel that made the floor of the platform, gripped his pistol, and waited.

No guards came.

He slowly rolled onto his back with his handgun still drawn and looked up to the top of the fire escape where it met the roof. No sentries there either.

He sighed deeply with relief and started to get up, checking the ground behind him. The ground path led to a courtyard-like opening beyond his sight. But directly before him, several meters away from the fire escape, was an enclosed crossing that bridged the building portions of the Fortress. It was lined with the same blue rippled steel siding but housed several window cutouts that remained black as the night sky. He waited for several minutes before climbing the stairway to the next landing, then another stairway to a second landing, and finally to the roof. He removed his hat briefly and peered over the roof ledge, scanning for sentries on the rooftop.

The sentry post was indeed unoccupied, a short barstool sat alone next to the metallic cylinder of a searchlight. It remained unlit, as the lookout box of hastily assembled wood and corrugated aluminum was unmanned. Durbin dared to hope for but a minute as he turned and looked out over the Gale Fortress. The compound was a series of blue square buildings, each taller than the last as they made an irregular boxy perimeter around an open courtyard. The courtyard showcased a meeting dais, unlit fire barrels —rusted with heat and overuse— loudspeakers mounted on twisted wooden poles, and another dais with pillories. The pillories did not hold Nick Nathanson in their wooden shackles. And the courtyard was void of guards or Gale Fortress inhabitants. Nick was in one of those structures, and Durbin was not certain which one, nor where to begin his search. He cursed himself at finally realizing the folly in his poor planning, his emotional rush to rescue Nick, and his denatured heroics. He stood on the ledge of the building, looking down desperately at the courtyard, the stockade, the empty dais.

What did you think you were going to do, you old fool? Bust in guns blazing? And against scores of armed men? You don't even know this Balon Charles, or what he is capable of, or just how much of a loose cannon he is.

"Your recklessness has gotten the best of you," Durbin muttered to himself under the moonlight.

"Indeed it has."

The answering voice was high-pitched.

The patrol guard from earlier.

They had stopped talking just long enough to sneak up on Durbin as he lamented his foolish choices. Durbin quickly pondered options, but not knowing how many patrolmen were actually behind him made any planning difficult. Resistance could be met with death. And even if only one or two patrolmen were with him on the roof —and he dispatched them— he would still need to make his way to the ground, or navigate whatever labyrinth awaited him inside the Fortress. He slowly turned around.

His movements were met with a series of metallic clicks and chunks as bolt pins were pulled as the two patrolmen that Durbin had evaded earlier raised their rifles and pointed them at his chest. The patrolmen were well out of his reach, but too close for him to draw his own firearm. There was little chance of him taking down both before one of them landed a bullet in his chest. But still, Durbin considered it. Then, he surrendered.

CHAPTER 25 — BALON

Balon Charles rolled a thin, frail paper square around coarsely shredded leaves of aromatic brown tobacco. He licked the edge of the paper softly, shaping the roll into a cylinder before bringing the handmade cigarette to his lips. A red wax candle sat on a tin plate on the table that held up his weary elbows. He used the flame of the candle to light the paper, drawing in a short breath as he did so. The paper crackled and sizzled as the leaves took fire, the scent of citrus and dirt mixing in the air. Balon reached for a brown tin can that held his tobacco, purchased from a trade caravan before the last winter. The supply of tobacco cost him a quality pair of boots. He shook it, mixing the dried orange rinds into the brown and tan shreds of leaves before rolling another cigarette. Then he closed the lid of the can tightly, preserving the leaves for another day.

Balon exhaled grey and white smoke as he looked up to the ceiling of a quaint office, dimly lit, featuring a bureau of chipped wood veneer and several fabric chairs that swiveled on casters. Nick 'The Mechanic' sat in one of those chairs, unbound and unspoiled. A couple of guards stood on either side of a heavy metal door with a long narrow glass window that rose from the latch. Jarvey sat on another chair, apart from both Balon and Nick. Balon's fingers worked gingerly with the rolling paper and tobacco, forming a tight white cylinder of luxury. He twirled the crafted cigarette between bony, grease-stained fingers before leaning out of the chair to offer the cigarette to Nick, who reached forward and cautiously snatched the stick before setting it down on the painted black end table beside him.

Snorting, Balon was displeased, but not surprised. "That holds some expensive leaves, there Nick. Comes from the south it does. I don't offer such a thing to just anybody."

Nick folded his hands, leaving the carefully made coffin nail on the table.

"Well, I don't know exactly where from the south, of course. Certainly not where I grew up. Not in the mountains of Blue Ridge, no. Tobacco never grew much there." Balon dragged slowly on his cigarette. "You ever been there, Nick? You know, before all of this?" Balon waved his hands in the air in careless circles, the exhaled smoke swirling with exaggerated character.

"This Collapse thing really has us in a bind, now, don't it, Nick?" Balon continued. Nick's persistent silence was not pleasing to him, yet he remained cool and composed. "But you know... -we could be the start of something new. With you, the Fortress could be a booming nexus of industry and commerce! We could maybe even make it as though the Collapse never happened."

Nick scoffed quietly, but it was not lost on Balon, who felt a hot twinge in his right ear, a flare-up of anger, at the point where the flesh met his skull.

"Look, Nick, you have had a day to yourself, to cool down. You have had some time to distance yourself from all those things at Windy Well. You have seen the excellent facility here. I have little else to share with you besides plans of making this world a better place. With you here, and Jarvey, of course, some of the greatest post-Collapse minds in one place could change the world. You don't have to be held back by that murderous snake any longer."

"Kimwu is not a snake..." Nick muttered under his breath; Balon pretended to not hear it.

"You could thrive here, Nick. I have nearly half a dozen working wind turbines compared to their measly, lonely *one*. And if you got the others working? Oh ho! Imagine the power they could produce!" Balon stood to his feet in excitement, pulling the remainder of the cigarette from his lip. "And a well? Oh, Nick, we have an entire reservoir that can supply us with water forever so long as the skies give rain. All you would need to do is find a way to purify it. Filter it at its source. And you —and this Fortress— could be the epicenter of re-growth that this fallen world needs."

Balon felt like taking a bow, impressed by his own bravado. But he was interrupted by a grumbling, a vocal quality that he did not expect.

"This is how you try to entice others?" Nick growled lowly, his hands still folded in his lap, the cigarette gift on the short table still untouched.

With mild confusion, Balon cocked his head sideways. This was not a question that he expected. He had expected Nick to inquire about how much he would get paid, or about his living quarters. And suddenly, Jarvey left the room, bidding the other two guards follow him.

"You insult our leader," Nick continued, and with a hissing tongue, he cast threatening looks at Balon. "You mock our settlement's loss, you assault our people, you take me hostage, you... expect me to willingly *help you*?"

Balon was torn between bringing his clenched fist to Nick's jaw and baring his woes to him in a last attempt to sway him. Deep down, he knew that more force would actually push Nick away. And he desperately needed Nick's engineering expertise to rally the Fortress around him and quell any rebellion being planned by Brody. He dragged deeply on the orange ember tip of the cigarette before dropping it into a metal tray beside the rolling papers on the desk.

"Look, Nick," Balon calmed his voice as best as he could despite his anger and frustration at the pressure of the situation. He forgot to unclench his fist. "I know that things didn't get off to a good start. But you have to realize that this goes much further than just you and Windy Well. This Fortress is the largest, most prominent settlement in the region. It sits next to a highly valuable water source that is worthless unless it is purified. As a result, I have a potential mutiny on my hands. War within this settlement would destroy it, and all of its value would go to waste. Join me, re-establish the flow of energy and resources here, help me stop this rebellion, and you will be one of the most powerful men in the Black Swamp, seated in the most powerful settlement."

"No," Nick said firmly.

The anger and rage ticked up furiously in Balon's chest.

"Are you even listening to me, Nick?" The sound of cracking knuckles interrupted the question.

"There is nothing you can offer me, that I would accept."

Raged ticked up again.

"Not even your *life*?"

"I will forfeit my life before bowing to a vile bigot like yourself."

Balon's vision turned red.

"Oh, you will bow."

With the clenched fist, Balon struck Nick's jaw, bones cracked and men grunted. Nick fell sideways out of the chair, onto his hands and knees, spitting blood from his mouth to the dirty tile floor. Balon kicked the chair away. It knocked over the end table and the handmade cigarette fell to the floor as well.

"I told you that you will bow, vermin lover. That black snake has poisoned your brilliant mind. Maybe I can knock the venom loose."

Balon leapt toward Nick, who was kneeling on hands and knees over the floor. Balon wound up a black boot before driving it into Nick's stomach with maddening force. Nick spit more blood while rolling onto his back from Balon's kick. Balon approached the defenseless man and stomped on his chest, audibly cracking ribs. Nick groaned in pain, trying to roll away from Balon, with nowhere to go, spitting blood from the mouth. Balon pulled his leg back for another kick to Nick's midsection when the door burst open.

One of the guards from earlier reappeared. He looked down at Nick's broken body with wide eyes. "I am sorry to interrupt, Balon, sir, but our patrol caught a man snooping on the roof of Building Three."

Balon looked down questioningly at Nick, who rolled slowly and tried to wipe thick red blood from his mouth, coughing and groaning in pain.

"Only one?" Balon scoffed. "You should have smarter friends, Nick. You *could* have smarter friends..." Balon drove the tip of his boot into Nick's face a final time before turning to the guard. "Where is the intruder now?" he asked.

"Jarvey has him in the detention center of Building Three." he responded.

Balon gave a dismissive wave. "Lock this one up here. Return my tobacco to my office." Balon knelt down briefly to pick up the hand-rolled cigarette that Nick insultingly refused. He placed it in his own mouth as he drew close to Nick's blood-covered face. "We are not done yet," he whispered slowly.

Balon rose and left the room as the guard shut the door behind him.

His boots echoed through long empty hallways as he made his way to Building Three, the rhythmic beat accompanied by his quiet murmuring.

"One man? Some rescue party. Stupid Well-dwellers. Must be why my parents died. They only do the minimum required work, and that is why they fail. That is why people die. That is why my family died. I swear to God if this Fortress regains its full potential, I will eliminate every single one of you... If Nick won't join me, then I will make an example of him. The Fortress needs to know that only Balon Charles is in control. Yes. These two Well-dwellers will be placed in the stockade in the courtyard. Examples indeed..."

He paused for a minute and turned around. Taking a different hallway, he made way to the armory of Building Two. A heavy grey steel door opened away from his hands. Inside were scores of firearms, rifles, pistols, handguns, and the occasional shotgun. He pulled from the wall a small handgun, checked the magazine, and placed the piece in his pants after clicking on the safety. Then he resumed his path back to Building Three to inspect the intruder who so boldly infiltrated his Fortress.

CHAPTER 26 – DARIUS

Darius's legs burned constantly from the bullet wounds in his thighs. Soma, a doctor at Windy Well, was surgically removing the bullet from his left thigh, and suturing the wounds on the right. She used corn liquor from Riverwide as an anesthetic and to calm his nerves as she plunged alcohol sterilized forceps into the bright red tissues in his legs. She worked quietly and diligently as she tore a hole in his flesh with a needle and thread to close the wounds. She ignored his grunts and yelps and his palm smacking on the surgery table as he coped with the stabbing pain that the whiskey couldn't seem to dull. Soma would pour corn liquor into and over the wounds. Darius winced with the burning sting as it bubbled slightly when contacting the raw tissue. Soma would shake her head disapprovingly and dab a clean cloth over the incision area. The suturing process went on for each wound on Darius's legs. Soma talked while she worked, telling Darius about her practice at the Medical College and the fact that bullet wounds like his were as common as broken bones in their emergency room.

He knew she was trying to distract him from the pain of the bullet excision procedure and suturing while she told him how fortunate she was to be out on a boating excursion at the height of Collapse rioting. During one wave of those riots, emotionally distraught mobs buried under undue amounts of medical debt and malpractice errors stormed hospitals and other health care clinics. Her sailing team got word of the violence befalling nurses and doctors and therapists and avoided port for as long as they could. They were told of health care professionals being hung in the streets, lynched, lined up in firing squads and executed. Others were dragged from their vehicles and beaten with pipes and bats. There was no quelling the rage in the mob scene for several days. Soma's team sailed along the lakeshore until the mob had turned their bloodlust onto each other during the final days of the Collapse. She and her team had docked their boat for one day —in order to collect supplies and leave the area. They then made sail for Cleveland. The team had arrived to see Cleveland in flames, the entire city burned to rubble. It would never recover.

"So, you came back here," Darius finally said, craning his head up and forward from his position lying on the surgical table.

"I didn't know much else," Soma replied, her springy scrunchy black and silver curls bouncing as she shook her head. "A few of my colleagues —we were some of the only medical staff to survive— went west to The Fort, Three Rivers, or Riverwide. I stayed around here. When the suburbs started falling to Loners and Marauders, I stumbled upon Windy Well. And I have been here ever since. Makes a good home, to be honest. All things considered, of course."

Soma snapped a thread with scissors, and patted Darius's leg, her dark hands soft but strong. "We are all done here, soldier." She dumped her instruments in a steel tray with a clamoring metal noise and set the tray on a warped steel counter that held more spirits and corn liquor. Darius then noticed more shelves that hosted medical books, and others that held what he assumed was medical observation equipment. His legs ached and throbbed intermittently and whenever he tried to move them. He grunted.

"Oh, don't you try to get up just yet. I need to find a wheelchair. And you'll be wanting some of that booze if you are to be going to the burial for Davide."

He intended to go to the burial of Davide. He did not know the Native American man very well, but he was happy to have worked beside him in the last few weeks. There was no one in Windy Well who treated Darius with malcontent, and Davide was no exception. Darius had found him to be old and crotchety, significantly more so than even Durbin, but he was pleasant enough to be around. He may have complained about driving the water carriage to Woodstock, but he never complained about the small jobs around the settlement. He also never complained about the company provided to him during said jobs. What he would complain about, with some frequency, was how things were so different now from when he was a youth. He would bemoan the loss of days of riding bicycles on the Reservation, and rolling cigarettes and cigars by hand until the callouses became unfeeling pads of leather. He complained about how the casino he worked at as a young adult was so much more comfortable than anything he had ever experienced since. Strangely, he talked as if the Collapse were not the worst thing that had ever happened to him, as if his life had already taken a drastic turn before the disaster...

When the door opened again, it was not Soma with a wheelchair, as Darius had expected. It was Trina, with tears streaked on her dirty face and a touch of rage gracing her crooked smile upon seeing him. To his surprise, she leapt to the table and hugged him. She looked at the fresh dressings on his thighs, "I'm glad you're okay. Will you be able to walk when you're healed?"

"Yeah, Doc Soma says I should be a'right in a few weeks to a few months." He grunted as he found the strength to set himself up to better see Trina, and the pain radiated throughout his legs like lightning, the very bones in his left trembling in agony. But the sight of her, no matter how the dirt from the road and hunt clung to her cheeks, made him smile in earnest.

"It sounds like you shot off your mouth and Durbin disappeared. Any ideas where he is?" she asked him.

"I like to think that my mouth saved Kimwu from being butchered right there by that hateful bigot." Darius forced a laugh, but in truth, he felt like the whole incident was partly his fault. "Durbin went out that day to scavenge and salvage. Said he didn't feel like he belonged in the process of digging a new well. He and Nick had some words. I was told that Durbin came back and talked to Kimwu before leaving again. But that was yesterday. A lot happened yesterday..."

Trina turned her head sideways, "You think he went after Nick? You think he is going to confront this Balon guy?"

"You never know with Durbin."

The door to the infirmary opened once more and Soma arrived pushing a brown and silver wheelchair with large spoked wheels and mismatched blue and black leg rests. The solid rubber wheels squeaked lightly on the floor as she positioned the chair for Darius to slide into it. He noticed that his right leg was far less painful, but he still stifled an agonizing yell as he put weight onto his legs and collapsed into the wheelchair.

"This will be your chariot until those wounds heal and you can stand again. I warn you, it won't be easy, and I need to see those incisions every other day to make sure you don't develop any infection. If you do, those legs will be gone permanently, and the chariot will be the only way you can get around.

"Thanks. And I got you Doc, you and I will get to know each other real good." He tried to smile at her, but winced, as moving the chair in a circle was just as painful as sitting up on the table. He clumsily propelled the chair out of Soma's infirmary and into the common area of Windy Well. The bumps in the ground jarred the bones in his legs and each wobble felt like taking another bullet, but he tried his best not to let it show.

Trina spoke again.

"What are we going to do? This place needs Nick. And I don't feel comfortable just letting Durbin go off like that. What if he *did* go to track down Balon? Do you think he has more than just those few guys he came with? Durbin can't take them all. And what if..."

"Easy, Trina," Darius said, trying to bring calm to his own voice. But between Trina's exasperation and the sudden intoxication of Soma's corn liquor, he found that difficult to do. "Let's go talk to Kimwu. I need to know that he is okay, and perhaps he knows a bit more about what Durbin is up to. Anything will be more definite than our speculation."

Trina followed Darius as he wheeled towards Kimwu's shelter in the shadow of the wind turbine. She offered to push when he grunted heavily with pain caused by bumps in the rough trampled earth. Not wanting sympathy, he focused more effort into stifling his noises. They passed Windy Well inhabitants who were trying to resume a sense of normalcy. They gave space to those who were mourning and nodded with quiet salutation to those whose eyes they had met. And soon they were joined by Raelynn, who asked Darius if he needed any assistance with his dwelling —which he had not thought about until now — or with attaining supplies to get him through the next few weeks. To Darius's surprise, Trina stated that she would take care of his needs, placing a hand on his shoulder. He looked up to her from his wheelchair and for the first time since Balon shot him, he felt no pain. When they arrived at Kimwu's dwelling, however, he felt a different kind of pain. Darius had forgotten that Kimwu's residence was atop a flight of steep metal stairs leading to stacked shipping containers. He looked up to the green, yellow, and red blanket covering the doorway to his dwelling then looked down at the bandages on his legs. His face fell.

"We will bring Kimwu down here. We should meet in the council room," Raelynn said in her typical mechanical manner. "You have my permission to enter. Wait for us there."

Darius had been in the council room before, but it felt quite different without the leading members of Windy Well present. It was still dark and stiflingly hot despite its emptiness. The yellow light suspended from the ceiling bathed the mismatched chairs in a sickly glow, casting heavy shadows about the re-purposed shipping container. A crooked chair with only one armrest sat at the far corner —Davide's chair. A metal chair,

Nick's, was an oddly welded conglomeration of steel and gears that sat next to Kimwu's humble but intact wooden chair, its worn cloth cushion so old its color was indeterminant. Raelynn's chair was wrapped in leather, faded and worn from being stretched over its hidden wooden frame. These chairs belonged to people who believed that the world could be better than it is. These were chairs that belonged to people who held Windy Well on their shoulders. Now, one was dead, and another abducted by a despicable man violently prejudiced against people of color.

A rushing wave of self-pity washed over Darius as he again realized that he was powerless to help. Bound to the chair for the foreseeable future, he could not launch a rescue mission. And Balon would not engage in recourse with Darius due to the color of his skin.

But I am half white, he thought to himself, *not like that ever counted for anything.* Darius fell into his old cycle of thoughts — those dark and lonely thoughts of never being "enough" for anybody. He was never black enough, or he was never white enough. He was never smart enough for other groups, and he was never 'street' enough for the inner-city boys. And now he couldn't walk enough to be of any use in saving one of the most important people in his new home. The liquor's effect rounded on him again, enhanced by the heat of the council room and he dropped his head into his hands in sadness.

Sometime later, Trina and Raelynn appeared in the room, joined by Kimwu. He looked unharmed, save for a several large scrapes across his knees, elbows, and forearms that were thickly covered in black and maroon scabs. With a long thin arm, he held his back where Balon had kicked him. Darius looked up to him from his meager seated position.

"Are you well, Darius?" Kimwu asked him, his accent thick. He pulled out a chair from under the table and sat, his knees and hips bent severely as the chair was so low to the ground.

"I think I will get by, Kimwu." He tried to mask his frustration and sadness, but was certain that he'd been unsuccessful. He forced a smile anyway and looked at Trina and Raelynn as they each took a seat on either side of Darius and Kimwu.

Once seated, with gangly limbs overflowing the humble wooden chair, Kimwu cleared his throat. "You ah in no position to mount a rescue effort for da 'Mechanic'."

Darius started to protest, but Kimwu raised a hand. "Balon's men ah well-armed. Dey has a well-guarded fortress and dare numbas ah great. I cannot allow you to go for negotiations because he does not like men such as you and I. He feels us inferia'."

Trina spoke from beside Darius, "But you would let Durbin go instead?"

"I did no such ting," Kimwu responded, shaking his head and looking down at the table. "But Paul tells me dat Durbin sought his council on approaching Balon's fortress. Durbin's actions were done wit'out my knowledge. I would have requested he go wit uddas and for a diplomatic solution. Not heroics."

Frustrated, Darius spoke, "A man like Balon does not do diplomacy, Kimwu. You should know that." He immediately regretted his disrespectful tone, but Kimwu gave it no attention.

"And so you see da predicament we ah in. War is not an objective to me in any circumstance. I lived tru genocide, and coups. I lived tru despotic rule and understand well its effect on people. I have vowed to do all in my powah not to let dat happen here."

With even less caution than before, Darius interrupted, "All the more reason for us not to bow down to this guy. If diplomacy isn't the answer, and full-on war isn't an option, then let's have a small team go in there and get our guy back. Nick deserves more than that gangrel. And this settlement needs him. Maybe we...they...-can meet up with Durbin before he gets there and..."

"He may have a point, Kimwu." Raelynn's cold and sharp voice cut him off. "I am willing to go to Gale Fortress covertly. I have been there when Nick has had conferences with Balon's man—Jarvey, I think. Perhaps we can survey the situation and decide there if diplomacy or rescue is the better option. For all we know, Durbin could have gone elsewhere. Or have been taken prisoner himself. Let a small group of us go, or not, but the truth is—we need Nick back at Windy Well."

For the first time in the few short weeks that Darius had known him, Kimwu showed a sign of despair and fatigue. His shoulders slumped, and his stoic expression that wasn't quite a smile—but not quite a straight face—faltered.

"I cannot, in good conscience, condone a non-diplomatic party to Balon Charles. If you wa' to fail, de price would be steep. De Well would lose valuable hands, and de risk of war upon our gates would increase." Kimwu folded his hands in his lap and licked his thick purple lips, pausing in thought as if to carefully choose his next words. Then he looked directly in Raelynn's eyes. "But I will allow you to lead a diplomatic party. I prefer it be made of de two of you, wit Caleb. De t'ree of you wa not here when Balon abducted Nick, and dat may be helpful to our ends."

Trina looked confused, her gaze moving quickly but subtly from Kimwu to Raelynn. Darius was confused, as well.

"I thought we just said that Balon is not interested in diplomacy?" he pointed angrily to the bandages on his legs.

"Raelynn is in charge of dis operation now. Darius, you will remain here and heal from your wounds, as will I. We will wait for da safe return of Nick with Raelynn's party."

"And Durbin?" Darius questioned as Kimwu rose from his chair.

"Durbin is responsible for his own choices," Kimwu said quietly as he walked out of the council room.

CHAPTER 27 — RAELYNN

Raelynn was nervous.

She tried to mask it by not engaging in conversation as she, Caleb, Trina, and —after much deliberation— she recruited two other volunteers from The Well. They followed railroad tracks from just west of their settlement towards Gale Fortress to the south. The last time she had tried to rescue someone, it had ended with her husband's death, and that consequence still weighed heavily on her. This time, she was playing leader to a group of fresh faces whom she barely knew, heading into an area that was home to at least one is hostile, where their mechanical engineer was being held captive. She knew that Gale Fortress was an inactive appliance factory, well to the southeast of Windy Well. She knew it was serviced by dozens of wind turbines unrelated to the Windfield Complex. She knew that there was a railyard nearby, as also a large reservoir, though she knew not the condition of either.

They were armed with bows, cross-bows, handguns, rope and bullet-proof tactical vests, one of the unfamiliar men — Gerald— insisted that he was more comfortable with a rifle strapped to his back. Before departure, Kimwu allowed her access to The Well's rarely utilized armory, where she equipped her team with gear that the settlement had salvaged over the years. She explained their objective: to rescue Nick 'the Mechanic' by whatever means necessary.

"I still think Durbin is there, too." Trina was sure to interrupt more than once as they were deliberating plans within the armory.

"He is not our objective, Huntress," Raelynn responded, assuring control of her team.

"He is my objective, Raelynn. He has looked over Caleb and me for weeks now, helped us escape certain death at least twice. He has taught us much about the world outside of our protected home. He has a big heart, and I just know that he went after Nick. If he is in trouble as a result, I will not let him go unaided. " She stood there, stern-eyed and stoic, not defiant, but firm in her argument. Caleb stood by her side, nodding in agreement. Flint sat on his hindquarters beside Caleb, looking up to him, mouth slightly agape with a tongue dangling out the side.

Raelynn conceded, "*If* we come across Durbin, do what you must, but do not compromise the welfare of Windy Well because of your personal focus. Nick is essential to the progress of this settlement, and he is the top priority. While Durbin's life is important, his short time at the Well has not made him essential to the big picture. I know this is not easy to hear. But it is the truth."

Nodding, Trina looked satisfied and Raelynn decided no more needed to be said about the matter. Supplies were distributed to everyone, backpacks were loaded, and boots were laced before the group left The Well.

After departing just after sunrise the day prior, they had nearly arrived at Gale Fortress, tensions high with anxiety and uncertainty. The railroad met up with dozens of others opening a clearing from their paths of trees revealing the Fortress ahead, with silvery windmills gleaming in the evening sunlight. Upon closer approach, they observed rubble and machinery, railcars, and sheets of corrugated steel forming a steel palisade around the inner blue buildings of the Fortress. It had a block fort formation to it, and if Raelynn were to trust her instincts, there was a courtyard type of field in the middle of the arranged structures. The windmill turbines were spread across the compound, guarding the corners, built in proximity to the defunct manufacturing facilities. Raelynn felt the complex to be a massive Windy Well, though made up of re-purposed permanent structures instead of a conglomeration of semi-trailers and shipping containers.

She scouted the rooftops, observing the unoccupied sentry posts, hastily constructed of random scrap and materials, housing unmoving searchlights, unmanned by guards. Her gaze moved across each of the wind turbines she could see, some rotating in the gentle breeze, others unmoving. Two of them were each missing a propeller blade and were unusable. An entry gate, also unmanned, sat closed and secure far to her right. The lack of guards was disconcerting. The others stood around her, awaiting instruction, also surveying the grounds of the quiet Fortress.

One of the young men spoke up, "Huntress, shall I try to find a higher vantage point? There are no guards at the gate. I see the sentries are also empty. Are we in the right place?"

"This is certainly it," Raelynn replied. She teetered with uncertainty about making decisions with these young individuals in tow but kept her face stonewalled. "A higher vantage point would help. Something must be going on in there for the

Fortress to feel this empty. Let's climb to the top of the barricade perimeter. Those railcars look solid. Be quiet. Take your time. If the space is clear, try to find a way to scale the buildings. Our objective is to free Nick. Let us not shed blood, if we can help it. Chances are high that we are greatly outnumbered..." She drew in her breath sharply and sighed as she exhaled away the building tension of making decisions in which there was no turning back. "Gerald, right?"

He nodded, "Yes, ma'am," as he fixed the faded blue baseball cap on his head. Black tactical armor covered a black T-shirt, and tactical pads adorned the knees and thighs of thick brown cargo pants with full pockets.

"I would like you to scout first. Signal to us positions to move on based on what you see. If the lack of guards is any indication, I think everyone in the Fortress is in a central location. And I fear it has to do with Nick. From your point, I will rely on your eyes and judgment. The rest of us will wait atop this barricade for your signal."

Gerald gave affirmation as Raelynn grabbed his shoulder. "Do be careful. Do be quiet. We need to know what we are looking at in order to rescue Nick."

He nodded once again, jumped quietly from atop the makeshift wall of rusted train cars and cargo trailers, rolled away, stood to his feet and dashed toward a blue building with vine-covered metal rigging climbing along its vertical face. Gerald silently scaled the vines and metal, his arms reaching deftly for higher and higher rungs until he scaled over the roof's edge. As he disappeared to the far side of the roof, Raelynn found herself missing such technology as radios and headsets for communication. Before the Collapse, with this situation, Gerald would be relaying everything he saw, and she could further develop her plan. But instead, she sat in silence, awaiting Gerald's signal to move to a rooftop of their own.

Some time had passed before Gerald reappeared. He nodded exaggeratively, then pointed twice to his right, and once to his left. She turned to Caleb and the others, trying to hide the nervousness that came with her leadership. "Caleb, come with me. Two buildings to the left. Trina, you and..." she paused as she blanked on the gentleman's name.

"Marcus, ma'am," he said.

"Marcus. The two of you go to the top of the building to the right of Gerald's position. Our plan will be to locate Nick. Free him from a cell, or whatever holds him. Nothing brash unless we create some type of diversion. Be smart. Be patient. We are only five."

She hated not knowing what the next step would be, or how exactly they were going to free Nick. She was not against silent infiltration and assaulting Fortress members, but she knew the risk involved if that were their task. As she urged them with further caution, they all made their way to their assigned points, deftly scaling the building and rickety scaffolding as though it were in their nature. Staying low to the surface of the rooftop, Raelynn and Caleb peered out into the courtyard between the defunct manufacturing buildings. She was partially correct about the populace of the Fortress being before them.

Centered on a wooden dais amidst four small sets of aluminum stadium bleachers were two pillories. In the stockades, bound and helpless, were Nick and Durbin. Scores of men sat in the bleachers, arranged to mimic an outdoor auditorium with the wooden dais on view. She motioned for Gerald to join her and Caleb, then she laid low, alternating her gaze from the dais —surveying the myriad of men around the courtyard— to Trina and Marcus. They were three rooftops away. Communication would be difficult. With her vision centered back on the dais and pillories, she watched a greasy man in black stroll across the wooden planks. He carried a white bullhorn as he walked past Durbin and Nick, occasionally pausing to grab one of them by their bloody and bruised face as he brought his close. Then he jerkily stood and resumed pacing. Gerald crawled close to her.

"That's Balon with the bullhorn. He's the one who shot Darius and beat Kimwu," he whispered to her between panting breaths from descending and scaling buildings. Raelynn didn't recognize him, but she did recognize Jarvey standing adjacent to the dais. He stood, looking disinterested in the proceedings, rubbing his hand across the chest of oil-stained button-down shirt. His gaze moved about the men sitting in the bleachers, to the stockade, and then to the building where she lay on the roof.

She and Caleb and Gerald ducked to avoid being seen.

A voice resounded over the courtyard, distorted and echoing between the buildings, amplified by a bullhorn. Raelynn risked a look over the ledge of the roof once more.

Balon continued to pace the dais but clamored loudly with his voice enhanced by the bullhorn. He would bring the piece close to Durbin and Nick's faces —with them being unable to move their heads away from the piercing sound— and berate them and their refusal to join his cause. Jarvey was not the only one present who appeared disinterested. Scores of men in the crowd looked like they were being paid to be present, unarmed and forced to remain in the seats or standing around the pillories under pain of consequence. Balon did not pay heed to their boredom and rambled on about mutiny and examples and loyalty and death and how the Gale Fortress should be the seat of power in the Black Swamp. Then Raelynn had an idea.

"Caleb," she said in a hushed tone, but loud enough to be heard over the reverberations of Balon's voice. "Nick told me about some of the mechanisms in the wind turbines. If you cross input and output on the capacitor of the turbine, you can cause the capacitor to explode. There is a safety harness and repel cord in every motor compartment of the turbines. Attach the harness and repel cable to yourself, and swap the capacitor inputs. It is a large cylinder, lying horizontally. After crossing the inputs, jump out of the engine compartment. It will be a strong enough distraction. I will make demands of Balon and bluff that we will destroy other turbines if they do not release Nick."

"And Durbin?" Caleb asked.

"Yes." Raelynn sighed. "Are my orders clear?"

"Absolutely," Caleb replied. "Give me time to scale the turbine over there." It was a working turbine, thrumming lightly and slowly. It sat far enough away that he would be able to scale the attached ladder without being noticed, but close enough to be an impactful distraction.

"Be safe. I will not make our presence known until you have caused the distraction. Be quick. Be safe."

"Got it," Caleb said, as he crouch-ran to the rigging they

had used to climb to the rooftops.

She leaned closer to Gerald. "Go to Marcus and Trina and inform them of Caleb's objective. Tell them I plan to threaten to destroy more turbines if my demands are not met. I am bluffing that we have more in our numbers than we actually do —but they have no way of knowing. After that, make your way to a working turbine and, if Balon remains hostile, destroy that turbine. Use the harness just like Caleb. That may be the only way we can pull this off without bloodshed and further escalation."

"Understood," Gerald said, and he too crouch-ran to the rigging to descend the building once more.

Raelynn was alone, relying on others now to make the plan work. She rehearsed her planned threats in her head. And she waited.

CHAPTER 28 — BALON

Balon had a captive audience.

He had two prisoners to use as fodder to convince the whelps in his settlement to drop their delusions of mutiny and follow him fully. For the sake of the Fortress. For the sake of protection. For the sake of their own livelihood. Balon had worked too hard over the last several years to lose his place of influence because of things outside of his control. And now was his opportunity for a show of force and direction. He did feel bad that it may end with the loss of a brilliant man, and that the Black Swamp would be without his technical genius. But Balon knew that sometimes, sacrifices had to be made. The death of the infiltrator, however, would be inconsequential to Balon. And the only purpose would be one last-ditch effort to get Nick to see reason and join Balon's cause.

His grip tightened around the handle of the bullhorn that he planned to use to make himself heard. He hiked a leg up high onto a wooden platform and caught a toe of his boot, causing him to stumble slightly, drawing muffled snickers from those who were watching. He cast glares in every direction simultaneously, unable to spot the culprits. Upon the dais were featured two rugged wooden stockades that held Nick and his friend, the infiltrator, Durbin. Balon didn't much like Durbin. He had nothing to offer but sneaky antics and unreasonable sharp words. He had no skills and no loyalty. He seemed to have an affinity for Nick, though, based on his foolish attempt to rescue him alone. Killing him would be easy. And then the other fools who thought about turning on him will realize that only death awaits them without his leadership, whether in the Fortress or out. Balon glanced at Jarvey who acknowledged his presence and looked away to survey the Fortress settlers sitting on the bleachers and standing freely around the dais. A few of the men fiddled with their hands, some stared at the captives in the stockades. Others looked to the ground at their feet, kicking at tufts of grass and patches of dirt.

Balon stepped up to Durbin, grabbing his chin and lifting his face, making certain to press his neck uncomfortably into the hole of the stockade. His cheeks were bruised and scratched deeply below his right eye, thanks to Balon's own boot. The left side of his face was scraped and embedded with dirt and gravel, thanks to the courtyard's surface as Balon's guards escorted them to the pillories. Balon shook his head dismissively in Durbin's face and then dropped it before turning around to face Nick. With a bloody chin, Nick raised his face to Balon.

"Still some fight in you, ay?" Balon said to Nick, he refused to crouch, deny Nick's neck any comfort. "I hope you use that energy to make the right choice in a bit. You will hope it is made before I end the life of your valiant friend, here."

Balon made certain to show off the belt sheath that housed a long bowie knife. "I shall reward his valiance with a coward's end, as this knife causes his throat to spill blood all over this stockade." He tapped the rim of the bullhorn to the top Nick's skull, then crouched low to get in his face menacingly while snapping, "But, you could ensure that it doesn't happen."

The bullhorn gave a heavily piercing sound that

morphed into a wailing honk as Balon pushed the button and brought the loudspeaker to his lips. He stood and addressed the crowd in the bleachers.

"Settlers and soldiers of Gale Fortress: for over eight years we have held this settlement in the highest esteem. We have fought for it. Some have died for it. And we have worked for its prosperity in this post-Collapse world that we have found ourselves in. I have granted you all physical power to squash your adversaries and protection within these fortified walls. I have held for you a location that is in the middle of plentiful hunting grounds. In the Fortress, you have electricity because of our numerous wind turbines."

"What about safe water?" a voice from a face unseen called out from behind the pillories. A few grumbles and murmurs rippled through the crowd, and the aluminum stadium benches creaked with the shifting unease of many of the attendees.

Balon lowered the bullhorn and leaned close to Nick again. "Did you hear that? They are thirsty. A man with the intelligence to provide them water would rank very highly in their eyes." He fiddled with the hilt of his sheathed knife, snapping and unsnapping the worn metal ring and button enclosure. His face altered to a look of disdain as he turned to Durbin. "Your time runs short, infiltrator."

"One of our captives here, responsible for the prosperity of Windy Well to the north, has been commissioned to help us revitalize the reservoir that sits upon our doorstep, granting us nearly infinite clean and safe water." Balon pantomimed with the bravado of a circus ringmaster as he marched to and fro across the dais. A scant few yelps and whoops were heard from the crowd. A heckler asked why he was bound in the stockade.

"But unfortunately," Balon's voice screeched through the bullhorn, "he has chosen his loyalty to an inferior leadership. He has chosen weak and stupid, unplanning, backward thinking, and murdering dirt-mongers as his post-Collapse king."

A small chorus of boos and pleas limped out of mouths in the crowd, but none had any conviction.

"Can none of you convince him to join us? Will none of you ask him to spare his own life? All he needs do is grant me his loyalty, as all of you have done. As all of you will continue to do, lest you find yourselves in his position..."

The mood of the crowd changed, silence falling over most, with the bullhorn making distorted echo noises as Balon let it lower to his hip. "They fear me, gentlemen." He said to his stockade prisoners. "You would do well to fear me, also."

Nick's head hung low, blood mixed with saliva dripped liquid tendrils from his puffy and bruised lips. None of the men from the crowd made an effort to approach the dais. Balon could feel a certain tension rise in the courtyard. No one really knew what to do. He turned in a slow circle, surveying the crowd surrounding the dais: the men seated uncomfortably stiff on the aluminum benches, the men standing at partial attention, some looking at their boots kicking the ground. He searched for Brody specifically, wanting to ensure that he was not going to be taking Balon's charge of the Fortress without a fight. But he could not see Brody in the crowd.

Insubordinate tool, Balon thought to himself.

Balon, after pausing for a bit more, pandered on in an attempt to rally and threaten his crowd.

"I would much prefer that all of you continue to serve me and the Fortress as most of you have for years. But the Fortress cannot maintain prosperity within the Black Swamp without the unfaltering loyalty to this leadership that prosperity itself requires. We cannot allow dissension to hold back this great settlement!"

Balon strutted behind Durbin —bent over in the stockade— and kicked his feet out from under him, causing him to be hung by the holes that held his hands and head. His legs scrambled wildly as he grunted, lifting his body again to maintain his airway. Then Balon swept Durbin's legs again.

"Mutineers WILL. NOT. BE. TOLERATED." he shouted into the loudspeaker, it protesting with screeches and distorted echoes as he yelled louder with each word. Durbin scrambled more in the stockade and Balon brandished his bowie knife and held it high above his head. "Those who mutiny will be put to death!"

An explosion blasted from a corner of the courtyard to Balon's right.

Surprised and startled, Balon twisted to see one of the wind turbines engulfed in a fireball, a large metallic blade charred and falling point first to the ground behind Building Four. People in the crowd gasped and turned in the direction of the fire. Quickly, Balon looked to other turbines, lowering his knife and bullhorn. The turbine to his left remained operational, its blades thrumming quietly in the dusk sky. He looked back to the burning turbine and halfway through the motion, he caught a glimpse of something shiny. A silver lining. A twinkle or a flash. He heard a faint rush of wind and then felt a sense of panic.

Balon couldn't breathe.

CHAPTER 29 — TRINA

Trina Hurst sat perched upon her rooftop post waiting. Every calloused threat from Balon to his crowd of apathetic onlookers found her gripping her bow more tightly. This man had shot Darius in the legs, potentially denying him the opportunity to walk again. He had abused Nick, the man responsible for Windy Well's prosperity and survival. And now he was kicking Durbin, the man who had given Trina and her brother newfound hope, and a new family by guiding them from Bridgetown to Windy Well. Balon was ruthlessly causing pain to a man who had shown her a father's response when her own father was no longer alive. Balon was choking and assaulting and threatening a man who helped to show her that there was more to this life than just crying about the Collapse.

Gerald had just informed her and Marcus about Caleb's intent to detonate a turbine several buildings to her left. Then he, too, ran off to the next turbine to perform the same detonation, if necessary. Her patience was running thin with every blow that Balon dished out, and without thinking, she drew an arrow from her belt sheath and nocked it in her black and silver recurve bow. She cared not if she was seen. Marcus whispered something to her from his cover of shadows, but she wasn't listening. Standing at the edge of the rooftop, her bow was drawn tight, and she aimed it steadily at Balon's head wherever he moved.

Then the explosion occurred. She felt the percussive

wave as the sound flew through her, yet still, she stood stoic and trained on her target. The fireball flashed to her left in flickering waves and called the attention of the crowd gathered on the bleachers and around the wooden dais. Even Balon was surprised. His eyes were wide and his face an expression of perplexion as one precious turbine was now in flames. He lowered his cowardly bullhorn and knife, then looked around the rest of the Fortress, searching for an excuse or a scapegoat.

Trina breathed. Sharp breath in, with a slow exhale through pursed lips.

She calmed her soul from the inside out, allowing her senses to take over, and her mind to go silent. She smelled the putrid stench of the stagnant reservoir nearby, the earthy bark of the surrounding forests, the greasy sting of clumped motor oil in the engines and wheel bearings of the junk that made up the fortified barriers of Gale Fortress. She could smell the sweat —mixed with dirt—that clung to the skin of every settler in the courtyard below. Then, the coppery smell of blood that dripped from Durbin and Nick's wounds. With that sensation, Trina focused more on Balon, her right hand pulling the bowstring back against tremendous tension that felt effortless to her. She heard nothing, and a swell of calm overcame her. Balon looked right at her as she adjusted her angle slightly then she sighed and loosed her arrow.

Balon looked directly at her as her arrow pierced his throat. His eyes and mouth widened in puzzlement. The knife fell from his grip, then the bullhorn, breaking Trina's silence with a piercing screech that reverberated throughout the courtyard. She could see Balon struggle for breath as blood trickled from the arrow embedded deep into his flesh. Trina, now aware of what she had done, shot a look to Raelynn a rooftop away. Raelynn also had a look of shock on her face, then she moved to the edge of her rooftop to make her presence known. Meanwhile, Balon fell onto his face, forcing the arrow farther through the back of his neck, the wooden platform resounding with a solid thump as his body fell, flat and lifeless.

Several of the Fortress settlers stood from their seats in the stadium benches, looking to the rooftops, and wind turbines, then to Balon's body on the dais. Jarvey did not look concerned. He looked up to Trina's position on the roof and nodded, almost approvingly. Then he noticed Raelynn, but she spoke first.

"Stand down Gale Fortress!" she shouted, with no need for an amplified speaker. Balon's use of the bullhorn turned out to be unnecessary. "I am Raelynn Tillebrand of the Windy Well. We have destroyed one of your sources of electricity and have several men stationed to destroy others if need be."

Jarvey centered himself within the settlers of the Fortress as best as he could, motioning for the men to lower their guard and allow him to speak.

"I regret that your leader, Balon Charles, had to be removed from the situation. But we require the return of our men to Windy Well. We want no further bloodshed." Raelynn gave a pointed look at Trina who lowered her bow and replaced an arrow in its quiver. Trina's suprised look in return indicated that she was unaware that she was readying another arrow.

"Raelynn, I am Jarvey Maines. Second in —" he glanced

down at Balon's body, "leader of Gale Fortress. I will send my men away to their barracks. I will release the captives. Come down and we can discuss a truce. I promise no harm to you or your men."

Trina exhaled a sigh of relief, not realizing she had been holding her breath in fear that she had made a mistake and sentenced herself and Durbin to death by the hands of the Gale Fortress. Raelynn looked at her approvingly.

"Give us some time. I will dismiss my men and bring a few cohorts with me and we can discuss truce at the dais where you stand. Can you please release your captives?"

Jarvey motioned for a few of the closest men to climb the stockade and undo the bindings of Durbin and Nick, both of whom had hardly the strength to stand. Trina had no clue how long they had been held in wooden shackles, or what physical abuse Balon had inflicted on them before having them bound. The top restraint of the pillories opened with a rusty creak and hollow but heavy thump as wood met wood. Jarvey directed his men to help Durbin and Nick, as their forms crumpled weak and beaten, helpless masses of abused humans at the foot of the roughly constructed pillories. With two men per captive, they carried Durbin and Nick to the stadium seats and laid them carefully. Several of the men had retired to their barracks, as ordered by Jarvey. Raelynn whistled sharply and indicated for them to convene in the courtyard to meet with Jarvey.

In the courtyard, they found an unarmed Jarvey staring at Balon's body, sighing heavily, and shaking his head. His eyes followed the shaft of the arrow that had pierced his neck. It was clear Jarvey was going to remain reliable in his word; no other

Gale Fortress men were around. Trina spied Durbin laying on the lower level of the bleachers and ran to him, sliding on her knees as she cradled his bruised face.

"Michael," she said, "we are here. You're free." Observing the bruises on his face and blood on his lips as he breathed heavily, struggling for air, she remembered her fear and frustration at his disappearance. "Why did you come here?"

Durbin opened his eyes and smiled at her. "Thank you," was all he said.

"No, that is not an answer. We are trying to find a home. A family. Windy Well is it. That's our new home, Michael."

He struggled to sit up and Trina helped him; he coughed and spat blood on the ground. "It is your home, now, but not mine. I came here for my friend. For Nick. But also for you, because Nick is part of your home, too."

"You foolish old man," Trina said sadly. She hugged him.

"Is Nick all right?" he said, looking around the empty courtyard, the wooden dais where Raelynn was approaching Jarvey.

Trina pointed to a set of bleachers to their left. "Marcus is tending to Nick over there."

Beyond the dais, Marcus had produced a small scrap of cloth and was wiping blood, dirt, and sweat from Nick Nathanson's face, helping him too, to sit upright.

Raelynn finally stood in front of a lamenting Jarvey. He looked up to her and rose slowly. He stepped over Balon's body and held a hand to her in an offering of peace.

"There is nothing I can do to repair this incident," Jarvey said, "but I will do all that I can to help the relationship between our settlements. I do not share the same values or lack of respect for people's differences as Balon held."

Raelynn looked at his hand. She looked around the settlement, observing the buildings. Trina held Durbin's arm as a child would, observing their discourse.

"I understand your position, Jarvey, " she said, and she took his hand as they shared a firm handshake. "The Well will not be trusting of the Fortress for some time. What will be done about those under your command that *do* share Balon's world view?"

"They will be allowed to seek refuge elsewhere, and will not be welcome here. And I understand, trust is not easily regained. I worked hard to orchestrate the relationship initially, and tried to keep Balon apart from it — for obvious reasons." Jarvey wrung his hands. "Truth be told, I had been trying to find ways to remove Balon from power for some time. I just didn't plan on it involving his death. And certainly not in a public fashion."

Raelynn gave a sharp look to Trina with that remark. And in a rare show of emotion, she even allowed Trina to see a glimmer of an approving smile.

"Did you do that?" Durbin asked Trina. He pointed to the arrow rising from Balon's neck. "Impressive."

Trina beamed at the compliment, but she realized she was not comfortable being responsible for the death of a human being. An image of Paul flashed in her mind, and she made a mental note to talk to him upon returning to the Windy Well. Upon returning home.

"If the Fortress is run by compassionate individuals," Raelynn said, "I feel that we can work on relations. We still have much to gain from each other, but it won't be easy. It will take some time for our people to heal from this."

Jarvey nodded then looked at Nick, who was standing with Marcus's help. Jarvy approached him and bowed deeply before Nick.

"I apologize for wrongs done to you in my home, Nick, and I know that my words are of little comfort. Please know, that while I am in charge of Gale Fortress, no one from this settlement will ever be responsible for the harm of another Windy Well settler."

Trina helped Durbin to his feet and they joined Nick, walking slowly as Durbin grunted in pain clutching his chest where the stockade had pressed into him. Nick smiled through a bruised face and bloody scrapes as Durbin approached. Jarvey offered both hands to Nick.

"After you heal, let us revisit repairing this: our situation, and this place. We are stronger and safer together." Jarvey released Nick's hands and looked him in the eyes. He then turned to address Nick and Raelynn together. "We have more space here than we have men. If for any reason, you need the space here in the Fortress, you are welcome here. It is the least I can do in an offering of peace."

Gravel crunched on the ground around them as men came from different directions. Caleb, Gerald, and a rather large man who Trina did not recognize approached. He was carrying a few backpacks. She recognized one as Durbin's. Caleb quickened his pace at the sight of Durbin and rushed to meet him with a hug. Trina braced them all to keep from falling.

"It worked," Caleb whispered to Trina during the triple embrace. "Nice shot."

"Brody," Jarvey spoke, "thank you for retrieving those." He took the backpacks from Brody and gave Durbin's worn pack to him. "I apologize for our wrongdoings. I ask for your forgiveness and for forgiveness from your home." Jarvey gave another backpack to Nick. "When you are healed, let us try again." Jarvey tried to smile, but Trina could see a burden of embarrassment upon his face.

Jarvey stepped away from them all, kicking dirt while chewing on his bottom lip. "The main gate will be open, and you all can walk from this place. I hope, in time, we can put these wrongdoings behind us knowing that the one responsible will bother no one anymore."

"Our apologies as well for invading your space. We will work to better both settlements. Await word from us, and perhaps we can establish an agreement for trade." Raelynn remained stoic throughout her apology, even as she looked Jarvey up and down. Trina thought Raelynn may even pity the man slightly, having to clean up a mess he did not make.

"Until next time?" Jarvey asked. He smiled nervously.

"Until next time," Raelynn responded in kind, her rare smile appearing just as nervous.

CHAPTER 30 — CALEB

Caleb tugged at the carabiner tied to the harness around his body and checked its security one last time. The windmill capacitor he had sabotaged was smoking and sizzling, years of dust and grime piled on the machinery had begun to combust. With his boots on the ledge of the cockpit-like entry to the turbine engine, he leapt backward, out into the empty air above Gale Fortress. The turbine rushed away from him, flames spewing from the open engine cockpit door before exploding into a great fireball. The force pushed him away, but the harness jerked hard against the belay cord. Then his backside hit solid ground. His body protested in pain. But above him the cord grew relaxed and began to fall towards him, flames dancing along its length, and at its end was the belay winch formerly housed in the turbine. He rolled away hastily, ignoring the pain in his back, as the winch smashed into the ground—the impact embedding it into the soft earth.

He detached the belay cord and carabiner, then unbuckled the escape harness while hoping that Raelynn's plan of distraction had worked. Caleb could hear nothing but the rippling of flames from the turbine high above him. A pain rang from the back of his head where he had hit the ground, and his back ached, causing him to twist stiffly as he surveyed his surroundings. Taking note of the rooftops above him and narrow passageway before him, he made way to where he hoped was the courtyard.

His boots scuffled the gravel as he turned corner after

corner before finally finding a large clearing. He recognized the bleachers and dais, and noted Durbin and Nick sitting on bleachers, finally relieved of their wooden bindings. Caleb approached Raelynn, who stood to talk to a man that Caleb recognized from his proximity to Balon on the dais. He did not see Balon but observed a mass of rumpled clothing and greasy hair lying on the warped wooden surface the dais. Caleb spied one of Trina's arrows rising from the mass. The men from the Fortress had dispersed and it appeared Raelynn had defused the captive situation as intended. Caleb surmised that their diversion had worked. Raelynn succeeded at getting Durbin and Nick released, and somehow only one man lay dead. Caleb was grateful but was unsure what to do next. Trina and Durbin stood from their bench, he looked beaten and broken and weaker than Caleb had ever known. But beyond them, another rather large man approached. He carried bags, and Caleb did not appreciate the stern look upon his face.

Hastening his pace, he wanted to warn them about the large man, but then the man Raelynn was talking to the one who called to the approaching large man.

"Brody," he said, "thank you..."

Caleb relaxed —*always vigilant*— and turned to embrace Durbin after also noticing the approach of Gerald. They had strength in numbers, and with Raelynn's control, he felt he could turn his attention to what was important to him. Durbin. Caleb's heart hurt at the sight of his friend bruised and bloodied, stumbling into Trina's arms with feeble steps. But Durbin's eyes lit up as they met Caleb's. He wrapped his arms around them both, an embrace not experienced since the attack on them near the Spire. Only this time, Caleb had a hand in their safety, instead of feeling like a coward.

"It worked." he whispered into Trina's ear. He nuzzled his nose into Durbin's ear, just as Flint had done to Caleb before their rescue mission, "I am so glad we found you, Michael. So glad you are alive."

Durbin took both hands and grasped Caleb's head. "It means a great deal that you came for us. We would not be alive if you hadn't."

The man called Brody handed Durbin's road-worn backpack to him, greeting him with only a nod and tight lips. He also gave a bag to Nick who was being aided to his feet by Marcus. Nick looked worse than Durbin, a trail of dried blood down his shirt, bruised eyes and swollen lips. Raelynn continued her diplomatic resolution with the man she referred to as Jarvey. Many words were said, few of which held any importance for Caleb until Raelynn called for the settlers of Windy Well to return home. Marcus assisted Nick, Trina with Durbin, Gerald walked beside Caleb as they all followed Raelynn, flanked by Brody and Jarvey as they walked to the main entry gate that was not unlike the one at Windy Well. Brody and Jarvey opened the gate —two large freight traincars pulled by chains and adorned with plates of metal to cover holes and ground clearance. Metal wheels ground and squealed upon rails that guided the freight cars into position, opening an exit for Caleb's crew.

Jarvey looked to the open exit, and then to Raelynn. His face was a combination of surprise and curiosity.

"The rest of your men?" Jarvey asked, greeted only by

trees and rubble and scrap.

Raelynn broke from her stone-faced nature and smiled. "A bit of a bluff in order to preserve lives," she admitted.

"Well done, Miss Raelynn. The Well is fortunate to have your leadership. I will aim to govern the Fortress with as much discernment as you."

"Good luck to you, Jarvey. Keep people who have earned your trust close by. They must share the same ideals as you. And all should be well."

Raelynn and Jarvey shared another handshake as a demonstration of good faith and a look forward to the comradery of their settlements, then the settlers of Windy Well bid farewell to Gale Fortress. They donned new titles such as heroes, rescued captives, and commander. They also carried hearts heavy with the knowledge of the events that had brought them there.

Caleb turned around and took in the sights of the Gale Fortress one last time. Its wind turbines stood as monuments over the appliance factory, but also as guards. Trina briefly shared the story of her bow, Panic, and the trance-like phase that took over her as she brought down Balon Charles. Raelynn informed him of the terms of peace that Jarvey and she discussed. Caleb hoped that those turbines held some sort of protective power over the Fortress, that Jarvey's promise of peace and acceptance would override any of the hate left in that compound, that neither Kimwu, nor Darius, nor anyone else would be attacked just because of their very nature ever again.

With Nick and Durbin's injuries, and without the urgency of rescue, return travel to Windy Well was much slower.

Frequent stops were made for resting, more level paths were chosen for safe footing. Ravines and riverbanks were avoided, and because of their numbers and fair armory, they felt safe to traverse open roads when they were present and intact. They each took turns carrying Nick's and Durbin's backpacks to ease their burden of travel, shared rations and fresh hunts, and slept in shifts overnight during the three-day journey home. In a rare showing of emotion, Raelynn sang praises of everyone, bestowing accolades of heroics to them. She focused heavily on the fact that none of them knew what details their mission held prior to embarking, and how each of them had volunteered to rescue Nick, knowing so little about the potential danger. And she also sang of Trina's resolve.

"How does it feel, Huntress, to wield a weapon and a will that can end the life of someone who threatens you or your kin?" Raelynn asked of Trina during her commendations.

"I don't really know." Trina's response was heavy with hesitation. "It doesn't give me joy to have ended Balon's life, no matter how malicious he was to our people. But it does give me joy that my people are safe because of it."

"That is fair, Huntress. Our world is full of things that we don't understand. Of feelings and consequences unknown to us. I think your answer is a responsible one."

Caleb noticed that his adventures recently had taken on the trait of the unknown. When he first embarked on the mission to find hope for Bridgetown, he had no real plan of action. Same with encountering Durbin. Then again when signing up to aid Sully with the water carriage to Woodstock. And, most recently, to rescue his friend. Though their time together has been short, Caleb found himself admiring Durbin. He forced away thoughts of how different things would be if the rescue mission had failed.

By sunset on the third day, they were greeted by the towering wind turbine standing like a monolith within Windy Well. They could hear the commotion at the gates as the parapet patrols spied their party amongst the tall field grasses and reeds. The gate had squealed open before they were within a thousand meters of the settlement. Then the party hastened their pace. Even Nick and Durbin seemed to forget their wounds at the sight of home. Waiting beyond the fence wall as it noisily slid open were many people. Kimwu greeted them, with bandages on his knees and elbows. Darius sat in his wheelchair; Doctor Soma stood behind him. Paul was nearby as Omar operated the gate machinery. Sully was running from somewhere deep in the settlement, with Flint barking wildly and leaping. Soma had left Darius to tend to Nick and Durbin, calling names and waving her hands and shouting orders to get others to assist with their injuries.

Caleb watched his sister nearly run to Darius in his wheelchair. She leaned over him and spoke quietly to him. Darius exclaimed. "You did what?" He lightly pushed her away and proceeded to fiddle very clumsily with the leg rests of the chair, swinging them out of the way. Then he stood up. He cringed, his legs trembled, and even stifled a yelp. But he stood and embraced Trina tightly.

Kimwu chuckled as he hugged Durbin and Nick while he kept repeating, "My friends, my friends," until Soma and her assistants pulled them away to her medical bay.

Paul approached Raelynn with praise for a successful mission, displaying a bit of disbelief mixed with amazement, before ending with, "Thank you for finding my friend."

And finally, Sully and Flint made their way across the common area of Windy Well, both of them bounding along like excited puppies. Caleb beamed watching the footrace between his two closest friends in the Well —*in his new home.* He crouched and wrapped his arms around Flint's fluffy, recently washed neck. Flint paid him with wet tongue kisses, licking the dirt from his face. He stood to greet Sully who lost the race substantially, gasping for breath with his hand on his chest. Sully hugged Caleb tightly and kissed his cheek lightly as Flint spun in circles and figure eights around their legs barking playfully. "No more dangerous rescue missions."

"No." Caleb said looking up at the silvery-white turbine as if it were his first time seeing it. "I think we are going to be all right."

EPILOGUE — DURBIN

Michael Durbin had spent the majority of the summer recovering from his injuries. He had made Windy Well his home during that time. Dr. Soma had tended to his cracked ribs with compression bandages and sutured the deep cuts in his face. In the evenings, he would offer counsel to the leaders of the Well, either personal or settlement business, while Paul offered spiritual guidance to those who sought it. He aided in Darius's learning to walk again, and then he began taking on occasional Windy Well jobs on his own. While Sully and Caleb delivered water to settlements like Woodstock and TreeTop, and Raelynn and Trina — along with a few other aspiring huntresses — gathered meat for winter preservation, Durbin had taken on scavenging. His years of nomadism equipped him well for scavenging. He understood safe locations and the risks of others. He knew how to identify salvageable materials as well as how best to hide larger goods that he and a team would return for and deliver later. Metal, fabrics, clothing, footwear, food-preservation supplies, or any weaponry was considered a boon —so long as the materials were abandoned. Durbin took no part in thievery, regardless of the value of the scrap.

The summer days had grown long and hot, with the sun hanging high in the sky for hours longer than the moon illuminated the night. Nick had offered to join Durbin on a scavenging expedition, having also healed from cracked ribs and a broken jaw. He talked with a half-clenched mouth and struggled to take bites of deer steak that was butchered too thick, but his recovery was mostly full. They were traveling north, towards the Irish Hills region to scavenge any abandoned farming communities between there and Windy Well. Durbin was mostly familiar with the territory, but the seasonal changes in overgrowth would occasionally make navigation difficult. Nick and Durbin discussed the use of primary roads, and after determining they had been through worse than a few ruffians and toll-bridge hijackers, they opted to stick to more established routes.

Nick and Durbin each carried a large hiking pack, its length beginning at their butts and the top rising above the tops of their heads. The packs were half empty, however; only a few days of food and water and a bedroll occupied them. The remainder was for collecting smaller goods. Their focus this time was to collect clothing and possibly ammunition for their firearms and for trade. All variety of rounds were becoming scarce, and even a half-empty box of common rounds could secure leverage when bartering with a trade caravan. They were each well armed themselves, bowie knives, pistols, and even rope. Though after the events at Gale Fortress, both Nick and Durbin had found themselves less fearful of roadside strangers. Those notions were put to test as they approached a bridge over a small river.

"Looks like a toll bridge up ahead," said Nick, his jaw unmoving on one side.

"Extortionists" cursed Durbin.

Nick looked downriver, then upriver. "Want to try and sneak some way around?"

But something about the toll bridge didn't look right to Durbin. When highway brigands held up bridges, they were often plentiful in men, guarding two and three wide along the road against the free passage of travelers, and more often, trade caravans. They were heavily armed, and possessed a constitution suitable to their methods of banditry. Though the crates and wagons confiscated through questionable means remained on the small bridge, no bandits could be seen. Durbin even thought he smelled charred wood and the air had a faint taste of scorched metal.

"There are no guards on the road. Let's check it out," Durbin said to his friend.

They cautiously approached the bridge to find it not necessarily abandoned, but not inhabited either. Among the crates and wagons, a few melted plastic barrels, charred wood, and ash-covered tents were bloodied bodies of bandits. Durbin wasn't sure who or exactly how many, as several were dismembered, burned, or decapitated. Food rations lay crushed in the road, tattered clothing was strewn about in a whirlwind of chaos, bullet casings laid out like copper confetti. Blood soaked the road, and the wood, and torn bedrolls. Severed limbs still clung to handles of crates or in heaps of clothed flesh at the base of the guardrail separating the bridge from the short plummet to the river below.

Durbin had seen this type of carnage before.

His stomach lurched as buried thoughts about Camp Moon exhumed themselves and flooded his mind. He suddenly struggled to hold back emotions he had long held dormant.

Sweat dripped into his beard as blood trickled down his chin from his own lip that he had pierced with his teeth.

He jumped in defense as Nick touched his shoulder. "You all right, my friend?"

Durbin noticed that his breathing had become erratic. "Yeah. No. No, I'm not." He looked around the toll bridge camp with jerky movements. "This place has me recalling memories that I don't want."

Nick's response was short. "Family?"

Durbin nodded, licking the blood from his lips, and wiping his beard with the back of his hand.

Then something caught his eye that was not covered in soot or blood. It was silver and reflected the light of the sun that was filtered through trees along the river-bank. It was nearly impossible to believe that there was any light to reflect at all. Durbin walked over to the silver object and kneeled beside a bloodied body propped up against fractured wooden crates. The head leaked blood from a square gash near the right ear.

But the shiny object was what really held Durbin's attention.

It was a gun.

And on the side, along the barrel above the slide stop, engraved in blocky calligraphic lettering was the word: EXODUS.

It was *his* gun.

Suddenly the body next to him heaved and coughed, sputtering thick blood on his lap as he reached for Durbin with red quivering fingers. Durbin scampered backward, slipping on blood as he dug the heels of his boots into the concrete to slide away from the outstretched hand. Then the hand fell, as wet coughing sounds erupted from the man's body. "Eric...cough...red..."

"Eric Red?" Durbin tried to follow along. "That's who did this?"

The hand raised again, at nothing this time, partly due to Durbin's distance, and partly because he was certain that the injured man could not see.

"Air...Erich—ch—ch—ch...cough...THE RED", and the injured man's body convulsed one last time before all breath left him in a long, slow gurgle of blood.

Durbin picked up his reacquired silver firearm, flipped the safety off and on, and slid out the magazine with a click only to find it empty. The butt of the grip stock had a square shape that matched the wound on the head of the man who had just gargled to death. Durbin imagined a bit of combat that entailed the firing of the last rounds into that man before the assailant struck him in the head with the pistol. *Was it his Eric the Red?*

His hands were cold despite the summer heat as if all blood had left him while he loosely held the empty pistol. Nick must have noticed. He placed his hands on each of Durbin's shoulders saying, "You don't look well, my friend. And I fear I know this look. What's wrong?"

Durbin stalled in giving an answer because once it was said, it could not be taken back. It would be out there for all of the world to know. But along with the words would also be emotion. Several of them. Most of which had been suppressed for more than ten summers.

"I have told you about my family..." Durbin said quietly, looking at the gun as if it could share secrets.

"You have," Nick replied solemnly. "And I am sorry."

"This is the gun that was stolen," Durbin said with an emotional quake in his voice. "Red was the word written in blood on the wall of our cabin at Camp Moon. The one who killed my family is still alive."

SPECIAL THANKS

To my editors: Taryn Lawson, and Andrea Altenburg for making me look good. For providing integral feedback and allowing the them and style to shine through. And for teaching me several things along the way.

To Jenifer M: who was an avid fan from the day I decided to seriously pursue this endeavor. "My biggest fan", or at least, my first.

BOOKS IN THIS SERIES

End of...

Years after the Collapse of society, pockets of civilization aim to rebuild. But the nature of human evolution, the fierceness with which the Earth regained her throne, and individuals thirst for power make survival difficult. As resources dwindle, human ingenuity must adapt if humankind is to survive.

End Of Reason

End Of Seasons (Coming Soon)

End Of Everything (Coming Soon)

Made in the USA
Monee, IL
17 June 2020